# THE RADAR JOB

by

JAMES BADDOCK

MALVERN PUBLISHING COMPANY LTD

Published by

Malvern Publishing Company Limited
P.O. Box 16
Malvern
Worcestershire
WR14 1UH
England

ISBN 0-947993-16-9

Printed and bound in Great Britain by
EntaPrint Ltd., Cranleigh, Surrey.

*To Mum and Dad who started it all*
*and Melanie who helped to finish it.*

# PROLOGUE

## GERMANY: NIGHT OF OCTOBER 10/11, 1942

The pilot gently eased the Ju88 night fighter through a 180 degree turn and began the next leg of his patrol. He resisted an impulse to call up Himmelbett Station Wolf; they would tell him soon enough if they had anything on the radar. It did seem inconceivable that they had nothing for him at the moment; the sky was illuminated by searchlight beams and flak explosions. Somewhere below him, he knew, there were probably over five hundred RAF bombers on their way to attack whichever target had been singled out for mass destruction tonight but, so far, he had not seen a single one of them.

The radio crackled into sudden life, startling him. "Wolf to Adler One."

"Acknowledged," replied the pilot, crisply.

"Order: turn port, ninety degrees."

The pilot responded immediately; he touched the rudder bars and hauled the stick over. This was the first rule of radar controlled night fighter interception: to react instantly to any order from the ground.

"Order: lose height. Come down three hundred metres."

The pilot eased the stick forward and concentrated on watching the altimeter. Alongside him, the observer scanned the night sky, although he knew that the chances of his seeing anything at the moment were virtually non-existent.

"Announcement: the target is five kilometres ahead of you," said the ground controller.

"Acknowledged."

"We'll bring you in below and behind him."

"Excellent."

"Prepare: ten degree starboard turn."

The pilot said nothing. Behind him, the radar operator would be watching the screens for the tell-tale blip that would be the enemy bomber. Until that happened, the pilot had to rely entirely and exclusively on the instructions from the ground station.

"Order: execute turn."

The pilot touched the rudder bars and settled on the new course.

"Announcement: range three thousand metres."

The radar operator cut across the controller's voice with an excited shout: "Got him! We've got him!"

"Good luck, Adler One," said the ground controller. From this point on, the aircraft would effectively be under the radar operator's control; he would guide the pilot onto the bomber.

"Down a hundred metres," said the radar operator. "Turn to starboard. Hold it. Range two thousand."

Despite himself, the pilot found himself straining his eyes into the darkness ahead. He was aware of the futility of the act; he would see nothing yet.

"Fifteen hundred. Turn to port a fraction. That's it."

"How far above is he?"

"Fifty metres."

The pilot grinned to himself in anticipation; any minute now . . .

"Two hundred and fifty metres."

"Where is he?" muttered the observer. "We ought to be able to see the damned thing by now."

The pilot pulled back on the stick and the Ju88 began to climb. Somewhere ahead of them was a British bomber, just ripe for the taking.

"Come on, come on, where are you?" He suddenly realised he had spoken aloud and mentally cursed himself for revealing his anxiety. Wouldn't do at all . . .

"There!" shouted the observer and, half a second later, the pilot saw them too: eight bright yellow flames in a line, the exhausts of a four-engined bomber.

"Kettle drums, kettle drums," the pilot intoned, giving the strange, almost ritualistic incantation that told ground control he was in visual contact.

"Lancaster," reported the observer.

The pilot flicked the gun safety catches switch and saw a row of red lights on the instrument panel: the three 20mm cannons in the nose were ready to fire. He checked the airspeed indicator and throttled back a fraction. The Ju88, with its unwieldy array of aerials for both radar and radio, had a high stalling speed and they were only just above it, but the pilot wanted to close with the bomber as slowly as possible so that he would have ample time in which to carry out the attack.

The pilot stared upwards at the monstrous shape of the Lancaster as he brought the Ju88 in behind and below it. This was going to be too easy; they had not even seen him yet. He pulled back on the stick and the Ju88's nose lifted abruptly; she was just on the verge of stalling now, hanging in the air on her straining propellers. "Opening fire," he announced and then pressed the firing button, feeling the aircraft shudder to the recoil of the 20mm cannons.

The pilot kept his finger on the button as the Ju88's nose began to fall away from the target, until there was a sudden silence: the ammunition drums were empty. He was distantly aware of the observer crawling into the nose to reload the guns but his entire attention was concentrated on the huge shape above.

The Lancaster was heeling over to starboard; the pilot moved the stick to port to take the Ju88 clear and then put the night fighter into a banking turn so that he could follow the stricken bomber down; he wanted to see this one die. The port outer engine burst into flames and the bomber began to side-slip; the pilot watched, mesmerised, as the port wing flapped like some colossal bird's and then the bomber's nose went down as the wing tore itself away in grotesque slow motion. The doomed Lancaster began to turn over, slowly at first, but the pilot knew that the spin was irreversible, that within seconds the bomber would be tumbling over and over too rapidly for its crew to have any chance at all of baling out. Like a gigantic sycamore seed, the dying bomber spiralled away into the darkness below.

"Announcing: bomber destroyed." The pilot's voice was expressionless.

"Congratulations, Adler One," said the ground controller.

“Good work, both of you,” said the pilot to his two crewmen.

Behind him, the radar operator patted the ‘Liechtenstein’ radar set. It had been installed only two months previously but it had already proved its worth; they had downed six bombers in the last month alone. “Thank the radar,” he said and then added, “Who said it wouldn’t work, Herr Oberleutnant?”

“I take it all back,” the pilot laughed. “Our wonder scientists have finally done something right.” His tone grew more serious. “Now we might even be able to shoot down enough Tommies with it to stop them turning out cities into piles of rubble.”

# CHAPTER 1

**LONDON: MARCH 1943**

Sir Gerald Cathcart finished reading the list of figures on the report in front of him and shook his head slowly before looking up at the two men facing him on the far side of the large desk. "I see what you mean," he said quietly.

"And the figures are getting worse," said the man in the Wing Commander's uniform. "We're losing a higher percentage of aircraft with almost every mission."

"So I see," said Cathcart, indicating the report. It contained details of last night's RAF bombing mission. Over seven hundred Lancasters, Stirlings, Wellingtons and Halifaxes had bombed Essen, in the Ruhr Valley; out of these, forty-three aircraft had not returned; six per cent of the bombing force had been lost.

"That's why we need your help," said the Wing Commander urgently. "We must have more information about their airborne radar."

"Well, I've sent for the man you need to talk to. Major Guthrie runs our Continental networks."

There was a knock at the door; Cathcart smiled at his two guests, as if to comment on the perfect timing of the interruption and then called out, "Come in."

The man who came into the office was dressed in an impeccably cut pinstripe suit, the uniform of the senior Civil Servant; but there was no disguising his military bearing. Major Guthrie was in his middle thirties with prematurely greying hair; he glanced at the two visitors and it was immediately apparent that he was on his guard.

"Ah, Major. Good of you to be so prompt. May I introduce Wing Commander Ryan and Professor Daniels? Gentlemen, this is Major David Guthrie, on temporary secondment from his regiment."

"I've been on 'temporary' secondment for the last four years," said Guthrie, smiling, as he shook hands with the two visitors. Cathcart motioned Guthrie into an empty seat; the major sat down, apparently relaxed.

"These two gentlemen have come to ask for our help," explained Cathcart, his tone somehow exluding Ryan and Daniels; they were outsiders. Ryan suppressed a smile; he had never had dealings with Cathcart before but he had been told that Cathcart tended to keep a possessive eye on his subordinates. Not that he was unco-operative, but his post of Deputy Director of the Secret Intelligence Service led him to be fiercely autocratic; he preferred to run things his own way, without outside interference or advice. But Cathcart would help; he had to.

"They would like us to obtain some information, if it's at all feasible," said Cathcart smoothly. "And the only source for this would be one of our Continental networks."

"I see," said Guthrie. "What sort of information?" He looked expectantly at Ryan, who replied:

"The Germans have developed a new kind of radar equipment, which they have installed in their night fighter aircraft. It would appear to be very effective and we need information about it urgently. At the moment, quite frankly, we know very little about it at all."

Guthrie exchanged looks with Cathcart. "And you think we can help you?" he asked Ryan.

"For several months, you have been passing on extremely detailed and accurate information concerning Luftwaffe night fighter operations in the Netherlands. Information of a type that could only come from an agent with access to a Luftwaffe air base. Am I correct?"

Cathcart cleared his throat. "I cannot comment on that, Wing Commander."

Ryan ignored this. "What I am asking is whether you could ask your source to obtain information about the Liechtenstein radar."

Guthrie looked at Cathcart again but there was nothing in his superior's face that gave him any hint as to what attitude to adopt. He decided to temporise. "Shouldn't you be talking to the Special Operations Executive about this? Dutch networks are their responsibility, after all." He thought he detected a slight smile on Cathcart's face, instantly suppressed.

Ryan gazed levelly at Guthrie. "Forgive my bluntness, Major Guthrie, but don't you think the SOE's made a bit of a cock-up in Holland?"

This time, it was Guthrie's turn to control his features. It was perfectly true; SOE had an abysmal record in the Netherlands. It was only too obvious to SIS that the Germans had penetrated SOE's Dutch networks as far back as 1941 and that these so-called 'Resistance' groups were being used by the Nazis for the purpose of sending back false or misleading information. However, SIS's repeated warnings to SOE had been greeted with cold disdain; SIS's own disastrous record in Holland had been cited, along with various comments about people in glass houses. Relations between the two services were, to say the least, less than cordial.

Guthrie realised that Ryan was still talking. "The point is, we have a good deal of respect for your source and we'd rather deal with him, or them, if at all possible."

"And the SOE?" asked Cathcart, with a mischievous glint in his eyes.

"Let me put it this way," said Ryan slowly. "Our total of worthwhile information from the SOE's Dutch networks has been negligible. But from yours—excellent."

"I see," said Cathcart. "Officially, of course, we have no networks in Holland, but—well—we may be able to do something for you." He smiled briefly. "Now—exactly what sort of information would you require?"

"Anything at all would be useful. Ideally, a photograph of the equipment or a detailed drawing. Even a verbal description would be better than nothing."

"So—" said Guthrie slowly. "Let me get this straight. You're asking for one of them to smuggle a camera or drawing instruments into a Luftwaffe base, past security checks and guards. If they're caught then not only will they be tortured and eventually executed, but the entire network will be blown wide open. You're asking them to risk their lives for this information; what I want to know is this: just how important is it?"

There was a heavy silence. Ryan, looking at Guthrie,

reflected that Cathcart was not the only SIS member who might be difficult to deal with. But he could see Guthrie's point . . . "I'm afraid it is absolutely vital, Major."

He passed over the typed report. "Last night, we lost forty-three bombers out of a total force of seven hundred and three aircraft. Three nights ago, we lost thirty-six out of eight hundred and twelve. That means that over the last four days we have lost nearly eighty bombers and over eight hundred aircrew. On average, on every bombing operation we carry out, we lose six to seven per cent of our force and the proportion is steadily rising. And a major factor in the Germans' success has been their night fighter tactics in which this airborne radar plays a vital part as far as we can ascertain." He gestured to Daniels, who, until now, had been a silent observer. "Professor Daniels here belongs to the Telecommunications Research Establishment; he can give you the details better than I can."

Daniels nodded. "Very well." He looked at Guthrie. "How much do you know about the German radar system?"

"I know a fair bit about the 'Freya' and 'Würzburg' systems," Guthrie replied. "After all, a good deal of the information came through us, didn't it?"

"Quite." Daniels did not seem to be at all discomfited by the ironic comment. "In that case, you'll know that our bombers can be detected by the 'Freya' radar while they're still over East Anglia. By the time they cross the Dutch coast, they can be picked up by the 'Würzburg' stations. Each of these stations locks on to one of our bombers and directs one of their night fighters onto the target. These ground stations are in constant contact with their aircraft by radio; the system seems to work very efficiently.

"However, the 'Würzburg' is only accurate to within about two miles; from then on, the fighter has to find the bomber by itself. Until about nine months ago it could only do so visually and, given a dark night, there was every chance that our bomber could give them the slip. But it is now evident that they're carrying their own radar equipment so that once they're within two miles of the target, they pick up the bomber on their own set. Using this, they can close to within visual range."

"Which is where our planes are at a disadvantage," said Ryan quietly. "The Jerries are using three main types of aircraft as night fighters—the Messerschmidt 110, the Dornier 217, and the Junkers 88. They're all twin-engined aircraft, not as fast or as manoeuvrable as the Me109s or the Fw190s, but they're still faster and more handy than our bombers. They're shooting a lot of our planes; too damned many. As I said, we're losing six or seven per cent of our aircraft on every mission. You can work it out for yourself, Major. Statistically, we lose our entire bombing force every seventeen missions. We can replace the aircraft, although the aircraft manufacturers have to work flat out to do so, but we can't replace the aircrew so easily. It's a vicious circle. We're losing men so we have to cut down our training schedules, which increases the chances of the new crews being shot down so we lose more men. Something like thirty per cent of crews going on their first three missions never come back."

Guthrie stared gloomily at Ryan, feeling a sinking sensation in the pit of his stomach. The picture Ryan was painting was only too grim; it was beginning to look as if he was not going to be able to refuse Ryan's request . . .

"One last point," said Ryan slowly. "Like the other figures I've quoted, it's not something for public consumption. Our aircrew are expected to do a tour of duty lasting thirty operations. The odds of surviving throughout that tour are less than five per cent."

Jesus, thought Guthrie. Twenty to one against. "Can't you try jamming their equipment or something?" he asked despairingly, knowing what the answer would be.

Daniels gave the answer. "We've tried. We're reasonably certain that they're using a wavelength of 62 centimetres or 490 megahertz. We've based this conclusion on pulse signals that have been picked up by RAF listening stations.

"On top of this, we have the information gained by a 'ferret' flight that was sent out in December. We used a Wellington, carrying special listening equipment and the crew deliberately invited attack by the night fighters. It worked, in that the aircraft was indeed attacked and strong signals on the 62 centimetre frequency were picked up. Fortunately, the Wellington, although damaged, managed to ditch in the sea. All of its crew were picked up safely.

"Subsequently, we tried sending out jamming signals on that wavelength but they have had no discernible effect. We need to know more about the equipment, about its range, its sensitivity, its accuracy and so we need either pictures of it or a detailed description. Once we have this information, we can see about neutralising or circumventing it but, at present, we are groping in the dark."

"And we're losing more aircraft all the time," interposed Ryan, a note or urgency in his voice. "We are utterly committed to the bombing campaign, the RAF by night and the Americans by day but if this loss rate persists, quite apart from the appalling consequences in terms of loss of life, there will be pressure brought to bear to end the campaign altogether. If that happens, if there is any break in the bombing of German industry, then the strategic consequences would be incalculable. The Second Front might be delayed or even called off altogether. The bombing has to go on; it is seen as essential to Allied strategy."

"Despite the losses?" said Guthrie.

"Despite the losses," Ryan echoed heavily.

Guthrie looked at Cathcart, who nodded wearily. "We'll do what we can, Wing Commander," Guthrie said quietly.

After Ryan and Daniels had left, Cathcart regarded Guthrie quizzically. "I hope our friends in Baker Street don't get to hear about this. They won't be too pleased."

"Treading on their patch, you mean? Too bad. They ought to get themselves better organised. Bloody amateurs."

Cathcart knew exactly what Guthrie meant, especially as regarded SOE's operations in Dutch territory; not that SIS's own record was exactly laudable. The SIS networks in the Netherlands had been virtually wiped out in 1939, following the Venlo Incident, in which two of SIS's top intelligence men in the Netherlands had been kidnapped on the Dutch-German border by German SS agents. This had not only destroyed the Dutch networks, but had also compelled SIS to withdraw agents from all over Europe. The task of rebuilding Britain's Continental intelligence networks had fallen to the newly formed SOE; in the case of the Netherlands, the results had been disastrous.

However, unknown to anyone but themselves, the SIS had almost inadvertently retained one agent in Holland. He had only just been recruited by Guthrie himself when the Dutch networks collapsed; only Guthrie had known the Dutchman's identity and so he had escaped the wave of arrests that had taken place as soon as the Germans invaded the Low Countries. The decision was taken to keep the existence of this agent hidden from SOE; SIS wanted this one for themselves. The agent had been given the codename 'Voltimand' and, as one SOE debacle in Holland succeeded another, Cathcart and Guthrie blessed their foresight. Indeed, these very failures on SOE's part only served to make Voltimand's position more secure: if the Germans felt they had the Dutch networks under control, then they would be less likely to be diligent in searching for unknown agents.

Voltimand had now built up a very efficient cell of agents, whose flow of information was steady, thorough and accurate. There was no way now that Cathcart and Guthrie would let SOE have Voltimand; it was not just a case of professional rivalry but was also a result of cold-blooded appraisal. If they let SOE have Voltimand, he'd be dead inside a month, judging by Baker Street's record to date.

"You'll contact Voltimand, then?" asked Cathcart.

"Yes. I just hope I'm not asking them to take on too much."

"Voltimand knows what he's doing. He won't do anything foolish."

"No, I suppose not. I hope to God nothing goes wrong, though."

Cathcart looked meditatively at Guthrie. He was a good man, thought Cathcart: capable, intelligent, one of the best men he had, in fact. But too—what was the word?—empathetic? Too liable to become personally involved. Unfortunately, the cold, hard truth was that Britain needed this information; and badly. If obtaining it meant the deaths of Voltimand and his entire cell, then so be it. It was the price one had to pay.

In the final analysis, thought Cathcart, Voltimand and his group were expendable.

# CHAPTER 2

**BERLIN: MARCH 1943**

"Congratulations, Major Behrens. The Fatherland is deeply in your debt." An outburst of applause greeted the Reichsmarschall's words but Behrens hardly heard it. Nor did he notice Goering's wide smile; the only thought that Major Anton Behrens had in his mind was that it was true what they said about Goering—he did smell like a Paris brothel, with all that cologne.

Behrens was fully aware of the inappropriateness of the thought; he ought to be overwhelmed by elation. He had just been awarded the Knight's Cross, the highest military honour possible, the medal that every fighting man in Germany longed for, and yet all he could think of was that this was all a massive waste of time. Why did he have to be presented with the damned thing at a lavish reception, for God's sake? He had never liked wearing full dress uniform in any case and to stand up here on what was effectively a stage to be admired by Berlin's elite was not for him at all.

"I was sorry to hear about your injuries, Major," said Goering quietly, so low that only the two of them could hear. Behrens was taken by surprise; Goering even sounded as though he meant it. Maybe he did, thought Behrens: he had been a pilot himself once and a good one, by all accounts.

Behrens glanced down at his left hand; or rather at the artificial hand enclosed in the black glove. "Thank you, Herr Reichsmarschall." Behrens grinned. "The worst of it is that it keeps itching, even though it isn't there."

Goering smiled sympathetically and clapped Behrens on the shoulder. "And even worse than that is the thought of not being able to fly again, isn't it, Major?"

Behrens nodded slowly, dumbfounded. He was beginning to see why the older pilots he knew swore by Goering; he might be a degenerate pervert, drug addict and sycophantic politician but, when all was said and done, he understood his flyers.

"Never mind, Major. Although it is probably no consolation, you should feel proud of yourself. You have done your part and more. And this medal is a symbol of that. Wear it with honour." Goering's voice had risen for the last three sentences of his speech; he was the politician again, speaking for the benefit of the audience, even bowing slightly as they applauded. As Behrens limped down the steps, the applause reached a crescendo; Anton Behrens, the Scourge of the Ivans, as he had been dubbed by the newspapers, was now being accorded a hero's welcome.

He made his way back to his seat, only distantly aware of the hands that reached out for him, some to shake his hand, others to pat him on the shoulders or back. As he sat down, he was absently fingering the coveted award; he felt absolutely nothing.

When he had been a novice pilot—how long ago that seemed now!—and he had seen Werner Molders wearing the Knight's Cross, he had vowed that one day he too would wear it. In the event, he had gone one better, gaining the Knight's Cross with Oak Leaves. And yet there was the taste of ashes in his mouth. What difference did it really make, after all? What good did it do him? He had already gained the respect and admiration of his fellow pilots; the medal would not change any of that. And it couldn't give him back his hand; it would not enable him to fly again.

And it wouldn't bring Anneliese back, either . . .

The orchestra started to play again; the speeches were over and the festivities could begin. Almost immediately, Behrens found himself surrounded by well-wishers; this was hardly surprising, as he was one of the five guests of honour, but he wanted none of it. Didn't these parasites know there was a war on, for God's sake? Out there, on the Russian Front, thousands of men were dying every day and they were sitting there, stuffing themselves with food and drink . . .

He stood up abruptly and broke away from the inane chatter, the fawning glances and words. He limped across the floor as fast as he was able.

"Major! Major! Wait one moment, please!"

Behrens turned around and saw who was calling him:

General Haller, one of the Air Staff. He waited for Haller to come over to him.

"Forgive me, Major Behrens. I should not have allowed you to be pestered. A man likes to be alone with his thoughts at times like these."

Behrens glanced at Haller's own Knight's Cross. How had he won that? he wondered bitterly, but said nothing.

"I mean, it's an unforgettable moment for you, isn't it?" asked Haller jovially. "You don't really want all these people hanging around you, do you?"

"Not really," Behrens admitted.

"Especially with you so recently out of hospital. A great strain . . . Perhaps you would do me the honour of joining us at our table?"

It was as good as an order. Behrens capitulated gracefully. "The honour will be all mine, Herr General."

Haller was accompanied by his wife and daughter; Behrens' heart sank when he saw the latter. Haller's daughter was staring at him with an expression he had seen several times recently from women, too often in fact; it was a mixture of admiration, curiosity and timorous fascination. He was not only a hero, but a disfigured one to boot; a new experience for jaded palates. Behrens groaned inwardly; Fräulein Haller looked as though she were about to pounce on him.

"This is Marthe, my wife, and Klara, my daughter. Marthe, Klara, may I present Major Behrens?"

"Charmed to meet you, Major," said Frau Haller. "Do sit down, please."

Klara Haller stared intently at Behrens; he had the uncomfortable sensation that he had just been mentally undressed. "You do us a great honour, Major."

"My pleasure," said Behrens stiffly.

"Come, come, Major!" said Haller expansively. "You should be happy! This is your evening, after all. Waiter! A drink, please, for our guest."

There was no escape, Behrens realised. He could not now decently leave the reception as he had intended; he would have to sit it out, endure it.

Suddenly, a thought struck him: Anneliese would have been completely at home here. She would have loved every minute of it. Not for the first time, he asked himself how much he had really meant to her.

Give her credit, he thought: at least she was honest about it. She had come to see him just once in hospital and that had been when he was looking better, but even that had been too much for her. She had written to him, saying, quite bluntly, that she thought it would be for the best if they were to stop seeing each other. Try as she might, she could not come to terms with his disfigurement. He couldn't blame her; apart from the missing hand and the limp, he was also badly burned down his left side from his ribs to his thighs. But the letter had hurt, all the same . . .

"Pardon?" he said; Klara Haller had asked him a question.

"Will you be staying long in Berlin, Herr Major?"

"I honestly don't know. It depends on what the Luftwaffe have in mind for me."

"I think we can take it as read that Major Behrens will be in Berlin for some time," said Haller, smiling. "There are one or two posts available that I'm sure he would be able to fill admirably."

"Then we'll be seeing a lot of you over the next few weeks, Major?" persisted Klara.

"I'm sure you'll be a very welcome guest at our house," said Frau Haller, smiling conspiratorially at her daughter.

Behrens knew how a prize bull felt while he was being examined at a sale. Was he being set up as a potential marriage prospect for Klara Haller? He could do a lot worse, of course: Haller's daughter was remarkably attractive. She was the archetypal Aryan woman, tall, blonde and blue-eyed, but it was the predatory glint in those large eyes that Behrens was worried about; she looked as though she could consume him for breakfast before she had properly woken up.

The orchestra started to play a waltz; Haller and his wife excused themselves, leaving Behrens alone with Klara. Not exactly subtle, he thought sourly.

"Do you dance, Major?" she asked and then continued, "Oh, do forgive me. I was forgetting—"

"Well, if you don't mind the limp—would you care to dance?"

"Of course."

As they moved around the floor, he was uncomfortably aware of her closeness, of her perfume. He also observed, with wry amusement, that he was experiencing great difficulty in keeping his eyes above neck level: she had a stunning bosom, most of which was revealed by the low cut evening dress.

"I do hope you'll take up our invitation to visit us, Major," she said, her eyes sultry.

"If my duties permit, I'd be glad to."

"You'll be very welcome." She smiled flirtatiously. "Especially if my mother and father are out."

"Really?" Behrens raised his eyebrows.

"Well, I thought it would be nice if we could have a little private chat, get to know each other. You know what I mean, Major."

I'd have to be exceedingly stupid or naïve, or both, not to know exactly what you mean, thought Behrens. And why not? He had seen the way she had reacted to holding his artificial hand; she seemed fascinated by it . . . "As I said, it will be a pleasure, Fraulein."

"Please, Major. Call me Klara."

She reached out her hand, and touched his cheek as she spoke. Behrens saw a look of almost feline triumph in her eyes and felt sickened.

"Excuse me, Fräulein. I'm afraid I must sit down. My leg, you see . . ."

"Oh, of course. How remiss of me. Please accept my apologies." She sounded contrite but there was no warmth or compassion in her eyes.

They returned to the table and, within minutes, the two women had excused themselves to 'powder their noses'.

"You seem to have made quite an impression on Klara, Major," said Haller. With all the finesse of a sledgehammer, thought Behrens.

"She's a very beautiful woman," he replied evasively. "You must be very proud of her, Herr General."

"Indeed I am. She is a good German. She knows what you have done for the Fatherland and respects you for it."

"I haven't done so very much."

"What? Are you saying that a hundred and sixty-eight

enemy aircraft shot down is not very much?"

"Not really. Some of the Russian planes we come up against are obsolete. Sitting ducks. And their pilots are untrained. And remember this: although we're shooting them down by the hundred, they're replacing them even faster than we can destroy them. Anyway, it doesn't matter how many we shoot down—we're still losing the war on the ground."

Haller looked nervously around him, fearful that anyone might have overheard Behrens' defeatist comments. "We must all do what we can, Behrens. Your victories are helping to slow the Russians down so that our counter-attack will be decisive."

Behrens stared at Haller, disbelievingly. "Counter-attack? What counter-attack? Try telling the front line troops about counter-offensives and strategic withdrawals and they'll laugh in your face. They're the real heroes, General, not me. They're facing overwhelmingly superior forces out there but they still carry on fighting, regardless. And they're dying in their thousands. How many did we lose at Stalingrad? Two hundred thousand men? More?"

"Major, you forget yourself! How dare—"

Something seemed to snap inside Behrens. "Two hundred thousand men! And we sit here stuffing ourselves and award each other meaningless bits of metal! We don't deserve men like that!"

Haller glared at him, the anger only too evident in his eyes. "We must all do our duty as we see it, Major! We cannot all have the honour of being in the front line!"

Behrens laughed; it had an ugly sound to it. "Honour? You call it an honour? I think there are many who would cheerfully forgo that honour, General, and who would gladly change places with you." His voice oozed contempt. "We must all do our duty, must we?" He picked up his glass and, without taking his eyes off Haller, poured the wine over the tablecloth. "It just seems to me that some of us have more of it to do than others!"

He stood up abruptly and walked away, ignoring the staring faces.

Behrens eyed his reflection in the mirror and smiled tiredly. He had really landed himself in it this time; he was finished, to all intents and purposes. Haller would never forgive him and Haller had the ear of Goering. But it had been worth it; it had needed to be said. Not that it would do any good; anyone who had overheard it would put it down to stress. It had all been too much for him, poor boy . . . Not surprising, of course, with those shocking injuries, a dreadful shame, wasn't it?

To hell with them.

There was a knock on the door. Behrens glanced at his watch; it was almost 12.30. Who in heaven's name could it be at this hour? Of course . . . it had to be.

"Fräulein Haller! This is a surprise." She was looking as coldly beautiful as ever, even though the cleavage that had so distracted him was concealed by an expensive-looking fur wrap.

"I'm sorry if I've disturbed you, Major." She didn't look sorry. "May I come in?"

"Of course." Behrens stood aside to let her pass, closed the door and took her wrap. "May I offer you a drink?"

"That is kind of you. Do you have brandy?"

"Coming up."

As he poured the drinks, she sat in the armchair and crossed her legs, elegantly. She smiled up at him as he handed her the glass; the smile was full of such blatant eroticism that it almost took his breath away.

"Prosit," she said, her voice husky.

He returned the toast and took a hasty mouthful, to calm himself down. He was behaving like a damned schoolboy . . .

"You're probably wondering why I'm here," she said in a matter of fact voice.

"Well, yes."

"I gather you rather upset my father tonight, Major."

"I imagine I did, yes."

"Serves him right. He can be a pompous ass at times. But I was intrigued when I heard about it. Very few men are prepared to stand up to my father and I was very impressed. Very impressed indeed. It only made me all the more determined to get to know you better, Major. So here I am."

Behrens was suddenly aware that his pulse was racing, that he was gripped by a tense excitement. He was being offered it on a plate, here and now, and he knew she would be good, very good. He also had no doubt that she had more in mind than just a night of kinky sex, that she wanted more from him than that, but if she was willing, then why not? "Indeed you are, Fräulein."

"Please. I'd rather you called me Klara."

"Klara, then. Actually, I was just about to go to bed. Would you care to join me?"

She smiled, almost ferally. "I'd love to, Major."

"Please call me Anton."

"Anton," she acknowledge and stood up. Quickly, deftly, she unbuttoned her dress and let it fall to the floor. Underneath, she was naked, except for her stockings, which were held in place by garters.

He moved over to her, watching her eyes, seeing the almost naked lust in them. He reached out with his artificial hand; her eyes followed it, alive with tense anticipation. He touched her breast, lightly; she moaned softly and closed her eyes.

Behrens smiled to himself as he pulled her towards him.

Klara Haller sighed and stretched herself luxuriously against Behrens. "That was wonderful, Anton," she said, her voice hoarse; probably from all the groaning and panting, thought Behrens sardonically. She ran her hand lightly over his chest. "Did you enjoy it, too, darling?"

He cupped her breast and kneaded it, none too gently; he had already discovered her liking for the caveman approach. "What do you think?" he replied, his expression unreadable in the darkness. Yes, he had enjoyed it, on a purely physical level. She was an enthusiastic partner in bed, totally uninhibited and very knowledgeable in the arts of pleasing a man; how could be fail to enjoy sex with such a desirable woman? But there had been something repellent in the way that she had begged him to fondle her with his artificial hand. It had made his flesh creep, even while he had wanted to possess her utterly. Which he had; and not just once, either. Three times already and it was not yet light outside. The woman was insatiable . . .

She was kneeling beside him now, holding his hand to her breast. Although he could not see her face, he was suddenly certain that she was deciding whether this was the moment to make her move; he had been waiting to discover the true reason for her visit ever since she had arrived. She bent over him, her blonde hair brushing lightly against his groin, and then he felt the soft pressure of her lips; he closed his eyes and concentrated on the sensations.

She waited until he was fully aroused and then sat back on her haunches, still gently caressing him with her fingers. "Anton?"

So this was it, he realised: she was finally going to lay her cards on the table. The charade was about to come to an end. "Yes?"

"This row you had with Father at the reception?"

"Yes?" he said again.

"He wasn't very pleased with you, you know."

"I don't suppose he was."

"I'm sure that he'll understand why you acted like that once he has a chance to cool down. I mean, he'll realise that you didn't mean it."

"Ah, but I did mean it, Klara. Every word of it."

There was a moment's silence; her fingers paused in their caresses and then resumed their feather-light attentions. "Even so, I'm sure that if I spoke to him and if you were to apologise to him, it would all be forgotten."

Behrens looked up at her. "I doubt that. Too many people overheard it."

"Put it this way, Anton. It would be overlooked; my father would see to that. He actually has a great respect for you and for your achievements. I'm sure he wouldn't want it all to go to waste over one ill-advised outburst."

He chose his next words very carefully "So you're saying that if I apologise to your father, it'll all be forgotten and I'll be offered a job here in Berlin?"

She nodded. "Yes, that is exactly what I am saying, Anton." She was staring intently down at him. "And then we would be able to see each other as often as we wanted to. Wouldn't you like that?"

He could see it all now, could see why she was here. Insult or not, Haller wanted him on his staff; as a ranking 'ace', he would be very useful to parade at receptions and conferences. Klara Haller wanted him for her own purposes; certainly for sex, to gratify her own bizarre appetites and, quite conceivably, for more than just that. Again, as a holder of the Knight's Cross, he would be a suitable consort for her, if he were to be returned to favour. And it would be done, of that he had no doubt. Haller probably knew his daughter was here; he had quite possibly sent her to him to 'explain' the situation. His future career would be assured if he accepted her offer.

And all he had to do was to apologise . . .

He sighed. It was a pity, really; Klara had been quite superb in bed and had excited him as much as, if not more than, any other woman. He would have liked to have enjoyed her body at least once more, but the price she wanted was too high.

"I think you might as well start getting dressed, Fräulein Haller," he said quietly.

"What do you mean?"

"I mean that there seems no further point in you staying here, Fräulein."

"No further point?" Her voice was as cold as a December wind; as she spoke, her hands moved away from his body.

"None at all, Fräulein Haller. I have no intention of apologising to your father or to anyone else for what I said last night. I meant every word of it. And, furthermore, I am not remotely interested in him or his job—please tell him that as well."

There was an icy silence that lasted for several seconds. "You bastard, Behrens!" she spat. "You'll be sorry you said that, you know!"

"Quite probably," he agreed calmly. "Shall I try to find you a cab? I presume you will not be wanting me to escort you home, now?"

The blow, a swinging open-handed slap, took him utterly by surprise. "You loathsome bastard, Behrens! May you rot in hell!"

Hell hath no fury, thought Behrens wryly . . . She sprang off the bed and reached for her clothes. "Call a car for me, if you please, Major," she said with frigid formality, not looking at him.

He sighed again, almost regretfully, as she buttoned up the dress. Perhaps he was a bloody fool, rejecting her offer, but he knew that he could never have accepted it.

This time, Anton my boy, he thought, you have really gone and done it, haven't you?

# CHAPTER 3

**LEIDEN, NETHERLANDS: APRIL 1943**

It was a bright Spring day but there was enough of a chill north wind to remind people that winter had not been left far behind as yet. Vim Schelhaas hunched his shoulders under his overcoat as he walked across the town square. He went into the shabby-looking restaurant opposite the Town Hall and was greeted by the proprietor. "The usual, Vim?"

"I suppose so." Schelhaas glanced around the gloomy interior and caught sight of a familiar face sitting by himself at a corner table. "And one for Jan as well."

The proprietor nodded. "He's been waiting for you for the last half hour, Vim."

"Couldn't be helped. I had to speak to the Headmaster again."

"Thinking of sacking you, is he?"

"He's been trying to do that for years." He took the two glasses and headed towards the corner table.

The proprietor watched him go. He would make sure that Schelhaas would not be interrupted; this was clearly Resistance business. The proprietor knew full well that Schelhaas was the leader of the local Resistance cell and that Jan Kuipers, the man in the corner, was one of his lieutenants, but he had no intention of informing the Nazis. He was no collaborator, not like that bastard De Jong across the square, throwing open his doors to those scum . . .

Schelhaas sat down. "Evening, Jan. Still cold outside, I see."

"You could say that, Vim. You said you wanted to see me?"

"Yes, I did." Schelhaas glanced around surreptitiously, although he knew that the proprietor would ensure that no-one would be able to overhear their conversation. "We've had a message from London. They want us to get some information for them."

"What sort of information?"

Schelhaas looked appraisingly at the younger man. Kuipers had been a pupil of his only six years ago. The war had ended Kuipers' studies as an aircraft engineer and designer; typically, the Nazis had decided to use his skills but only as an assistant mechanic on a Luftwaffe airfield. Kuipers was brave and resourceful—he had already provided the Voltimand group with a good deal of valuable information which had then been passed on to London—but he was also young, with the impetuosity of youth. He might take unnecessary risks . . . Schelhaas sighed; he had no real choice. It had to be Kuipers. "You work on the night fighters, don't you?"

Kuipers nodded. Verwijk airbase, where he worked, was about eight kilometres from Leiden and was used by a Staffel of Junkers Ju88 night fighters.

"Do you know anything about any radar sets being carried by the aircraft?"

Kuipers frowned slightly and then nodded as if he had just found the answer to a problem that had been bothering him for some time. "I think I know what you're talking about. All the Ju88s are carrying quite large antennae on their noses nowadays. It must make them bitches to fly. I always assumed they were part of their radio gear—it's not really my speciality—but yes, they could be part of a radar installation."

"According to London, these aerials would be quite complex, much more so than ordinary radio. Is that the case?"

"Yes."

"It sounds as though they are what London is after. They would like more detailed information on the equipment. Not just the aerial array but also the actual electrical gear."

"What—a description or pictures?"

"Ideally, a photograph or a drawing."

Kuipers blew out his cheeks. "Not easy. I can get a good look at the external aerials but I'm rarely allowed inside the fuselage and then only when under supervision. You'd have to arrange for the supervisor to be called away, or something."

"That might be arranged. The point is, could you smuggle a camera or drawing instuments into the base?"

Kuipers looked dubious. "I think it would have to be a camera. It would take too long to sketch the equipment accurately."

"A camera would be more dangerous. You'd never be able to explain it away if it's found."

Kuipers shrugged. "A pencil and paper would be just as incriminating, as far as the guards are concerned."

"Could it be done? Without taking too many risks?"

Kuipers nodded. "Security is not very tight, really. We're searched at random intervals when we come in and go out but if we wait until the day after one of these checks, it should be safe enough. They've never yet had a check two days running."

"You're sure of this?"

"Well, no," Kuipers admitted. "All I'm saying is that the odds are very heavily against it. Worth the risk, I'd say."

"Unless they tighten up security."

"Not with Gottlieb and Halldorf in charge."

Schelhaas nodded agreement. Gottlieb was the Luftwaffe Area Security Officer, responsible for all the Luftwaffe installations in the Leiden area; Halldorf was in charge of security at Verwijk itself. Neither man was exactly enthusiastic about his appointment. Gottlieb preferred to spend his time indulging his pleasures in Leiden's restaurants and brothels, while Halldorf seized every available opportunity to go riding or shooting; as a result, security at Verwijk was lax. "There is one thing, though," said Schelhaas. "There's a rumour that Gottlieb is due to be replaced. Marika's picked up a whisper at Gestapo HQ but we can't be certain. If it's true then his successor might be less dilatory."

"Then we'd better set it up as soon as possible then, hadn't we?"

Schelhaas stared at Kuipers for several seconds and then nodded. "I'll try and devise a way of distracting your superior. Who would it normally be?"

"One of three. Heynckes, Niedermann or Schramm.

Depends on which shift is operating. Why? Will that be relevant?"

"It could be," said Schelhaas enigmatically. "But I think I know how we can do it once you get the camera inside the base."

Kuipers grinned in anticipation.

Behrens looked gloomily around the office, ignoring the man who had escorted him up from the street entrance. So this is what you get for upsetting Luftwaffe generals and their daughters, he thought sardonically. A piddling little office on what used to be the premises of a Dutch law firm. Luftwaffe Area Security Officer; hardly what one would expect for a holder of the Knight's Cross but there it was. Still, he reflected, it could have been worse; if it had not been for that coveted award, he might now have been en route to a concentration camp.

He became aware that his escort—what was his name? Ludwig?—was talking. "The black telephone is your outside line, Herr Major. The red one is a direct link to Luftwaffe Headquarters in The Hague and the green one is the internal line."

Behrens nodded absently. Ludwig was one of his assistants, an overweight, balding Unteroffizier who, he suspected, had managed to ingratiate himself with Gottlieb. Behrens had two assistants: Ludwig and a man named Ziegler, who was apparently at Gestapo HQ in Leiden at the moment: "We were not expecting you until tomorrow, Herr Major," Ludwig had said almost accusingly.

Which was why Behrens had arrived twenty-four hours early, of course: he wanted to see how his subordinates behaved when unsupervised. Thus far, he had not been over-impressed. Ludwig gave the impression of feathering his own nest, of liking a quiet life. One thing that Behrens had been told back in Berlin was that Gottlieb was being replaced because of his negligent attitude: Ludwig certainly did not appear to be the sort of man who might have encouraged his superior to be more conscientious.

"And this is your filing cabinet, Herr Major. The key is in the top left hand corner of your desk."

"Do you have a duplicate key?"

"Naturally, Herr Major." Ludwig seemed surprised at the

question.

Behrens stared intently at the other man. He supposed it made sense for Ludwig to have keys as wells but—was it normal practice? He decided to let it go for the time being. "Very well. And these files contain—?"

"Details of the installations that are your responsibility, Herr Major. The main one is Verwijk Airfield, of course, but there are also three Himmelbett radar stations as well as various anti-aircraft emplacements. We have personnel lists as well as details of equipment for each of them."

"And the local Resistance?"

"I beg your pardon, Herr Major?"

Behrens sighed testily. "What information do we have on them? Where are the files?"

"Oh, I see, Herr Major. That's the Gestapo's jurisdiction. They handle that side of things."

"Are you saying that we have nothing on file about the Resistance?"

"That's correct, Herr Major. As I said, we leave all that to the Gestapo."

Behrens turned away. It sounded as though Gottlieb had succeeded in arranging a cosy, untroubled existence for himself; let the Gestapo look after the Resistance, by all means—less work for himself that way.

The internal telephone rang suddenly. Behrens moved to answer it but Ludwig was right next to it; before Behrens could take a single step, Ludwig had picked up the receiver. Clearly, he was used to doing so; Behrens began to wonder if Gottlieb had actually done anything at all.

Ludwig spoke a couple of brief sentences and then replaced the telephone. "Apparently Sturmbannführer Kreissner is on his way up, Herr Major. He is the head of the Gestapo in Leiden."

"I am fully aware of his identity, Ludwig," said Behrens curtly. "In future, Unteroffizier, you only touch these telephones at my specific request unless I am not actually here. Is that clear?"

Ludwig was taken aback by the silky menace in Behrens' voice. "Why—yes—of course, Herr Major."

And another thing, thought Behrens: how did Kreissner

know he had arrived? Had Ludwig been in contact with the Gestapo?

Sturmbannführer Kreissner was of medium height, with a stocky build; he would never have been accepted for the Waffen-SS, Behrens noted sourly. He would probably run to fat in a few years' time but now, in his mid-thirties, Kreissner looked fit and muscular. It was the eyes that Behrens especially noticed; they were grey, icy cold and calculating. Behrens suspected that Kreissner was ambitious and probably unscrupulous. Mind you, he thought, one had to be both to become a Strumbannführer in the Gestapo.

"May I take this opportunity of welcoming you to Leiden, Major Behrens?" Kreissner's gaze settled briefly on the Knight's Cross. "It is indeed an honour to have someone with such a distinguished record working here in Leiden."

Which is a pretty unsubtle way of reminding me that I'm in disgrace, thought Behrens. "I'm pleased to be here, Sturmbannführer Kreissner."

"Major Gottlieb and I succeeded in establishing an effective working relationship, didn't we, Unteroffizier?" said Kreissner, glancing at Ludwig, who nodded uncomfortably.

"Yes, you did, Herr Sturmbannführer."

"We drew up clearcut areas of responsibility," Kreissner continued. "It saved duplicated efforts, which, I'm sure you will agree, Herr Major, are such a waste. Much more efficient to have as few overlapping areas as possible. I like to think it worked very well and that the arrangement will continue to operate."

"I am always in favour of efficiency, Herr Sturmbannführer," Behrens replied, wondering if Kreissner would realise he was being evasive.

"I understand that this is your first security appointment, Herr Major?" said Kreissner smoothly. "If you need any help or advice, please do not hesitate to ask me. I shall be happy to oblige."

And that puts me firmly in my place, thought Behrens; the seasoned professional talking to the novice. "You are too kind, Herr Sturmbannführer."

"Well, I shan't take up any more of your time," said Kreissner. "I'm sure you'll be wanting to find out what's what. But remember what I said about contacting me. Unteroffizier Ludwig knows my number."

"Thank you."

After Kreissner had gone, Behrens realised that he had developed an immediate dislike for the Gestapo man; he did not trust him one little bit. Behrens was convinced that Kreissner would not be completely open about any information he might possess; he would only pass on whatever he thought the Luftwaffe ought to know, which might be nothing at all. Evidently, Gottlieb had been happy about the situation but Behrens was not.

Like it or not, Behrens decided, Ludwig was going to have to work for a living from now on. The Leiden Area Security Office might be only a backwater as regarded the German war effort but it was going to be run as efficiently as possible; and one of the ways this could be achieved would be by making it as independent of the local Gestapo as possible.

Kreissner would not like it, of course, but Behrens was totally unconcerned about that; indeed, the thought of annoying Kreissner was a positive incentive.

Kreissner was aware of a quiet glow of satisfaction as he returned to his office at Gestapo Headquarters. He felt he had put Behrens in his place rather well; he had not had to resort to any unpleasantness but had still left Behrens in no doubt as to who would be calling the tune. Damned fighter ace, thought Kreissner; probably thought he could come down here, throwing his weight around, just because of that bloody medal round his neck. So what difference had it made if he'd shot down a hundred and fifty Russians? It hadn't had any effect, had it? The Russians were still advancing, despite all these pampered heroes of the sky, while the real work of the Third Reich was being done by men like himself, true Party members. Well, this glory fly-boy would soon find out what was what . . .

Kreissner sat down at his desk and picked up the typed report that had been left there. He skimmed through it rapidly and then threw it down in disgust. Nothing. Not one single damned lead at all. A month of investigation and there was still no evidence available concerning local Resistance activities; but Gestapo HQ in The Hague was convinced that there was a partisan cell active in Leiden and Kreissner agreed with this analysis.

The problem was that this cell was not attracting attention to itself; fuel dumps were not being blown up, nor were trains being derailed, but it was increasingly obvious from counter-intelligence sources that information was being passed to the Allies concerning military installations in the Leiden district. No death or glory tactics, just a quiet, effective information gathering operation; that was the hallmark of this cell.

Moreover, they were avoiding contact with any other Resistance group; had they done so, they would have been arrested long since. But this group worked alone; indeed, Kreissner was not even certain if it was a group or just one man; he tended to favour the group theory because the information being obtained was too diverse for one agent but he had no proof either way. Not only were they not connected with any other Dutch cell, it was increasingly likely that they were not even being run by SOE. Every line of enquiry had come to nothing; he had absolutely nothing to give The Hague but they expected results, and fast.

He sighed. They were going to have to widen their enquiries. Every single Dutchman employed on or near military installations would have to be investigated as well as those working for the Occupation civil hierarchy; a time-consuming task.

There was a knock on the door. "Come in," he called.

An attractive young woman entered, carrying a bundle of files. She was of medium height with blonde hair, very blue eyes and an excellent figure. "Scharführer Kunne asked me to bring these up to you, Herr Sturmbannführer."

"Thank you. Fräulein Schuurmann, isn't it?" Kreissner had seen her several times around the building; she was one of the Dutch workers, employed as a typist in the pool on the ground floor.

"Yes, Herr Sturmbannführer." Her German, he noted, was fluent, albeit with a definite Dutch accent. She really was quite beautiful, he thought . . .

"And your first name, Fräulein?"

She blushed prettily. "Marika, Herr Sturmbannführer."

"Well, Marika, it's nice to see a pretty face around here for a change. It brightens the place up."

She flushed a deeper red but her pleasure at his compliment

was evident to Kreissner. For a second, her eyes met his and he saw an unmistakable look of invitation in them. It was only for the merest instant, then it was gone, but he knew it had been there.

"Thank you for bringing these up, Marika." He deliberately stressed her name.

"My pleasure, Herr Sturmbannführer." And there it was again, that look of sultry invitation as well as the barest emphasis on 'pleasure'. Then she left, closing the door behind her.

Kreissner started at the door. Interesting. And intriguing. He would consult her file; one could never be too certain when dealing with a beautiful Dutch girl but if all went as he expected, then . . .

He had been thinking for some time about appointing a personal secretary, purely to handle the non-secret correspondence and documents; it would be an ideal opportunity to get to know Marika Schuurmann more—intimately.

# CHAPTER 4

**VERWIJK AIRFIELD 10.15 hours**

Jan Kuipers wiped his hand across his brow then picked up his toolkit and walked under the fuselage to the starboard engine. He glanced at Obergefreiter Schramm, who was lounging against the side of the hangar, smoking a cigarette, and looked quickly around to see if anybody else was in sight. His face was inscrutable, betraying none of the tension gnawing at his insides.

It looked as though this was the chance they'd been waiting for. The Ju88 was parked on its own around the side of the hangar, out of sight of the Command huts and barracks. Only one man on the airfield could actually see Kuipers at the moment and that was Schramm himself. There might never be a better opportunity . . .

The camera was in his tool box, where it had been for the last five days since Kuipers had smuggled it past the guards at the main gate, concealed in his jacket pocket. There had been a full-scale security check the day before that, which was why Kuipers had chosen that day to bring the camera in. Even so, despite his confident assertion to Schelhaas that there would not be full-scale searches two days running, he had felt a dryness in his throat as he had walked up to the gates. If they had gone through his pockets, he would have been finished . . . but the guards had merely glanced at his pass and waved him through.

Since then, he had lived on tenterhooks; he had left the camera in his tool case together with a large throwing knife, about which Schelhaas knew nothing, and he had been expecting to hear the Gestapo knocking on his door at any moment. All anyone had to do was to open the box and he would be a dead man.

But nobody had done so. Not for the first time, Kuipers

blessed Major Gottlieb and his subordinate Halldorf for their incompetence. It remained to be seen how this newcomer Behrens shaped up, though . . . He could hardly be as negligent as Gottlieb, thought Kuipers as he began to unscrew a nut on the engine cowling.

He muttered a low curse as the wrench slipped from his grasp and fell with a clatter on the tarmac. He bent down to retrieve it, his back to Schramm, and made a thumbs up gesture, apparently to the empty sand dunes, before straightening up and turning back to his work.

The gesture was seen by a man lying full length in the spiky grass some three hundred metres away. He had a pair of powerful Zeiss binoculars glued to his eyes; like Kuipers, he had realised the potential of the situation. His name was Piet De Briess and he had spent the last five days at that precise spot, waiting for excactly that signal. He scrambled back down the slope out of sight of the airfield and began to scrabble amongst the tufted grass, taking out a portable radio transmitter/receiver. He flicked it on, holding the headphones to his ear.

"Prodigal calling Father," he said into the microphone.

"Father here," replied the voice in the 'phones.

De Vriess said only one more word: "Schramm."

"Acknowledged. Out."

Schelhaas switched off his set and replaced it in its hiding place behind a false panel in the wall. He picked up the telephone on the desk and gave a four digit number to the operator.

"Hallo? Leiden Station," said a woman's voice.

"May I speak to Mynheer Schrijvers, please?"

"I'm afraid he's out at the moment. Can I take a message for you?"

"No, thank you. I'll call back later."

"Very well."

Lena Maas broke the connection and took a deep breath. This was it, then. The brief conversation on the telephone had, in fact, been a coded exchange. The use of the name Schrijvers had identified Schramm and her reply that Schrijvers was out would tell Schelhaas that she was alone in the office and could thus place the call. Had this not been the case, the entire operation would have had to be aborted.

But not today. Lena worked in a small office next to the Station Supervisor's, her duties being to man the switchboard in addition to typing and acting as part-time secretary to Kriek, the supervisor. Normally, Kriek was always finding excuses to drop in to see her but today he was down at the Town Hall. She had the place to herself.

She plugged in an outside line and gave a number to the operator. Within seconds, she heard a voice replying:

"Hallo, Luftwaffe, Verwijk."

Normally, Lena spoke fairly good, but accented, German but this was a pretence; when she wished, she could pass as a native German. This was one of those occasions . . . "This is Gestapo Headquarters, Leiden. My authorisation is Isar Four Two."

"Authorisation confirmed. How may I help you?" Even over the telephone, Lena could hear a distinct tone of unease in the man's voice; nobody liked dealing with the Gestapo.

"I understand you have an Obergefreiter Schramm stationed on the airfield. Would it be possible for him to be brought to the telephone for a few moments?"

"It may take a few minutes," said the voice dubiously.

"I'll hold on."

"Very well. I'll try to get hold of him."

"Thank you."

Kuipers heard the bell of the telephone clamped to the hangar wall as he finished replacing the cowling; all in all, the whole process had taken only five or six minutes from his original signal. Schramm went to answer it, lifting the receiver off its wall mounting. As he listened, Schramm's expression changed visibly to one of apprehension; he then replaced the telephone. Without a word to Kuipers, he walked around the corner of the hangar and out of sight.

Kuipers wandered, apparently aimlessly, away from the aircraft until he could see Schramm's receding figure walking hurriedly towards the main buildings; he then walked back to his tool case and opened it. He took out the camera and, after a moment's hesitation, the throwing knife; he slipped the knife into his boot.

Kuipers inhaled slowly, deeply, to calm his nerves and then

began to take photographs of the aerial array around the night fighter's nose. After he had taken several from different angles he looked around again.

There was still no-one in sight.

Kuipers hesitated an instant longer and then climbed up the ladder to the cockpit hatch. Taking one more look around, he disappeared into the aircraft.

Schramm was so preoccupied with wondering what the Gestapo wanted with him that he was about halfway to the Command Building before he remembered that he had left Kuipers working alone on the Ju88. Strictly speaking, of course, he was not supposed to do that, although Kuipers was reliable enough and had worked unsupervised before without mishap. But there was a new Security Officer in Leiden and, by all accounts, he was an entirely different proposition to Gottlieb. Better if he covered himself, just in case . . .

His problem was solved as he saw Oberschutze Dorfmann.

"Hey, Dorfmann!"

"Yes, Obergefreiter?"

"Go and keep an eye on Kuipers. He's working on the plane round the other side of Number Two Hangar. Make sure he doesn't go inside, right?"

Dorfmann nodded sullenly and set off towards the hangar.

Schramm went straight to the main switchboard as soon as he reached the Administration Building; it did not do to keep the Gestapo waiting. He picked up the telephone, took a deep breath and said, "Hallo? Obergefreiter Schramm speaking."

"Did you say Schramm?" said a woman's voice.

"Yes, I did. Obergefreiter Schramm."

"There has been some mistake. I asked for Obergefreiter Schrantz."

"Schrantz? I don't know of any Schrantz here."

"You're certain of that?"

"Of course I am," said Schramm testily and then remembered who he was talking to. "There is no Obergefreiter Schrantz on this base," he added carefuly, in a more respectful tone.

"I see. I'd better check again. Goodbye," the voice said curtly. The line went dead.

Schramm stared at the receiver in a mixture of indignation and relief. Rude cow, he thought. Still, what else could be expect from the Gestapo?

Kuipers took one last photograph and then moved towards the hatch; be began to climb down the ladder. It had been relatively easy to find the radar equipment; the operator and the pilot sat back to back. He had taken half a dozen pictures before deciding that he had pushed his luck far enough. This would have to be sufficient for London; he slipped the camera into his overalls.

He had just reached the ground when he heard the shout.

"Kuipers! What do you think you're doing?"

"Shit . . ." Kuipers murmured. He saw the soldier about fifty metres away; it looked like Dorfmann and there was no doubt at all that he had seen him emerging from the plane. There were only two choices; he could either run or bluff it out. But the first option was no option at all; Dorfmann had a Schmeisser machine pistol slung over his shoulder. Kuipers would be lucky if he got twenty metres before being cut down.

He waited while Dorfmann came up, unslinging the Schmeisser.

"Well, Kuipers? What were you up to?"

"Faulty circuit," said Kuipers glibly. "Been trying to trace it for ages. Has to be inside so I went and had a look."

"You know damned well you're not supposed to go inside the aircraft without authority."

"Yes, I know. I'm very sorry." Kuipers' voice oozed contrition; Dorfmann looked to be in an ugly mood and had to be placated.

Dorfmann glared suspiciously at Kuipers. "Move away from the ladder," he said curtly. "I want to see that you haven't been up to anything in there."

Kuipers shrugged and did as instructed.

"Further. Go on, move!"

Kuipers backed away until there were ten metres between himself and the other man. Dorfmann clambered up the ladder and then looked inside. It was only a brief glance, lasting no more than two seconds. Kuipers bent down as if to tie his shoelace. Dorfmann glared at him again but, seeing the innocence of the action, said nothing. He looked through the hatch once more.

Kuipers' hand closed over the throwing knife and pulled it out of his boot. As he straightened up, he felt a momentary hesitation: this was cold-blooded murder.

There was no alternative. Dorfmann was clearly suspicious and would probably take him to the guardroom for a thorough search; it would only take seconds for them to discover the camera. Even if, by some improbable chance, Dorfmann accepted his story, he would still report the incident to Schramm when he returned and that bastard would undeniably insist on the search.

No; Dorfmann had to be dealt with. It was Kuipers' only chance.

But it was still murder . . .

Kuipers' right arm whipped forward; the knife glinted in the sunlight and then buried itself in Dorfmann's back. Dorfmann gasped and sagged heavily against the ladder. He looked over his shoulder at Kuipers, an expression of incredulity on his face and then toppled slowly backwards.

Kuipers never knew if the dying man's finger tightened on the Schmeisser's trigger through sheer reflex or whether Dorfmann was making one last attempt to shoot his killer, but the final result was the same: there was a deafening staccato clatter as the machine pistol fired a three-second burst into the air. The sound must have been audible all over the airfield.

Kuipers sprang forward, scooped up the Schmeisser and began to run.

Gefreiter Karl Mundt had just finished checking and cleaning the MG34 on the Kubelwagen. It was his pride and joy, that machine gun, which was normally bolted onto a tripod mounting in the back of the vehicle. Nobody really knew how the weapon had come to be on the base at all but Mundt had claimed it for his own and, by constantly badgering the Feldwebel, he had been given permission to mount it on one of the base's four Kubelwagens—provided he looked after the damned thing himself. Mundt had needed no second bidding; daily, he stripped, cleaned and reassembled the gun with loving care.

"Finished?" asked Dehner, the driver.

"Yes. She's ready for action."

"She? It's only a bloody gun, not a woman. Mind you, you treat that damned thing better than a woman. I reckon you'd—"

Dehner never completed the sentence: it was interrupted by the unmistakeable sound of gunfire. "What the devil—?" said Dehner, twisting round in the direction of the sound.

Mundt saw the running man first, as he sprinted towards the perimeter fence about four hundred metres away. "Get that engine started!" he yelled but the order was redundant; Dehner was already cranking the starter handle.

The engine caught first time. Dehner leapt into the driving seat and was accelerating away as Mundt fed the ammunition belt through the breech, feeling a burst of exhilaration: this was it, this was when he'd show everybody who'd laughed at him . . .

He looked ahead, seeing the running figure; their quarry was almost at the perimeter fence, some two hundred metres away. The Kubelwagen was lurching from side to side on the uneven surface; accurate shooting would be impossible but he lined up the barrel as best he could and squeezed the trigger.

Kuipers heard the Kubelwagen's engine behind him, the sound rapidly increasing in volume, and glanced over his sholder. As he did so, he saw Mundt taking aim and threw himself to one side as the MG34 opened up. Kuipers rolled and then loosed off a short burst from the Schmeisser.

Dehner cursed and swerved instinctively, throwing Mundt's aim off as the Schmeisser's bullets screamed past. Kuipers scrambled frantically towards the fence, looking for the hole he and De Vriess had cut eight days before. Glancing behind him again, he saw that the Kubelwagen had swung round and was only about fifty metres away now. He ducked as Mundt opened fire again, the shells flinging up earth and sand all around the young Dutchman.

Kuipers tasted the bitter tang of defeat. He was lying in a shallow depression and so was momentarily safe from the machine gun, but all they had to do was to keep him pinned down for the next ten seconds or so; after that time, they would be virtually on top of him. There was only one chance left—but he had to move fast.

He twisted round until he was lying on his stomach facing

the oncoming vehicle and lined the Schmeisser up on the Kubelwagen's windscreen. Ignoring the bullets that were slamming into the soil before him, he fired a long burst, holding the machine pistol firmly as it kicked in his hands.

The windscreen shattered; Dehner reeled back, clutching his head, his face a bloody mask. The car slewed round and heeled over, rolling onto its side and slithering to halt. Kuipers saw Mundt as he was thrown into the air but he was back on his feet before Mundt crashed into the earth.

Where was the bloody hole? Where was it?

There!

Almost sobbing with relief, Kuipers pulled the wire mesh strand apart and plunged through the gap. He began to clamber up the slope of the sand dune beyond the fence, grinning fiercely in exultation.

He had done it.

Mundt had landed awkwardly but he had rolled with the impact, absorbing the worst of its force. As he picked himself up, he was aware of only one thought: to stop that Dutch bastard. He ran back to the overturned Kubelwagen, ignoring Dehner's shrieks of fear and agony, and bent over the MG34.

It took less than three seconds to unclip the weapon; he had practised this countless times already in idle moments and could have done it blindfolded. He hefted the gun onto the car's body and swivelled it round until it was pointing at the fugitive on the far side of the fence. He'd get the bastard yet . . .

Kuipers was almost at the top of the dune when he heard the burst of machine gun fire; a split second later, he screamed as two bullets slammed into his right shoulder throwing him forward, still screaming, as he clutched at his shattered shoulder. He could feel himself slipping downwards, inexorably, could sense his consciousness ebbing away and tried to reach inside his overalls for the camera. If he could throw it into the dunes, perhaps De Vriess . . .

But the blackness came first and his inert body rolled untidily down the slope, in a tangle of arms and legs, to lie sprawled against the perimeter fence.

# CHAPTER 5

**VERWIJK AIRFIELD 11.15 hours**

Behrens climbed out of the car and cursorily acknowledged the salutes, heading straight towards Oberleutnant Halldorf, the senior security officer at Verwijk.

"Well, where is he?" asked Behrens without preamble.

"In the hospital quarters, Herr Major. He was hit twice in the right shoulder but he's still alive. The bullets smashed the bone, which is why he passed out, but the surgeon's stitched the wound up. He'll live." As he spoke, Halldorf was leading the way to the airfield 'hospital'; in reality, it was nothing more than a simple corrugated iron hut.

"Is he conscious?"

"Yes, Herr Major."

"And fit to answer questions?"

Halldorf's surprise was only too evident. "Yes, Herr Major."

Behrens looked intently at him. "Is there something wrong, Oberleutnant Halldorf?"

"Well, Herr Major, I assumed you would leave all that to Sturmbannführer Kreissner. He's on his way, after all."

Behrens halted in his tracks. "He's what?" he demanded in a low, menacing voice.

Halldorf glanced uneasily at Ludwig, who was following them some two metres behind. "He's on his way, Herr Major, to interrogate the prisoner."

"And how does Sturmbannführer Kreissner know about this incident?" asked Behrens icily.

"Standing order, Herr Major," Halldorf replied nervously, glancing again at Ludwig.

Behrens turned round slowly and glared at Ludwig. "Explain, Unteroffizier."

"Standing orders from Major Gottlieb, Herr Major. Any security infringements were to be reported to Sturmbannführer Kreissner immediately. The order is still in force, Herr Major."

"I see," said Behrens expressionlessly. "Cancel that order, Unteroffizier, as from this moment."

"Jawohl, Herr Major!"

Behrens turned back to Halldorf. "Take me to see the prisoner, if you please, Oberleutnant Halldorf." He spoke with exaggerated formality.

Behind him, Ludwig and Ziegler exchanged significant glances. They had already suspected it but now they knew; Behrens was no Major Gottlieb.

Kuipers' face was pale and drawn but his eyes, as they stared up at Behrens, were alert, expectant, defiant. Behrens doubted if the prisoner would reveal anything useful. Not here, anyway; no doubt Kreissner would be able to extract information from him at Gestapo HQ but Behrens wanted answers now.

"Very well, Kuipers. Let's get straight on with it, shall we? What were you doing with that camera? What exactly were you photographing?"

Kuipers said nothing; he merely glared up at Behrens in mute defiance.

Behrens nodded slowly. "I see. Then let me point out one or two facts of life to you, Kuipers. If you refuse to co-operate, then I shall be compelled to hand you over to the Gestapo. I'm sure I don't have to tell you how they behave, do I? You'll talk then, believe me—or what's left of you will. You know that as well as I do. On the other hand, if you co-operate now, I'll arrange for you to be transferred to military custody."

Still Kuipers said nothing but now his eyes showed not only defiance, but also contempt.

Behrens looked away. It had only been a forlorn hope at best; he had no experience of interrogations, after all. It was at this moment that the door opened and Ludwig came in. "Sturmbannführer Kreissner's just arriving, Herr Major. His car's outside."

"Very well, Unteroffizier. Ask him to wait in Oberleutnant

Halldorf's office for a moment." He turned back to Kuipers. "Did you follow that, Kuipers? The Gestapo are here. Now make your mind up, once and for all. Who is it to be? Me . . . or them?"

Kuipers still said nothing but his eyes, grim, determined, said it all. Behrens nodded heavily in unspoken understanding and went out.

Kreissner was standing at the window in Halldorf's office as Behrens entered. "Ah, Major. There you are. Is the prisoner ready?"

"Ready for what, Sturmbannführer?" asked Behrens, as if bewildered.

"To be taken to Gestapo headquarters," said Kreissner irritably. "That is why I have come here, as you no doubt know."

"I'm afraid that is quite out of the question," said Behrens firmly. "Kuipers was a Luftwaffe employee and is now a Luftwaffe prisoner, arrested on a Luftwaffe airfield. As far as I can see, he falls under my jurisdiction."

"Then let me point out to you the actual situation, Major. Kuipers is quite clearly a member of a Resistance group and thus comes under the jurisdiction of the Gestapo, whose responsibility it is to investigate any such activities."

"Really?" asked Behrens levelly. "Would you mind telling me what evidence you have that Kuipers belongs to any Resistance group? I was under the impression that there was no Resistance activity in this area; certainly you have led me to believe this. If you had any suspicion that a Resistance group was, in fact, in existence, then I could have taken appropriate measures. Is this your idea of shared information?"

"Your security should be cast-iron at all times, in any case. Which, quite evidently, it was not, as Kuipers managed to smuggle a camera past your guards, didn't he? I call that lax security, Behrens."

"At least we caught him, which is more than the Gestapo seem able to do!"

Both men were angry now, glaring at each other. Each man now knew that they were confronting a determined enemy; the battle lines had been drawn.

"Very well, Major Behrens. If that is the way you want it,

so be it. I take it you refuse to hand over the prisoner?"

"Correct."

"Then I shall have to gain the necessary authorisation—which I'll get, mark my words. Your lack of co-operation in this matter will be noted."

"Then do so. Until then, Kuipers stays here under my jurisdiction."

Kreissner went to the door. "You'll regret this, Behrens. You're treading on very dangerous ground. Just remember that."

"I shall take your words to heart," Behrens replied ironically.

Kreissner flung the door open and stormed out, brushing past the astonished Ludwig in the corridor.

Behrens let out his breath in a long sigh. Why the devil had he done that? He knew damned well that Kuipers would have to be handed over eventually, so why stir up unnecessary trouble? To give himself a little longer to question Kuipers?

No. That was not it at all.

It was nothing more than pure bloody-mindedness. A trial of strength, one he knew he would lose, but which would let Kreissner know he was a different proposition to his predecessor.

Marika Schuurmann had been sitting on the park bench for about ten minutes when Schelhaas appeared, walking slowly along as if enjoying the crisp Spring day. To anyone watching as he sat down on the bench, it would have appeared to be an entirely innocent meeting but a closer observation would have revealed the agitation on her face.

"They've got Jan," she said tersely. "Kreissner's put him in a cell at Gestapo Headquarters."

Schelhaas nodded heavily. So now they knew. De Vriess had seen the entire incident from his vantage point but had been powerless to intervene. He had not been able to say whether Kuipers had been dead or alive but now they knew the truth: Kuipers was alive and under interrogation. The entire cell was in jeopardy for the first time in its existence.

"What happened, exactly?"

"He was captured by the Luftwaffe but then Kreissner

pulled rank and took him to Gestapo Headquarters. I gather he and Behrens—he's the new Luftwaffe Security Officer—had a full-scale row about it but Kreissner won in the end, unfortunately."

Schelhaas stared bleakly at the ground. Kuipers was bound to talk sooner or later; he was a brave man but the Gestapo knew their business. It might take days, it might take weeks or even months, but they would break him and he would betray his comrades, not because he was a coward, but because such things as patriotism and loyalty would lose any meaning for him. All that would matter to him at the end would be how to prevent the next crippling blow from the rubber truncheons, how to stop the current being turned on again . . . There was a breaking point for everyone and he would reach it, ultimately. It was only a matter of time.

Which left Schelhaas and his cell with only two alternatives. They could just disappear, using the Lifeline organisation: they could be in London inside a month at the most, safe and sound. No-one would blame him. No-one.

But he knew how effective his cell was. Guthrie had told him how much they relied on the cell's reports in London and Schelhaas knew, ignoring false modesty, that Guthrie was telling the truth. If they ran for it, then all their good work would come to nothing.

And they would be running away.

But the alternative . . .

"How are you getting on with Kreissner, Marika?"

If she was surprised by the question, she gave no sign of it. "I've been transferred from the typing pool to his office. I handle his non-secret mail but I can often manage to look at the more important material."

"That's not what I meant, Marika."

"No," she sighed. "I don't suppose it was. You mean, is he trying to seduce me? Yes, he is. Nothing too serious at the moment but there have been a few not so subtle hints."

"Can you take the relationship further?" Schelhaas' voice was totally without inflection, as if he were discussing the weather.

"Now just a minute, Vim. The idea was that I was just to become his secretary so that I could get into his office. Just to flirt with him. No more than that."

"I know, Marika, but the situation has changed. I want you to gain his confidence, to be able to exert some influence over him."

"You know what you're asking me to do, Vim?"

"Yes, I know."

"You're asking me to seduce him! To sleep with him!" she protested. "He's loathsome!"

"It is essential, Marika," said Schelhaas gently. "Somehow, you've got to get inside Jan's cell. If you can manage that any other way, fine, but I think you'll have to become more closely acquainted with Kreissner to do that."

"Stop mincing words, Vim! 'More closely acquainted'! You're asking me to become his mistress, for God's sake!"

"I know I am, Marika. But it is essential. You must find some way to get into Jan's cell."

"Why?" Then an awful wave of realisation swept over her. "Oh God, no, Vim! You can't mean that! He's your friend, Vim! How can you?"

"Because there's no alternative, Marika!" She was taken aback by the look in his eyes; cold, determined. "He can blow the entire network."

"But—isn't there any other way?"

"I wish to God there were. We can't mount a rescue operation, Marika. We just don't have the weapons or the training. We'd lose more than just Jan if we tried it and we still might not get him out. And that would blow the whole cell wide open, anyway."

"Damn the bloody cell! Not only are you asking me to go to bed with that pig Kreissner but you're asking me to kill Jan as well! Who the hell do you think you are!"

"What would you have me do, Marika? Each and every one of us knew the risks when we joined the cell. If Jan talks, then we're finished. We could all end up in Gestapo Headquarters with him. We could simply run away, yes, but what good would that do Jan? They'll still have him and they'll still torture him. He'll die anyway, but slowly." He paused and then added heavily, "At least this way it'll be quick."

She stared at him, hardly able to believe what she was hearing. Vim Schelhaas, the kindly schoolmaster, was calmly discussing the murder of a friend and colleague, someone he had known for years. Did she really know Schelhaas at all? Could he actually be as callous as he appeared?

But the sickening thing was that he was right. If the cell were to remain in operation, then Jan had to be silenced.

Permanently.

She shook her head. "I don't know if I can do it, Vim."

"I'm not asking you to do it yourself. All I'm asking is for you to smuggle a capsule into his cell. The rest will be up to him."

"They're bound to suspect me, though, Vim. Haven't you thought of that?"

"True," said Schelhaas slowly. Even if Kuipers delayed taking the capsule, Kreissner would still remember that she had been in his cell; she would be the number one suspect. "Unless . . . unless we implicate someone else." He thought for a few moments and then said, "Leave it with me. I think I can offer Kreissner a more convincing suspect. You'd be left in the clear."

"It's not only that, Vim. It's Kreissner. Having to—you know."

"It may not come to that. You may be able to gain his confidence with—I don't know—vague promises, perhaps. But remember—" he added gently, "this was your idea in the first place."

"I know, I know." She herself had suggested the notion of leading Kreissner on so that she could get closer to him and to his papers. "Don't remind me." It had always been a possibility, she knew, that she would have to take it further. But this . . . "My God, Vim. What's happening to us? What are we turning into?"

"I know, Marika. It's this bloody war." He looked around at the park as if needing reassurance, some indication that what they were fighting for was worthwhile. You had to cling to that thought, she knew. Especially now—especially now. "I don't think we'll ever be the same again, Marika. But it has to be done."

There was a long silence before she spoke, very quietly. "All right, Vim. I'll do my best. Just tell me it's right."

"We're doing a good job here, Marika," Schelhaas said,

not looking at her. "You know that. In London, they're relying on us to keep the information coming through. It may not be much but it's our contribution to getting rid of these Nazis. We all made our choice, Marika. We could all have done nothing, left it to someone else, taken the easy way out. But we didn't. We decided to fight, even though it might cost us our lives. A soldier in an army isn't given the chance to run away at the first sign of danger but that's our only alternative if we don't do anything about Jan. Can we run away and live with ourselves afterwards? Leaving Jan in the hands of the Gestapo, just to save ourselves? If we want to carry on fighting, then we must do this dreadful thing."

She sighed deeply. "I know, Vim. I know. I just wish—" She broke off.

"Yes?"

"Nothing," she said, her voice artificially brisk. "I'll try and get the capsule to Jan, whatever it takes. The point is, Vim, will he take it?"

Schelhaas nodded. "Yes, he will," he said bleakly.

Marika stared at him for several seconds. "I suppose knowing that ought to help me feel less guilty, Vim." She looked away and said, almost to herself:

"But it doesn't."

Behrens stared incredulously at the printed card; it was an invitation to General Neuberger's birthday reception in three days' time. It was not so much the invitation itself that amazed him; as a ranking Luftwaffe "ace", he could hardly have been left off the guest list, even though he was in unofficial disgrace. It was the menu that staggered him; clearly, no expense had been spared to provide virtually every exotic delicacy imaginable. Quail's tongues, for heaven's sake! Caviar and pheasant! No wonder we're losing this bloody war.

Ludwig, sitting opposite him as they sorted through the hefty pile of documents that Gottlieb had left behind and which still had not been cleared, saw his expression. "Is something the matter, Herr Major?"

Behrens was about to voice his disgusted disapproval of the extravagant menu when he had second thoughts. Ludwig was far too liable to pass on snippets he had overheard, if he thought it might do him some good. He was not slow to report the shortcomings of others and there was no reason to suppose that he would not repeat any rash statements made by his superior officer. Behrens modified his comments accordingly.

"This menu for General Neuberger's reception on Friday. It's very impressive."

"Indeed, Herr Major?"

"Indeed. I wonder where they get it all from?" Behrens mused idly.

Ludwig hesitated and then his natural ingratiating manner asserted itself; that, and the desire to stir up trouble for someone else. "Unteroffizier Ziegler might be able to answer that question, Herr Major," he said with a slight smile.

"Really?" asked Behrens, his tone utterly indifferent.

"Well, I can't say for certain, of course, Herr Major, but Ziegler does seem to know where to—ah—find various items, if they're in short supply. If you know what I mean," he added as a sly afterthought.

"I know exactly what you mean, Unteroffizier," said Behrens sharply. "Are you suggesting that Ziegler is involved in illegal activities?"

"Good heavens, no, Herr Major," Ludwig replied unconvincingly. "I make no accusations at all."

No, you wouldn't, reflected Behrens, staring at Ludwig as if he had just found him under a stone. All you do is make nasty little insinuations without ever committing yourself.

All the same, Behrens decided, it might be worth talking to Ziegler . . .

Ziegler was a stocky, cheerful man, with a ruddy, open face; Behrens had found him quite likeable, as well as efficient, but he had learned never to rely on first impressions; he had once met Reinhard Heydrich and he had had the face of a choir boy.

"You sent for me, Herr Major?" said Ziegler, closing the door behind him.

"Yes, I did, Unteroffizier. Do sit down." He indicated the chair in front of the table and waited until Ziegler had taken his seat before continuing. "I'd like to discuss the arrangement you had with Major Gottlieb, in fact."

Ziegler frowned. "Arrangement, Herr Major?"

Behrens smiled good-naturedly. "I can understand your—ah—discretion, Ziegler, but, believe me, it isn't necessary. Major Gottlieb has told me all about the various items you obtained for him. The food, the cases of schnapps at, shall we say, bargain prices? The addresses and telephone numbers of available young ladies? He was very impressed by your abilities, you know, Ziegler. Very impressed indeed." He smiled warmly at Ziegler, who had a definite air of indecision. "I'm a man of the world, Ziegler. I know these things go on—we all do, don't we?—and, to be perfectly honest about it, I'm glad they do. I mean, life would be pretty unbearable if it weren't for these little luxuries, wouldn't it? All I'm saying is that I see no reason why the arrangement you had with Major Gottlieb should not continue."

Behrens could almost read Ziegler's mind as he struggled to come to a decision. Thus far, Behrens had been bluffing, taking a gamble that there had been some sort of unofficial arrangement between Gottlieb and Ziegler. It was a reasonable bet, given what he knew about Gottlieb, but it would be difficult for him to maintain the pretence if Ziegler decided to call his bluff.

"Well, Herr Major," said Ziegler slowly, "it is true that Major Gottlieb did ask me to obtain some items from time to time."

"Items that were, shall we say, difficult to obtain through the usual channels?" asked Behrens, smiling conspiratorially.

"Well—yes, Herr Major."

"And would you be willing to obtain these items for me, Ziegler? For a reasonable fee, of course."

"I'd be glad to, Herr Major."

Behrens' voice changed abruptly. "On your feet, Unteroffizier! Stand to attention!" he barked.

Completely bewildered, Ziegler shot to his feet and snapped to attention. Behrens stood up and walked slowly around the desk. "Do you realise, Unteroffizier, that you could be shot for what you've just told me?"

Ziegler swallowed nervously. "Yes, Herr Major."

"And you damned well will be, if you don't answer my questions! Is that clearly understood?"

"Yes, Herr Major."

"I hope it is, Ziegler. Firstly, who else is involved?"

Ziegler hesitated.

"I mean it, Ziegler. I'll have you shot! You know the punishment for black market activities as well as I do. Well?"

"Oberscharführer Brandt, Herr Major. He works at Gestapo headquarters, Herr Major."

"Oberscharführer Brandt," repeated Behrens. "And who else?"

"Major Gottlieb, Herr Major."

"He took part as well?"

"No, not exactly, Herr Major. He took a cut from us—for turning a blind eye, you see."

"Yes, I do see," said Behrens grimly. "This Brandt—what does he do?"

"He's on Sturmbannführer Kreissner's staff, Herr Major."

"He is, is he?" Suddenly, it was crystal clear what he should do with Ziegler; the Unteroffizier could be put to very good use now . . .

"Very well, Ziegler," he said, after a pause calculated to be lengthy enough to make the Unteroffizier sweat. "I have a proposition to put to you. From time to time, I too shall require items from you—items of information from Gestapo headquarters, to be precise. I want you to obtain these items from Brandt. I don't care how you do it, just get that information. Understood, Ziegler?"

"Yes, Herr Major."

"And if you don't, Ziegler, then I report you. Is that also understood?"

"Yes, Herr Major."

"Good. Now, the first item I shall require is a report on the interrogation of a Dutch prisoner being held there. His name is Jan Kuipers."

# CHAPTER SIX

## GENERAL NEUBERGER'S RESIDENCE

"Major Behrens!" the ornately uniformed major-domo announced in stentorian tones. Behrens was aware of two things in the same instant; that every eye in the hall was focussed on him and that his missing left hand was itching again. The outburst of applause took him by surprise; evidently, his fall from grace was not widely realised. As far as the majority of the guests was concerned, he was still a celebrity: the Scourge of the Ivans.

"Welcome, Major! Good of you to come!" said a corpulent man in the uniform of a Luftwaffe General; presumably, this was General Neuberger, in whose honour this entire junket had been staged.

"My pleasure, Herr General," Behrens replied formally. He could sense a certain constraint behind Neuberger's bonhomie; exactly how did you deal with a holder of the Knight's Cross who was in unofficial disgrace? Your problem, General, not mine, he thought savagely. "May I wish you a happy birthday?"

"Thank you, Major. You are very kind." He seemed to see someone behind Behrens. "Please excuse, me, Major." He left Behrens to greet some new arrivals. Behrens drifted across the floor, heading towards the bar.

He was overwhelmed by a sense of *déjà vu*; the ornate fittings, the velvet drapes, even the guests themselves seemed to be carbon copies of those at the Berlin reception. He decided that he would only stay as long as courtesy demanded.

He caught sight of Kreissner, in full SS dress uniform. Momentarily, their eyes met and a look of naked hostility passed between them. Kreissner bowed sardonically and then pointedly turned away. Behrens wondered how his interrogation of Kuipers was progressing; Ziegler had not yet been able to uncover anything.

"Er—Major Behrens?" The voice was hesitant; Behrens turned to see a fresh-faced Luftwaffe Leutnant with two other pilots behind him.

"Yes?"

"Leutnant Brinkmann, Herr Major. Stationed at Verwijk." He held out his hand; Behrens shook it, feeling vaguely uncomfortable. There was no mistaking the hero-worship in Brinkmann's eyes, which seemed irresistibly drawn to the Knight's Cross at Behrens' throat. Did I stare at Molders like that? Behrens wondered. Probably did, come to think of it.

"Pleased to meet you, Leutnant Brinkmann. And your two friends?"

"Leutnants Grabowski and Jurgens," said Brinkmann, carrying out the introductions. "We've heard a lot about you and your achievements, Herr Major."

Behrens shrugged awkwardly, by now thoroughly embarrassed. "I merely did my duty, Leutnant." Good God, he thought, I sound as pompous as old Haller! "And what aircraft are you flying?"

"Ju88s, Herr Major. Night fighters."

"I see. Rather more difficult to spot your targets, then? I never had that problem, of course."

"Well, the 'Liechtenstein' radar does make it easier, Herr Major—" Brinkmann broke off guiltily and glanced around, aware that he had been indiscreet.

Behrens let it pass; he doubted that there were any Allied agents listening to the conversation. "How long have you been at Verwijk?" he asked, to fill the awkward pause.

"Four months, Herr Major."

"Any successes?"

"Well, actually, yes, Herr Major. A Lancaster."

"And Leutnants Grabowski and Jurgens?"

They shook their heads mutely.

"Ah well. Maybe soon." God in heaven, he sounded like a benevolent old uncle. Behrens doubted if he was much more than five or six years older than any of these three. Yet they seemed so young, idealistic. Was I ever like that? Behrens wondered. I suppose I was, two or three years back, staring wide-eyed at Molders. What will these three be like in two years' time?

Probably dead, he thought with a chill.

Neuberger's voice cut across the conversation abruptly. "Telling them how to become an ace, eh, Major?"

"Trying to," said Behrens, turning around.

"Excellent, Major. Actually, there's someone I'd like you to meet." Neuberger indicated the young woman by his side. "My daughter, Trudi."

This can't be happening, thought Behrens incredulously; this is Berlin all over again. "Charmed, Fräulein Neuberger," he said formally, clicking his heels and kissing the proffered hand.

"Pleased to meet you, Herr Major."

The three pilots had somehow melted into the crowd, aware that their presence was not required.

"Look after Major Behrens for a moment, would you, Trudi?" said Neuberger and then he too disappeared.

Trudi Neuberger was about twenty-five or six and tall, with long, very dark hair. Her eyes were green but with gold flecks; they were the most striking feature of a face that was pleasant, rather than beautiful. The black evening dress showed off a trim figure. She wore no rings; remembering Klara Haller, Behrens was immediately on his guard.

"Well, Major, do I pass?" Her tone was cool, amused; Behrens realised that he had been staring at her like an adolescent. He flushed, cursing his gauche behaviour.

"I'm sorry, Fräulein Neuberger. I didn't mean to be rude."

"Please don't apologise, Major. It's not every day I get such admiring looks, especially from such a celebrity as yourself."

Behrens winced, inwardly; he was convinced she was mocking him, even though her voice seemed to contain no more than a light bantering tone. "You surprise me, Fräulein. I would have thought that you would be accustomed to receiving admiring glances from all sides." He would give as good as he got, he decided.

"Thank you, Major. You are too kind." Her voice was neutral; formally polite, Behrens decided.

There was an awkward silence, before Behrens said, "Do you like Leiden, Fräulein Neuberger?" He cursed himself; he was about as suave and sophisticated as a sixteen year old boy on his first date. Out of practice, or had she unsettled him? he wondered.

"I don't really know," she replied. "I've only been here about ten days. I'm staying with my parents for the next few weeks. It certainly seems very different from Berlin."

"True," agreed Behrens, wondering how he could extricate himself from this conversation: he knew he was handling it badly. "Rather quieter."

"Indeed. Although this seems on a lavish enough scale. Quite as big as in Berlin."

Behrens wondered how many receptions she had attended in Berlin and felt a sudden flush of resentment. She was another Klara Haller, a high-living parasite. All the bloody same, he thought viciously, but said nothing. There was a further strained silence; he felt he ought to say something but had little inclination to do so.

The orchestra had stopped playing; the couples dispersed, making their way from the dance floor back to their tables. The music began again, a foxtrot.

"Aren't you going to ask me to dance, Major?" she said, looking directly at him, her expression unreadable.

Condescending bitch, thought Behrens. "I'm afraid I would make a poor partner, Fräulein Neuberger," he replied with icy formality. "I regret that my injuries have put an end to any such activities. Now, if you'll excuse me?" He bowed with exaggerated courtesy and then spun on his heel. As he headed away from her, he deliberately accentuated his limp, aware of the childishness of the gesture but unable to restrain the impulse.

Enough was enough. He was damned well going home, now. He would probably be in it up to his neck anyway with Neuberger when his precious daughter told him about the way she had been treated, so leaving the reception early would make little difference.

Despite himself, he began to smile wryly. This was becoming a habit, this walking out of official functions . . .

"Listen, Kuipers. Listen to me. I am rapidly running out of

patience. Do you understand me?" Kreissner glared down at the moaning figure strapped into the chair. Kuipers' face was a ruin, a mass of bruises and blood. He could no longer open his left eye, his lips were puffed and swollen and he had lost several teeth; he had already undergone numerous beatings. On top of that, his interrogators had worked mercilessly on his wounded shoulder; it had now been damaged so badly that it was unlikely that he would ever be able to use or even move that arm again.

And yet he had not told them anything. Not one solitary fact, after days of intensive—"sharpened"—interrogation.

Kreissner shook his head in reluctant admiration. Kuipers was a determined man; but so was Kreissner, even more so now that Gestapo Headquarters in The Hague were putting pressure on him. Von Krug, his superior, wanted concrete results, positive information and so far, Kreissner had nothing to give him.

"You may think that what we have done to you so far is bad enough," Kreissner said dispassionately. "Believe me, Kuipers, we have hardly started. Do you understand?"

"Go to hell, Kreissner," Kuipers mumbled wearily.

Kreissner sighed and nodded to one of the SS guards standing behind the chair. The guard raised his rubber truncheon and smashed it down onto Kuipers' right shoulder.

The scream was deafening; Kuipers' entire body arched back in agony but as he sank back into the chair, he still said nothing. Kreissner muttered a low curse. Kuipers would break, eventually; he would only be able to take so many nights without sleep, so many beatings, but it was a question of whether this happened before von Krug took over. Kreissner could not permit that to happen; he wanted the kudos himself.

And this Dutch bastard wouldn't talk . . .

He was aware of an intense rage building up inside him and controlled it with an effort. Blind, unreasoning anger would serve no purpose at all here; indeed, it would probably be counter-productive. If Kuipers so much as suspected that his continuing defiance was provoking frustration in his interrogator then it would stiffen his resolve. All the same, Kreissner found it difficult to restrain himself from smashing his fist into Kuipers' face.

The door opened and an SS trooper came in. "Yes?" asked Kreissner impatiently as the trooper saluted.

"There's an internal call for you, Herr Sturmbannführer. From your secretary."

Kreissner sighed. What the hell did she want? Then, his irritation at being disturbed gave way to a sense of pleasurable anticipation. What, indeed, did Marika want? And why was she still here this late in the evening? Suddenly, all sorts of interesting possibilities presented themselves: the message itself would probably be unimportant but her actual presence here was an unexpected cause for optimism. As he left the interrogation room to take the call, Kreissner had a vivid mental image of Marika, naked . . . Perhaps those enigmatic, inviting glances were about to fulfill their promise.

"Sturmbannführer Kreissner speaking."

"Herr Sturmbannführer, this is Marika Schuurmann. There's been a signal for you from Standartenführer von Krug. It's marked Urgent, but someone's just put it into your mail tray and left it. Shall I bring it down to you?"

She really had a very sensual, husky voice, thought Kreissner. "Er—no. I'll come up." He replaced the telephone and turned to the trooper. "Take the prisoner back to his cell."

Marika swore softly as she replaced the receiver; she'd been foiled. The message from von Krug had, in fact, arrived that afternoon but she had held it back, waiting until she knew that Kreissner would be interrogating Kuipers. It had been worth suggesting she bring the message down; Kreissner might have been so engrossed in the questioning that he would not have wanted to leave.

But it had not worked; now, she would have to think of some other way to gain access to Kuipers. Deliberately, she did not allow herself to think beyond that, to admit that she was arranging Jan's death. She was simply trying to arrange that, for a few moments, she would be in the same room as him.

Easier said than done, however . . .

Kreissner came in, smiling at her. His expression was only too easily read and she felt her stomach turn over. This might be it; the time when she would have to stop flirting with him and go on to the next logical, if unpleasant, step.

"You're working late this evening, Marika?" He glanced at the clock; it was almost eight o'clock.

Marika smiled in return, trying to make it look as natural as possible. "I had a lot of things to do, Herr Sturmbannführer. I had just about finished when I noticed the letter. I thought you'd probably want to see it immediately." She held out a sealed envelope. "I hope I acted correctly, Herr Sturmbannführer," she added demurely.

"Of course you did, my dear Marika." He opened the message and rapidly scanned its contents. It was nothing vitally important, merely a copy of the proposed new security restrictions, along with a request for any comments or suggestions he might care to make. It could easily have waited; had he been making any progress with Kuipers and had it been anyone else but Marika, Kreissner would have been furious at the interruption. As it was, however . . .

Marika went to the door, where her coat was hanging. "If you'll excuse me, Herr Sturmbannführer?"

"You're not leaving?" asked Kreissner with an air of mock levity.

"Well, I've finished for now, I think. Unless the Herr Sturmbannführer requires me for anything?"

Dear God, thought Kreissner feverishly. As if the words themselves were not suggestive enough, the tone of voice, the expression on her face, even the way she held her body spoke volumes. He was virtually being propositioned, he realised. "Perhaps there is something you could do for me, Marika," he said carefully.

"Certainly, Herr Sturmbannführer. What is it?"

Dammit, thought Kreissner, aware of the sudden loss of nerve that always seemed to afflict him at moments like this; I can't just ask her outright to come to bed with me. "I was wondering if perhaps I could escort you home?" He winced inwardly at the stilted tone of his voice; he had never been very sure of himself with women, even at the best of times. He saw the instant confusion in her eyes, mingled with surprise, pleasure—and fear. "We could perhaps stop for a meal on the way. Or have you already eaten?"

Marika shook her head. "No, Herr Sturmbannführer, I haven't. You are too kind. But—" She broke off and looked down at her feet, plainly embarrassed.

"But what?" His voice was flat, expressionless.

"Well—what if we were seen together? I mean—" She paused. "What I mean is—well—you know what people say about Dutch girls who go out with German officers." She spoke in a low mumble, her words barely audible, her eyes apparently glued to the floor.

Kreissner stared at her. The bitch was turning him down. Unless she genuinely was worried about being seen in public with him . . . "Very well, Marika. How about a dinner for two, in my quarters? My batman is an excellent chef. You won't be disappointed by the meal and nobody will see you."

She shook her head slowly, firmly. "I'm sorry, Herr Sturmbannführer. It just wouldn't be right." Her tone was one of righteous virtue.

Kreissner felt the fury boiling up in him. First Kuipers and now this. The little cow had been leading him a dance, egging him on with her provocative looks and veiled innuendoes . . . a right tease. Only she'd gone too far this time. He'd show her.

"Come with me," he said curtly, seizing her wrist and pulling her after him.

"What—what are you doing? Let go, you're hurting me!" she protested.

"I'll do much worse than this if you don't co-operate, you little bitch!" he snarled, half dragging her out of the office and down the stairs. "If you think you can play games with me—"

Marika said nothing despite her agitation. It was beginning to look as though her hastily improvised plan might actually work, after all . . . Kreissner was responding exactly as she had hoped.

And yes, they were going down to the underground cells. She saw the look of shocked amazement on the guard's face at the foot of the stairs as they went past but the young trooper evidently thought better about saying anything. They passed through a heavy iron door; beyond it was a second guard, seated behind a table, who shot to his feet, astonished. Kreissner ignored him as he yanked Marika after him.

She had never been down here before; the entire basement had been rebuilt and now consisted of six prison cells with a central corridor. At the far end of the passageway was the interrogation room; for one heart-stopping moment, she was convinced that Kreissner was taking her there but he stopped in front of the last cell door on the right. He gestured impatiently to the second guard, still rigidly at attention; he marched briskly up to them.

"The keys, Hauser," said Kreissner curtly.

"Herr Sturmbannführer!" Hauser held out the bunch of keys as though he were still on parade.

Kreissner unlocked the door and flung it open. He was still holding her arm and he propelled her through the door with such force that she nearly fell. A prisoner was lying on the bunk, his back to them. Kreissner nodded to Hauser, who had followed them in; Hauser barked,

"Kuipers! On your feet!"

Kuipers turned over slowly and sat up on the bunk before hauling himself slowly, laboriously, to his feet. Marika cried out involuntarily as she saw his face; he was almost unrecognisable. He had obviously been beaten up several times, judging by the livid bruises and welts, not only on his face, but also across his chest and shoulders; what was left of his shirt was saturated with blood. She felt the bile rising in her throat; she had known it would be bad but not as dreadful as this . . .

"One of your countrymen, Marika," said Kreissner, a note of silky menace in his voice. "He has been unco-operative, you see."

Marika's hand was up to her face, stifling a scream; very little of it was play-acting, she realised distantly.

"So you can see," Kreissner continued theatrically, enjoying the situation, "it might not be too wise to antagonise me, Marika."

Suddenly, without any warning at all, Kuipers hurled himself at Kreissner, his left fist slamming repeatedly into the SS officer; Kuipers was yelling incoherently in rage as Kreissner fended him off awkwardly. Hauser grabbed Kuipers and hauled him away but the Dutchman spun round and lashed out with his foot, catching Hauser on the hip. Hauser swore and swung his rifle at Kuipers, the butt slamming into Kuipers' already broken jaw. Kuipers reeled back, gasping in pain and fury and then lunged in again at Hauser, his left arm flailing wildly.

Marika forced herself to act; Kuipers had realised why she

had come and was deliberately distracting attention from her but the fight would surely be over in a matter of seconds. She moved sideways as though avoiding the struggling men: three steps and she was next to the bunk. Her hand dived into her jacket pocket and closed on the capsule; she removed her hand and put it behind her back.

Kreissner was holding his chin, staring at Hauser and Kuipers; he had not noticed her movement at all. He took his Luger from the holster at his waist and moved towards the two men. As he raised it to bring the butt down on Kuipers' head, Marika turned away abruptly, her hands to her face. She dropped the capsule and flicked it under the bunk with her foot.

Kuipers cried out and she saw him fall heavily forwards. Kreissner kicked Kuipers in the ribs as he lay helpless on the floor; she hid her face again. Kuipers lay very still as if dead.

Kreissner went over to Marika, his earlier smooth urbanity had completely disappeared, to be replaced by pure venom. "Don't cross me, girl, or you'll be in for a dose of the same treatment. Is that clear?"

She nodded, trembling almost uncontrollably.

"And—?" Kreissner said impatiently.

She said nothing: she was shaking too much.

"And—?" Kreissner said again, but more loudly.

Her reply was almost inaudible. "All right," she whispered. "You win. I'll do" she took a deep breath, "anything you want."

"Good." Kreissner's tone was brisk, businesslike. "Then let's go, shall we?" He pushed her gently in front of him. She walked out unsteadily, averting her eyes from the huddled form on the floor. Kuipers had not moved at all after that kick in the ribs. Perhaps he was dead, after all, perhaps he would not need to take the capsule . . . She felt disgusted by her thoughts; she was actually hoping that kick had killed him so that her conscience could be clear . . .

Kreissner ignored Kuipers as he left; he would repay him the next time round. And he had more important business to attend to, anyway . . .

As they walked along the corridor, Kreissner slipped his arm possessively around Marika's waist.

Kuipers lay motionless for several minutes after the cell door closed. He was not actually unconscious, although the blow from the Luger's butt had almost laid him out, but it was as well to let Hauser think that he had been badly hurt, otherwise the bastard might just come in to finish the job . . . In any case, it would make his next move all the more convincing.

Slowly, painfully, he dragged himself across the floor until he reached the bunk. He attempted to haul himself up onto the bed but evidently the effort was too much for him; he collapsed, his left arm flopping lifelessly under the metal frame.

Kuipers could only see out of one eye but it was sufficient: the capsule was about half a metre under the bank. Reaching out, he grasped it, pulling his hand up to his face.

He could do it now, end the whole thing . . . They couldn't stop him now, just put the pill into his mouth, bite once and the cyanide would take effect in seconds. He would be dead, even before Hauser could get the door open.

And then Marika would be dragged into the interrogation cell, screaming. It would be only too obvious how he had obtained the poison . . . He had to wait until enough time had elapsed to divert suspicion from Marika or it would all be for nothing. At least forty-eight hours, he reckoned.

Two more days, then. Probably four beatings, maybe more. But he could take them now, knowing that he now had the means to escape, that he could end it whenever he wished.

He shivered involuntarily as he realised just what that 'escape' really meant.

Kreissner sat back on the sofa and watched Marika undress, relishing the look of terror on her face. Like a frightened rabbit, he thought, with a tingle of pleasurable anticipation. And she really did have a superb body as was becoming increasingly evident.

Marika removed her petticoat; now, all she wore was a brassière, panties, stockings and a suspender belt. She bent forward and began to unfasten the suspenders.

"No. Leave them on. The stockings."

She straightened up, aware of his eyes on her body. He gestured impatiently: she understood and unhooked the brassière, dropping it to the floor, revealing her breasts without any coquetry or any hint of invitation. She was not acting the part of a wanton seductress but that of a reluctantly compliant possession. Not that she needed to act, she thought, with an inward shudder.

"And the rest," said Kreissner softly, hoarsely.

She slid her panties down her legs and stood before him, naked, staring at the floor. Marika could not meet his eyes but knew that they would be on her body. Again, she wondered if she could go through with it . . .

She pushed the thought away; she had to, that was all there was to it. Kreissner must not be permitted to think too clearly about tonight's events, about the fact that she had been in Kuipers' cell. He must, at all costs, be distracted and the only way to do that was to let him think he had been successful in his treatment of her, that his threat had worked . . . She had to go through with it, so that when Jan—did—what he was going to do, then she would not be implicated. Think of it that way, Marika, she told herself. You're doing it to save your own life.

Even so, it was not easy, when his hands started to caress her body, pawing at her. It was even worse when he finished undressing; she almost cried out, no, I can't do it, not for Jan, not even for myself, no . . . But she said nothing, just stared at him as he came towards her as a rabbit would look at a snake. He pushed her onto the sofa, his weight pressing down on her. She could feel the tears on her cheeks; it was even worse than she had imagined. Yes, she had foreseen the pain, the disgust, but not this feeling of utter self-loathing; how could she be doing this with a man like Kreissner, after what he had done to Jan?

And what had she, herself, done to Jan? She had given him the means to kill himself. She was an accomplice in his suicide: she was helping to kill him . . .

Marika closed her eyes tightly. Had she really come to this? It was no good telling herself that Kuipers had to die, that he would take the capsule willingly, gladly. Useless to tell herself that she had given Jan his only means of escape. Useless; as far as Marika was concerned, she had helped to kill Kuipers and had then gone to bed with his torturer.

In her own eyes, she was a murderess.

And a whore.

**LONDON**

Cathcart decided that Wing Commander Ryan looked even more harassed than he had on his previous visit. Not surprising, perhaps: by all accounts, last night's air raid had suffered unprecedented casualties. Nevertheless, Cathcart's face showed no expression at all as he shook Ryan's hand and motioned him to a seat. Ryan nodded to Guthrie, the only other person in the room and then looked expectantly at Cathcart.

"We've bad news for you, I'm afraid, Wing Commander," Cathcart began without preliminaries. "Guthrie has received a message from our contact in Holland. An attempt was made, several nights ago, to obtain photographs of the radar equipment on one of the German night fighters. The agent was, unfortunately, captured as were his camera and films, and he is being interrogated."

"Poor wretch," said Ryan softly and instantly went up in Cathcart's estimation. Ryan must be aware of the wider implications of the information, yet his first reaction had been concern for a man he had never met and whose name was unknown to him.

"It rather torpedoes your request, however," Cathcart prompted gently.

"I know," Ryan said. "Is there no chance of a second attempt being made?"

"None at all," said Guthrie flatly. "They can't possibly try again—they'll be more concerned with survival at the moment. Their entire network could be blown. On top of that, they've queered the pitch for any second try anyway; the Jerries will be on their guard now. Any further attempt would be suicidal and certain to fail."

There was a heavy silence when Guthrie finished speaking. Eventually, Ryan said slowly: "Nevertheless, something must be done. Last night, we lost nine per cent of our bombing force. Fifty-four aircraft. There are now quite definite doubts being voiced by some very influential figures about the bombing campaign and whether it should be continued. We must find out more about that equipment."

Guthrie spread his hands expressively. "And I'm telling you it can't be done. Not by our Dutch contacts."

"You could ask SOE, Wing Commander," said Cathcart.

Ryan glanced sharply at him as if suspecting that he was being mocked but Cathcart's expression was utterly serious. "Much though I hate helping our opposite numbers, they might be able to get something going in Belgium or France."

"Where the Nazis would be just as much on their guard as they will be in Holland, I suppose," said Ryan testily. He thought for a few seconds. "What about a commando raid, like the Bruneval operation?"

Cathcart and Guthrie exchanged looks before Cathcart said, "That's not really our pigeon, Wing Commander."

"I know, I know," said Ryan, "It would have to be cleared through Combined Operations but you have liaised with them in the past. Could it be done, working with your group in Holland?"

"I honestly couldn't say," said Guthrie. "At the moment, I'd say no, not while our contacts are in danger of being blown. However, they are taking steps to preserve their security."

"What exactly do you mean by that?"

Guthrie stared bleakly out of the window as he replied. "They'll try to ensure that their man, the one who's being held by the Gestapo, doesn't talk."

"I see," said Ryan, as he deduced Guthrie's meaning. "If they can . . . do . . . what you say, would they be in a position to help such a raid?"

"We'd certainly be prepared to provide assistance and information, yes," said Cathcart.

"In that case, I shall put the proposition to Combined Ops. I'm afraid that we need the information on that radar badly. And if you or your contacts can't get it, then a full scale raid it will have to be. I'll get over to Combined Ops and see what they say."

Cathcart waited until Ryan had gone before turning to Guthrie. "Well, David? Is Ryan's idea a non-starter?"

Guthrie shook his head. "I doubt it. He'll probably get support from Combined Ops—it's exactly the sort of operation they go for."

"Would it succeed?"

"That's another matter. They'll have to attack a Luftwaffe airfield, which means, almost certainly, a parachute assault.

These airfields have troops stationed to defend them from just such an attack. Not to mention the anti-aircraft batteries; their flak shells would make mincemeat of any descending paratroopers. It could be the biggest disaster of its kind."

"That's if they try a full-scale assault," said Cathcart thoughtfully. "But what about a covert operation? A small commando unit, trained in undercover work, operating with the local Resistance?"

Guthrie considered the idea for quite some time before answering. "It could work, yes. They'd have the training for such an operation and the weapons to fight their way out of it got tough. Given the right leader then, yes, it would be a possibility. Hazardous but feasible."

"I see. I'd better contact Steadman then and see if we can work something out. We'd better present it to Combined Ops before one of their fire-eaters decides to stage a practice invasion of the Low Countries. Or before SOE get wind of it."

Guthrie looked discreetly down at the desk top, barely suppressing a smile. Patently, Cathcart wanted it to be an operation under the auspices of the SIS. That way, Cathcart would gain the kudos and in addition much of the damage to the Service's reputation that had been caused by the Venlo Incident would be repaired.

"Come to think of it," said Cathcart suddenly, "We might even be able to suggest a possible leader of this group. We've used him before now and he speaks fluent Dutch. Damned good record, too."

"Of course," said Guthrie, snapping his fingers. "Cormack. The very man. He'd be ideal."

# CHAPTER SEVEN

**NORMANDY, FRANCE.**

12.53. Seven minutes before the rendezvous and still no sign of the Germans. Despite himself, Cormack felt his hopes rising. Perhaps they would get away with it after all . . . Somewhere out to sea a motor torpedo boat should be groping its way through the darkness towards the beach, its engines on dead slow. It had to be there; they were finished if it was not. Anything could have happened to it; a drifting mine, an engine breakdown, faulty navigation; anything. But it was their one life-line; sooner or later, the Germans would search the beach and if they had not been picked up by then . . . Where was that bloody MTB?

He looked back at the two shadowy figures behind him. Squires was half-sitting, half-lying against the base of a sand dune; his right leg was bandaged at the thigh and he was breathing stertorously. He had lost a good deal of blood and was only just conscious. The other man, Elliott, was pouring a trickle of water down Squires' throat; in a moment of callous anger, Cormack wondered if Elliott was satisfied now. He suspected that the young Lieutenant had been rather disappointed with his first undercover operation in enemy territory; until an hour before, it had all proceeded without a hitch. Cormack was certain that Elliott had volunteered for the SOE out of a belief that their operations were habitually examples of derring-do and reckless courage. Cormack knew better; if you had to shoot your way out of trouble, then it was because something had gone badly wrong. Such as, what had happened at the farm which had cost Marshall his life . . .

They had been landed on the Normandy coast five days before from a submarine and had made contact with the local Resistance group, led by a tall, morose-looking man named Leguin. They had been given a simple brief: they were to examine the coastal defences in the Arromanches area. It didn't take all that much intelligence to deduce that the area was being surveyed as a possible invasion site; Cormack had no doubt that similar exploratory missions had been carried out all along the French Channel coast.

With this in mind, it meant that the fourth member of the party, Lieutenant Squires of the Royal Engineers, was the most important individual in this operation. Squires had made dozens of measurements, sketches and recordings, all of which had been entered in a small pocket notebook. Pages and pages of notes; but there would be even more filed away in his head, observations, opinions, theories. Squires was an expert, that much was obvious; and Cormack respected professionals, which is why he had so much time for him.

And so little for Elliott, but that was by the by. Elliott would learn, given time. And he had certainly behaved well enough at the farmhouse, when those bloody Germans had suddenly appeared in their half-tracks and they had been obliged to run for it. Squires had been hit as they had pelted across the farmyard; Marshall had picked him up single-handed and had virtually thrown him over the low wall behind which Cormack had taken cover, seconds before. And then Marshall had staggered to one side as a volley of bullets tore into him. Elliott had stood in the centre of the yard, coolly returning fire, until he and Cormack had shot out the headlights and the entire scene had been plunged into darkness.

Then Leguin's men had opened up from the farmhouse, raking the German vehicles with automatic fire, lobbing Molotov cocktails from upstairs windows, putting up a devastating covering fire so that the British agents could escape . . . Cormack and Elliott had carried Squires to safety, stopping only to bandage the shattered leg. Yes, Elliott had done well; given a few more missions, he would learn discretion, would learn the tricks of the trade.

And would he then end up like himself? Would he be living continually on his nerves, jumping at noises in the night, telling himself that this was the last time, that he'd had enough? Wondering why he was here at all? Elliott would have no doubts at the moment, of course: he was here on a secret mission that was vital to the war effort and that was more than enough justification.

Not enough for Cormack, though. Not any more. Oh yes, the information they brought back would be . . . helpful. It might even save a few lives, although there would be no way of knowing that: but was that reason enough to stick his head in the noose again? He'd done his share . . . This would be the last time: his nerves were so frayed, he'd be a positive danger if they sent him in again. Or so he told himself.

He shook his head to clear the brooding thoughts. Where was that damned boat?

There. He'd almost missed it, a pinpoint of light out to sea, winking on and off irregularly, flashing a Morse signal: "AC" four times.

Cormack scooped up the flashlight and spelt out the prearranged reply. Seconds later, he read out the MTB's second signal; they were lowering a dinghy to pick them up.

"Right," said Cormack, grinning with relief. "Our transport awaits us. Let's go." Between them, he and Elliott lifted Squires to his feet, each putting one of the wounded man's arms round his shoulders and then the three of them began to make their way awkwardly down the sloping beach towards the sea.

They had travelled only ten yards when Elliott hissed: "Wait! I heard something!"

Cormack froze into immobility. For several seconds, he listened intently but heard nothing beyond the sounds of the sea. "What—?" And then he heard it too; a shouted command.

In German.

Jesus Christ, thought Cormack savagely. To get this close, and then . . . While the despairing thought crossed his mind, he and Elliott were pulling Squires back into the shadows at the foot of the dunes.

Cormack took out the flashlight again and, hooding it with his hand so that it would only be seen from seaward, flashed out a message telling the dinghy to stay put for the moment. He could only hope they'd see it and that they'd have the sense not to acknowledge.

"There they are, sir," Elliott murmured, pointing eastwards along the beach. In the moonlight, the Germans, about thirty of them, were plainly visible, about two hundred yards away. They had come to a halt and one of them was shouting out instructions: Cormack spoke German fluently and found that he could understand every word, the sound carried so clearly.

The orders were quite simple and obvious; Cormack would have issued precisely the same ones had he been in charge of the search party. The soldiers were to spread out along the beach to east and west and were then to move inland at twenty metre intervals. The western edge of the patrol line would find them, without question. Cormack was aware of a sudden dryness in his throat; they had only one option left to them now. The contingency plan.

The suicide run.

Without taking his eyes from the approaching soldiers, Cormack said in a low voice, "You make sure you get Squires into the dinghy, Elliott. I am going to stage a diversion, to draw them away from you. As soon as they start following me, signal the dinghy to come in and then get the hell out of here." The soldiers were beginning to spread out now, half of them heading towards their hiding place. "Is that understood, Elliott?"

There was no reply.

Cormack spun round, suddenly aware of what Elliott had done, knowing what he would find.

Elliott had gone. Disappeared. While Cormack had been watching the Germans, the young lieutenant had slipped silently away.

Cormack had his mouth open to call after Elliott before he realised the utter folly of making any noise at all in the present circumstances. Equally foolish and futile to go after him; someone had to look after Squires and Elliott had decided who that would be. Cormack shook his head slowly in reluctant admiration; he'd see that kid was recommended for a VC, if it was the last thing he did . . .

He crouched down behind Squires, who was clutching his leg, face screwed up in agony. Cormack felt for his pulse, aware that he was merely doing it to take his mind off Eliott; it was strong and regular. He should be all right . . .

The soldiers were coming closer. The Germans were approaching along the shore, guns at the ready, spread out so that they could only be picked off one by one. Every twenty yards or so, the rearmost one would peel off and head towards the dunes: Cormack could not see if they were already moving inland or if they had gone into cover, awaiting an order to proceed in a single line abreast. It was irrelevant, anyway; the nearest German soldier was less than fifty yards away now and their probing torch beams would be certain to pick out the two fugitives.

Come on, Elliott, for God's sake! As the thought framed itself, Cormack felt a wave of self-disgust; the instant Elliott opened fire, he would be signing his own death warrant . . .

All the same, thought Cormack coldly, if nothing happens within the next sixty seconds, then Elliott might as well do nothing, try to make his own escape, because it would be too late . . . Cormack lined up the barrel of his Sten on the leading German and began to edge silently away from Squires. The instant that torch beam came within ten yards of the wounded man, Cormack had decided he would open fire. He might just be able to draw them away and then Squires might have the slenderest of chances to escape, even wounded as he was. A thousand to one against? Or more?

But better than no chance at all.

Cormack flicked off the safety catch, switching his aim to the left hand soldier, the one nearest to the sea. A rapid traverse to the right, keeping his finger on the trigger . . . He might get three or four before the others reacted. Then sprint into the dunes, still firing, letting them know where he was going, hoping they'd come straight after him. How long would he have then? Five minutes? Ten? Sixty seconds?

And he'd never know if it had been in vain, if Squires had escaped or not.

Twenty yards now; nearly time. The torch beams were swinging to and fro, ever closer to where he had left Squires. Cormack took a deep breath, squinted along the barrel and began to squeeze the trigger . . .

The sound of the exploding grenades, three in rapid succession, took Cormack completely by surprise, he had utterly forgotten about Elliott. The detonations were about two hundred yards away to the south-east, Cormack guessed; Elliott had covered a good deal of ground.

As one man, the German soldiers froze into immobility and then spun round as they heard the unmistakeable sound of a Sten being fired in a long burst. Seconds later, Cormack heard more weapons joining in: Schmeissers.

To the Germans, it was only too evident that gunfire was being exchanged in the dunes; the British agents had been discovered. The leading soldier bellowed an order; within two seconds, the Germans were pelting away from the two concealed men.

Cormack let out his breath in a long sigh. Elliott had done it, had bought them the time they needed . . . He scrambled back to Squires and took up the flashlight again, aiming it out to sea to send out the recognition signal a second time. A grin of blessed relief creased his lips as he saw the acknowledgment; they were coming in again.

He bent down, putting Squires' arm around his shoulder and lifted him to his feet. Slowly, he half-carried, half-dragged Squires to the water's edge and waited.

The dinghy came looming out of the darkness and then changed direction as its occupants saw the two men standing in the shallows. Cormack began to wade out towards the dinghy. When it was about ten feet away, he recognised the man sitting in the stern; Pollard, the Major who had briefed him on the mission. Willing hands helped Squires into the dinghy as Pollard asked:

"Just the two of you?"

"Yes," said Cormack flatly. "Marshall's dead."

"Elliott?"

Cormack turned his head in the direction of the gunfire. "That's him."

Pollard nodded in understanding. "I see. Then we'd better get out fast."

Cormack made no move; he seemed to be listening to the clatter of automatic weapons inland. Abruptly, ominously, the gunfire was cut off, the echoes reverberating around the dunes. Cormack waited for several seconds to see if there were any more shots and then nodded, almost curtly. "Yes, we'd better go. No reason to stay here, now." His voice was soft but there was no mistaking the bitterness in his words.

He climbed into the dinghy and sat looking out to sea as they pulled away from the now silent shore.

Cormack never once looked back.

**GESTAPO HEADQUARTERS, LEIDEN.**

Marika was aware of a dryness in her throat as she pushed open the street door and walked into the lobby. She went over to the desk and signed in, using the time thus spent to glance around. There were two troopers on duty, one at the foot of the stairway, the other by the door that led down to the basement cells. She ignored them; it was the person standing behind the desk that was important. Thank goodness, it was that pig Brandt; he ought to be easy enough to fool.

She put the pen down and looked up at him; he was blatantly staring down the front of the summer dress she had decided to wear with just this situation in mind. It was easy to read the thoughts running through his mind as he eyed her figure, shown off to good advantage by the tight dress; Marika would have to be searched, before leaving the lobby and normally this would have been done by one of the women SS officers but Brandt often forgot this regulation . . .

Wearing a resigned expression, she held up her arms for the search. Brandt gave a leering grin and came round the desk to her. He took his time over the frisking, his hands fondling the moulded contours of her body.

"Don't let the Sturmbannführer catch you doing that, Unterscharführer," called out the trooper by the stairs, grinning. "He might get jealous."

Brandt smiled good-naturedly. "Nonsense. I'm only carrying out my duty. I have to make sure she isn't smuggling anything in." He looked appreciatively at Marika. "Although I don't see how she could."

"Try between her legs!" the trooper called out.

Brandt grinned lasciviously and put his hand up under her dress, ignoring her sharp intake of breath. "No. Nothing there that shouldn't be," he laughed and then reluctantly withdrew his hand. He looked at her face for several seconds, savouring her expression of fear and disgust and then nodded to her. "Very well, Fräulein," he said formally. "Go on."

She picked up her handbag from the desk and walked hurriedly to the stairs, not meeting anyone's eye; plainly, she wanted to escape her humiliation as rapidly as possible. The three men watched her as she ascended the stairs.

"I'd have that from now to breakfast time," she heard one of the troopers say behind her.

"She'd eat you without even drawing breath," said Brandt. "Takes a real man . . ."

She was careful not to let any of her inner triumph show. She had hated the touch of his hands pawing at her but it had been necessary; he had been so engrossed in fondling her, he had not so much as glanced at her handbag, far less look in it, as he should have done. If he had, it would have been fatal.

Because, in the handbag, she was carrying a wad of banknotes tied together by string. Had it been discovered, she would have been hard pressed to explain why she was carrying a thousand Reichsmarks in used notes . . .

**LEIDEN: THE CANAL.**

Jongbloed glanced at his expensive Swiss watch and began to pedal harder. If he was late then Hauser would be in a foul mood. He was a bastard to deal with at the best of times but a man had to make a living somehow. The Gestapo were hardly the most desirable employers around but Jongbloed would far rather have them on his side than not . . .

Though why Hauser was in such a hurry, God only knew. Jongbloed had found the scribbled note pushed through his letter box that morning, telling him to be on the canal wharf round the back of Jansen's Mill at five o'clock sharp. Jongbloed knew the area; it was a derelict strip of land, once used as a store yard for the mill, but disused ever since the mill had been virtually destroyed by shellfire back in 1940. It was a lonely, desolate area but it suited Jongbloed; he preferred to meet Hauser as far as possible from any prying eyes. He would rather not have the fact that he was a Nazi collaborator become public knowledge.

There was nobody to be seen in the yard as he rode in. He dismounted and propped the bicycle against the yard wall; there was no sign of Hauser. He'd said the wharf, however; Jongbloed walked rapidly across the concrete, which was already fragmenting, with grass growing through the cracks. The wharf was some fifty metres away, partly hidden from view by a ramshackle hut that had once seen service as a watchman's shed; Hauser would probably be waiting behind it.

He heard a sound behind him and turned to see two cyclists riding across the yard towards him. With a start of surprise, he realised that the leading man was Vim Schelhaas, the teacher. What was he doing here?

Realisation struck him then. It was a trap. He began to run back towards his own bicycle but the second rider was already braking to a halt, cutting him off. Jongbloed came to a halt, staring at Schelhaas as he pulled up, and dismounted. The other rider stayed on his bicycle, ready to pursue Jongbloed if he made a run for it.

Jongbloed could feel his heart pounding as Schelhaas came towards him. He began to back away.

"Waiting for someone, Jongbloed?" Schelhaas asked, almost pleasantly.

"W-What do you want?" Jongbloed stammered.

"You," replied Schelhaas and Jongbloed cried out involuntarily as he saw the silenced automatic in the other man's hand. "Now just do exactly as I say, Jongbloed. Keep your hands down by your side. Turn around and walk towards the wharf."

Jongbloed obeyed, forcing his legs into motion; they were beginning to tremble violently. He knew what was going to happen: they were going to kill him, here and now, and there was absolutely nothing he could do about it . . . Ahead of him was the abandoned shed, while beyond it, he knew, was a stretch of open ground leading to the wharf. The canal was only about twenty-five metres away to his left; they were approaching it at an angle.

Jongbloed forced himself to remain calm as he realised that he had been granted one last chance to escape. He was about five metres ahead of Schelhaas and they would be passing very close to the shed. If he were to drive round the far corner and run for the canal, he would be hidden from Schelhaas' view for perhaps two or three precious seconds; time enough to reach the canal and dive in. He was a strong swimmer and, given luck, he could escape underwater. A long shot, perhaps, but better than nothing . . .

He was passing the hut now. It was only then that he noticed that he was hidden from view to any observer across the canal. Indeed, he was screened from virtually any vantage point.

Oh God, no . . .

Jongbloed raised one foot to run and then the bullet

ploughed into the base of his spine. He pitched forward onto the concrete, made a feeble effort to lift himself up and then collapsed, to lie unmoving.

Schelhaas gazed impassively down at the dead man. The bastard had been a collaborator, after all; Schelhaas felt no remorse over his killing. His death had been essential, if the plan he had worked out with Marika were to succeed.

He turned as De Vriess came over, riding Jongbloed's bicycle. De Vriess dismounted and then walked over to Jongbloed's corpse; he stared at it for two or three seconds and then spat at it.

"Come on," said Schelhaas. "Let's get rid of him."

They dragged Jongbloed into the hut and wheeled his bicycle in after him. Schelhaas closed the door and then padlocked it. They would return after dark and the body would be thrown into the canal, weighted down by his bicycle and a large slab of concrete that Schelhaas had already earmarked for the purpose.

Jongbloed would simply disappear from the face of the earth, his whereabouts an utter mystery.

Especially to the Gestapo . . .

## GESTAPO HEADQUARTERS

Marika placed the newly typed letter in Kreissner's "In" tray and then took a deep breath. She looked at the wall clock: 7.15. She was due at Kreissner's quarters at eight; she had perhaps thirty minutes. Ample time, if all went well . . .

Picking up her handbag, she went to the door. She glanced around the office, checking that all was as it should be and then flicked off the light. Marika pulled the door closed behind her and locked it, using the duplicate key De Vriess had made for her after she had taken a wax impression of Kreissner's original, several days before.

The corridor was deserted; she had banked on this being the case at this time of the evening. She went to the next door but one along the corridor and, looking uneasily around, tried the duplicate key in the lock. Two seconds later she was inside, closing the door gently behind her.

This was the office of Hauptsturmführer Opitz, Kreissner's subordinate. Knowing Opitz, there were bound to be classified documents on his desk: he tended to leave them there overnight if he had not yet finished with them. Silently, Marika crossed to the large desk. Even though the blackout curtains were drawn, there was still enough evening light spilling around the edges of the drapes for her to read the contents of the files strewn untidily across the desk-top.

The actual contents were irrelevant; all she wanted was one of a sufficiently high security classification. She sighed in satisfaction as she looked inside a buff-coloured folder; she folded it over carelessly and crammed it into her bag before going back to the door. Opening the door a fraction, she checked the corridor carefully before emerging; she pulled the door closed behind her.

Taking her time, she walked to the stairs and descended them, only too aware of the SS trooper on duty at the doot of the stairway. Random security checks were few and far between but you never knew . . .

He merely glanced at her as she passed and then she turned to the right and went through the door at the rear of the lobby; beyond was a corridor that led past the Ladies' toilets. She went in and selected the nearest cubicle, listening intently for over a minute to ensure that none of the others were in use. Then, methodically, she tore the typed sheets of the file into tiny shreds and dropped them into the pan. Repeating the procedure with the manila folder itself, she flushed the toilet several times until the last scrap of paper had disappeared.

Emerging from the cubicle, she went to the fly-blown mirror on the wall. She began to apply her make-up, noting, without surprise, that her hand was none too steady; but the ritual had a calming effect on her. Might as well do it, she told herself, grimly: she still had to meet Kreissner at eight . . .

By the time she came out of the Ladies', the trembling in her limbs had ceased but, instead of heading towards the lobby, she turned in the opposite direction until she came to the door at the far end of the corridor. It was ajar and a light was on beyond it.

This was the Locker Room, which led through to the NCOs Mess. The Mess was probably occupied but the Locker Room should be empty . . . She hoped.

Slowly, she pushed the door further open and went in. If anyone saw her, she was looking for Brandt, she reminded herself; but there was nobody in the room. The Mess door in the far wall was half-open; she could hear a radio and the low murmur of conversation that was punctuated by a sudden, raucous laugh.

Marika made her way rapidly along the rows of metal lockers, reading off the names. She had checked half a dozen before she realised that they were in alphabetical order; typical Germanic organisation, she thought, absently.

Gross, Gunthardt, Hahn . . .

Hauser. The one she was looking for.

And it was locked. Damn!

She rummaged in her handbag and took out a large paper clip which she straightened out and inserted into the lock, remembering how many times De Vriess had coached her at lock-picking. Child's play, he had said. Easy as falling off a log.

But not with who knew how many SS NCOs only feet away and with no conceivable explanation as to what you were doing if any of them were to come through that door . . . Not when your heart's pounding away and your hands are beginning to shake and the damned lock still won't open . . .

She froze as she heard the creak of a chair in the next room. Somebody sitting down? Or standing up? Her eyes were fixed on the doorway but still her fingers manipulated the wire, delicately probing, twisting, testing. The conversation had ceased: were they about to come out? They could not fail to see her . . . Come on, damn you! Open!

There was another laugh, the abrupt sound making her jump, and the low mutter of voices began again. Simultaneously, the locker door swung open.

Only one last thing to do now. She took the wad of banknotes from the handbag and placed it inside the locker, pushing it well to the back under a pin-up magazine. She closed the door and locked it. Ten seconds later, she was back in the corridor, breathing rapidly.

That wouldn't matter; she had nothing incriminating for the guards to find now. And if anyone noticed her agitation, then she was hurrying so as not to be late for Sturmbannführer Kreissner . . .

That one thought was enough to dampen any feeling of elation she might have had.

# CHAPTER EIGHT

**GESTAPO HEADQUARTERS, LEIDEN**

Kreissner glared at Hauser and then held up the banknotes. "And you're saying you know nothing at all about this, Hauser?"

"Nothing at all, Herr Sturmbannführer."

"Then what was it doing in your locker?"

"I swear to God I don't know, Herr Sturmbannführer!" There was an edge of panic in Hauser's voice; Kreissner ignored it.

"And I suppose you know nothing at all about the documents that went missing from Hauptsturmführer Opitz's office last night? Well?"

"I swear—I know nothing, Herr Sturmbannführer!"

"And you expect me to believe that?"

"It's the truth, Herr Sturmbannführer! You must believe me!"

"Why? Give me one reason why I should? I find that a secret file has been stolen and, the morning after the theft, a thousand Reichsmarks are found in your locker—your locked locker, may I add—and you honestly expect me to believe that you know nothing about either fact?"

"It's the truth, Herr Sturmbannführer."

Kreissner snorted in disgust. "On top of that, you were on duty last night, with—correct me if I'm wrong, Hauser—with a complete set of keys. You left the building at ten o'clock, correct? What did you do then? Meet your Dutch contact? Did you hand over the documents in return for the money?"

"I did none of those things, Herr Sturmbannführer. I returned to my quarters. You can check it with the log in the barracks."

"I already have. But it only takes a minute to exchange

documents for money. And you went back to your quarters alone, did you not? In other words, there is a space of some twenty minutes where you have no witnesses to account for your actions. Now, I'll give you one last chance, Hauser. Either tell me what you did with the documents or I'll send you down for interrogation. Which is it to be?"

Hauser's face paled; he knew, better than most, what Kreissner meant by 'interrogation'. "I swear, Herr Sturmbannführer, by my oath to the Führer, that I know nothing about any of this!"

Kreissner sighed and spoke to the two troopers flanking Hauser. "Take him down!"

After Hauser had been frog-marched away, Kreissner stared at the banknotes. Damned stupid place to leave the money, really. Probably didn't think we'd discover the theft so rapidly; under normal circumstances, the file would not have been missed until Opitz had returned his pile of folders to Records. Say 5 p.m. at the earliest, possibly not even then, if Opitz had been running true to form and had kept them overnight. The uncovering of the theft had been pure luck. Kreissner had wanted to take another look at Kuipers' file and had asked Marika to collect it from the Records Section. Marika had said that she thought Opitz had it and so she had gone to Opitz's office. He had been certain that he did not have it; Marika had been just as sure he did and so they had searched through the folders on his desk. It was then that he realised that a priority file was missing and the alarm had been raised, instantly. Kreissner had been informed and within minutes a full-scale search of the building was under way. Half an hour later, the money had been found in Hauser's locker.

Yes. A stupid place to hide it, thought Kreissner. Hauser had, presumably, brought it with him from his quarters when he had reported back on duty at eight that morning. He had probably not wanted to leave it in the barracks; not surprising, thought Kreissner, with the amount of pilfering that went on there. He would have been off duty again at two p.m. and then—a black market deal? A gambling den? A night with a local whore? All three?

It was a damnable mess; and the evidence was by no means conclusive, of course. Kreissner had sent Opitz out to bring Jongbloed in, to see if he knew anything of this. Jongbloed had been supplying Hauser with low-level information for over two years now. Hauser had arrested Jongbloed for black market activities and had given him a straightforward choice: face trial or collaborate. Jongbloed had offered his services with almost indecent haste but now Kreissner began to wonder about that. Who had recruited whom? Was Hauser a double agent in Jongbloed's pay, rather than vice versa? It would be a good trade from the Dutch Resistance's point of view: pass on relatively unimportant or misleading information in exchange for inside knowledge of the Gestapo's activities. It would explain why their enquiries into the local Resistance had not made any progress at all . . .

And why had that particular file been taken? It had contained dossiers on leading collaborators in Leiden, Delft and Haarlem. It would undoubtedly be of use to the Resistance but why had they stolen the documents rather than copying them?

Pointless to speculate. He'd see what Jongbloed had to say.

The telephone rang; he scooped it up impatiently. "Yes?"

"Haupsturmführer Opitz is on the line, Herr Sturmbannführer. He wishes to speak to you."

"Put him through."

"Opitz here, Herr Sturmbannführer. Jongbloed's disappeared."

"He's what?"

"He hasn't been seen since yesterday afternoon. He left his home at just before 4 p.m. and he has not returned since, Herr Sturmbannführer. He's disappeared."

"Right. Round up all his cronies and acquaintances. I want him found, Opitz."

"Yes, Herr Sturmbannführer."

Kreissner replaced the receiver. That settled it; Jongbloed had made a run for it, taking the documents with him. But they'd find him. There was nowhere he could go once his description had been circulated.

And, in the meantime, he still had Hauser to work on . . .

Behrens stared absently at the sheet of paper in front of him; it was covered, for the most part, with meaningless doodles but in the centre there were three lines of writing. One line read simply: "Kuipers". Underneath was written "Radar—K an aviation engineer" and on the third line, in block letters, "ZIEGLER?".

The film that had been in Kuipers' camera had been developed and had confirmed that he had been taking photographs of the 'Liechtenstein' radar equipment. Behrens had not been at all surprised about this; there was nothing else about the Ju88 that would have caused him to take such a huge risk. Behrens could well imagine that the Allies would be desperate for any information about the new radar sets.

Which, in turn, made it extremely unlikely that Kuipers had been working alone. Whether Kreissner wanted to admit it or not, all the evidence indicated that there was a Resistance cell in the area. The very convenient telephone call to Schramm, for example: he doubted that it was mere coincidence unless it had, in truth, come from Gestapo headquarters. Thus far, Kreissner had refused to give him any answer as to whether this was the case or not; as far as the Gestapo were concerned, it was nothing to do with Behrens now. All of his enquiries had met with a blank wall from Gestapo HQ. Which left Behrens with Ziegler and his unofficial sources of information; Behrens had no intention of being frozen out of the affair.

Behrens was aware that he was almost certainly cutting right across boundaries of jurisdiction, but he didn't give a damn. It wasn't just that he resented Kreissner and the way he had taken over the investigation, although he was honest enough to admit that this was at least part of the reason: no, there was more to it than that. Kuipers had killed one of Behrens' own men and maimed another for life; Dehner's jaw had been smashed to a bloody pulp and he would never again talk properly. Although he had never even heard of either Dorfmann or Dehner until eight days before, Behrens felt responsible for them. Security had indeed been lax; Kreissner had been right there and the airfield's security had ultimately been his, Behrens', responsibility. It did not matter that Gottlieb and Halldorf had allowed things to slide; the undeniable fact remained that he, and not Gottlieb, had been the Security Officer when the incident had occured.

So, for his own peace of mind, Behrens had to know what was going on but, to his intense frustration, he knew that there was very little he could do until Ziegler came up with some concrete information. Which might take days or weeks, assuming he could come up with anything at all . . .

There was a knock on the office door. "Come in," said Behrens abstractedly.

It was Ludwig. "There's someone to see you, Herr Major."

Behrens looked up. "Does this someone have a name, Ludwig? Who is he?"

"It's a she, Herr Major. Fräulein Neuberger. General Neuberger's daughter," he added helpfully.

Behrens stared at him, perplexed. What the devil did she want? "You'd better show her in, Ludwig."

She was wearing a pale blue dress, quite simple in design but pleasing to the eye; it suited her, Behrens decided, without quite knowing why. He held a chair ready for her; as she sat down, he dismissed Ludwig, ignoring the latter's raised eyebrows.

"Well, Fräulein Neuberger, what can I do for you?"

"I have come to offer my apologies for my behaviour on Friday night, Major Behrens. I honestly did not know of your injury when I made that insensitive remark about dancing. I really am deeply sorry."

Behrens, taken aback, said nothing for several seconds and then mumbled, "There's absolutely no need for you to apologise, Fräulein. It was my behaviour that was boorish and unforgiveable. It is I who should apologise and I do, with the very deepest regret if you were offended." He was aware that he sounded stilted but was unable to keep the pomposity out of his voice.

She smiled faintly. "Apologies accepted, Major," she said. "I imagine that we both found the occasion rather wearing, perhaps."

"True," he conceded. "That still does not excuse my behaviour."

"Please, Major! Can we not just forgive and forget? I think we would both much rather do that."

Brehrens nodded, relaxing slightly. "If you insist." He grinned wryly. "It's just that I seem to be making a habit of offending people at official functions."

"You don't like them?"

"To be honest, no." Behrens looked at her, considering. He had already realised that she had not actually said anything unpleasant to him at the reception; it had been in his own mind. "I'm glad I've had the opportunity to speak to you, Fräulein Neuberger. I think we—ah—got off on the wrong foot, so to speak."

"Yes, I think we did. Perhaps it would be better if we were to start afresh?"

"An excellent idea," said Behrens airily. "Would you think it very presumptuous of me if I were to invite you out for dinner?"

She smiled again. "I'd be very offended if you didn't,Major. I think it would be a splendid idea."

**LONDON**

Ryan was late, which was unusual for him, but he apologised to Cathcart and Guthrie; he had been detained by an unscheduled meeting with Air Marshal Harris. "You said you've found someone for the radar operation, Sir Gerald?"

"We may have," said Cathcart. "A Captain Alan Cormack.He's a Royal Marine Commando, assigned to Combined Ops and, at the moment, attached to SOE. His record is outstanding; he's been on several undercover operations in France and Belgium and is regarded as one of their top operatives."

"SOE, you say?" said Ryan doubtfully. He hesitated and then continued, "I rather gathered that SOE would be kept out of this."

Cathcart and Guthrie exchanged momentary glances. So it was true: the powers–that–be were finally beginning to perceive SOE's shortcomings, at least as far as their operations in the Netherlands were concerned. "That is precisely the problem," said Cathcart urbanely. "A transfer could, of course, be arranged, or Cormack could simply be returned to Combined Ops, followed by a temporary attachment to SIS—say, as a liaison officer. The point is, Cormack seems ideal. He's resourceful, experienced— and speaks fluent Dutch."

"Does he?" asked Ryan, the sudden interest evident in his voice.

"Not well enough to pass as a native," Cathcart conceded, "but probably good enough to fool a German."

"I see. And you say you can square his transfer with SOE?"

"Well, actually, this is where you come in," said Cathcart with a slightly embarrassed air. "Or, rather, your superiors. It would attract far less suspicion and comment if Cormack's transfer were to be seen to come about as a result of Allied Services bureaucracy, rather than as a consequence of a direct request from ourselves. If you want to circumvent SOE, that is."

"Yes. I see what you mean. Very well, I'll see to it," Ryan replied.

Cathcart looked mildly surpised. "You're sure your superiors will go along with this?"

Ryan stared levelly at Cathcart. "Last night, Sir Gerald, we attacked Duisburg and lost just under ten per cent of our force. At the moment, I think Bomber Command would sign a pact with the devil himself if it got us information concerning this radar. Yes, they'll go along with it, all right."

The first thing Guthrie noticed about Cormack was his eyes: they were icy-blue and penetrating but with the haunted look of a man under considerable strain. They also looked utterly exhausted; but he had only been back from France for forty–eight hours so this was hardly surprising. By all accounts, he had been lucky to get out alive.

Guthrie waited until Cormack had sat down and then began, "I'm sorry to call you back so quickly from your leave, Captain, but the fact is that we need your services rather urgently."

"I wondered what all the rush was about," said Cormack ironically.

"We want you to go into Holland for us, Captain."

"Holland?" Cormack sat bolt upright. "You've got to be kidding. Holland's a disaster area, a suicide run. No chance."

"I agree that the record of the Special Operations Executive in the Netherlands is not very good—"

"You can say that again," Cormack muttered.

"—but this operation will be run entirely by ourselves."

Cormack stared at him, naked suspicion on his face. "I didn't know SIS had any networks left in Holland. I thought they'd all been wiped out."

"Almost all, but we do have one left. SOE knows nothing at all about it and it reports only to us. Using our codes—not SOE's. You'd be working with them and you'd only be in contact with us."

"Not SOE?" asked Cormack, smiling faintly.

"Not SOE," echoed Guthrie firmly.

Cormack sat back, suppressing a laugh. It was obvious what was happening: SIS were trying to score points off SOE by running a successful operation in SOE's back yard. Talk about inter–service rivalry. . . Just which side were they all on, anyway? On the other hand, if this SIS cell in Holland were really separate from the SOE networks, then it might just be feasible. . . "What is the mission all about?"

Guthrie paused, marshalling his thoughts and arguments. "How much do you know about German radar?"

"Bugger all."

Guthrie opened a drawer in his desk and took out a buff manila folder, which he passed across to Cormack. "Read this as soon as possible; it contains details of the German air defence radar system. Basically, what we're interested in is the airborne radar carried by the German night fighters. We need information about it,"

"Information?"

"Photographs or accurate drawings."

"Not the equipment itself?"

Guthrie shook his head. "Too bulky to move. It's not just the set, there's also a complicated aerial array as well."

"So you want me to go in and take photos of it?"

"Exactly."

"And I'm to work with this cell?"

"Yes."

"Tell me about them."

"It's led by a man called Schelhaas. He uses the codename Voltimand. He's very capable: he's been active for us since 1940 and he's built up a very useful network in and around Leiden."

"You're certain they haven't been blown and turned?"

"Feeding us back false information, you mean? No, there's no hint of that. On the contrary, all of their material has been consistently shown to be accurate and reliable when verified by independent sources."

"I see." There was no mistaking the doubt in Cormack's voice. Guthrie was not offended; indeed, he was encouraged. Cormack was a professional, accepting nothing at face value, constantly questioning, evaluating, a man who relied on his own judgment and resources.

Cormack tapped the folder. "Why can't this Schelhaas, or Voltimand, or whoever, get the photos?"

Guthrie hesitated and then said slowly, "To be perfectly honest, he has tried or, rather, one of his men did. He was arrested by the Gestapo. They're interrogating him. Schelhaas is trying to get a cyanide capsule to him. At the moment, he doesn't appear to have talked; certainly, none of the other members of the cell have been picked up or are even under surveillance."

"But he could crack at any moment," said Cormack disgustedly. "And you want me to go and make contact with a network that could be rounded up at any time? For God's sake, that's no better than SOE."

"You would not be sent in until we were as certain as it could be that it would be safe."

"You mean when the poor sod's taken the cyanide," said Cormack bitterly. "Even then, the Jerries will be on the alert."

Guthrie stared at Cormack. "Are you refusing the mission, Captain?" He stressed the rank to emphasise his own seniority.

Cormack shrugged. "Not yet—Major. But I'll have to think about it. Who draws up the operation, for one thing?"

"You do. We can only give you the broad outline of the mission but a good deal will depend on what you discover when you get there."

"If I get there."

Guthrie smiled thinly. "You'll have to use your own initiative but that's why we asked for you in particular. Your record stresses your ability to work alone in tight situations."

"You mean my bloody–mindedness and insubordination? I expect that's how they put it. Right, give me the outlines and I'll start thinking about it."

Guthrie looked away. He could not understand Cormack at all; the other man seemed to be full of contradictions, not least of which was his attitude towards the mission. On the surface, he seemed extremely reluctant to take it on and yet, Guthrie sensed, there was also some deep inner motivation that would make it impossible for him to refuse it.

An enigma.

But also the best man for the job, judging by his record, which was undeniably impressive. Even so, Guthrie wondered. . .

He turned abruptly to face Cormack. It was not his decision, after all. "Very well. The cell is also codenamed Voltimand and there are seven members, apart from Schelhaas, so I understand. . ."

Kuipers screamed, his body arching backwards in the chair as the electricity slammed through him. He was no longer capable of coherent thought: his entire being was totally consumed by white hot shafts of agony. And then, as suddenly as it had come, the pain was gone; he flopped back down into the seat. He couldn't take much more of this, he realised distantly; he doubted if anyone could—the torment was unimaginable, beyond endurance.

Kuipers had wondered why they had not used the electrodes before; certainly, he admitted to himself, if they had done so, he would have broken by now, would have told them all he wanted to know. It was not just the pain itself, which was hideous, far worse than the rubber truncheons and steel–tipped boots; no, it was the cold impersonality of it. A flick of a switch and he was in agony; another flick and it had gone. This detached, mechanistic inhumanity was far worse than the sadistic beatings from the SS guards.

As if from a great distance, he heard Kreissner's voice: "Well, Kuipers? Had enough? Or do you want another dose of the treatment?"

"Fuck off, you fat shit," he hissed and tensed himself for the pain.

It did not come; in a way, that was even worse. Kreissner had not reacted to the insult, had met it with a cold detachment that made him seem like one of the electrical devices he was using.

"Don't be foolish, Kuipers. How much more of this can you take? And all I want are some names, Kuipers. The names of your accomplices and then you can go back to your cell and all this will be over. No more pain. No more suffering."

Christ, it was tempting. . . No more pain. . . "Shove it up your arse, Kreissner."

Kreissner signed. He disliked using electric shocks; there was too great a risk of killing the prisoner, especially if he had already been subjected to intensive—"sharpened"—interrogation. He had misjudged Kuipers' powers of resistance, he conceded grudgingly. He had thought he could beat a statement out of the young Dutchman in a few days; he had been sadly mistaken. Kuipers had held out for ten days now and von Krug at The Hague was demanding a report. Perhaps if he'd started off with the electrodes. . . but that was water under the bridge now. Kreissner nodded to the technician, who pushed the switch forward. Kreissner winced at the high–pitched animal scream that was wrenched from Kuipers' throat; his face grimaced in distaste at the smell of burning flesh. He watched in abstracted fascination as Kuipers' back arched higher and higher until it seemed the spine must break. Kreissner gestured again and the current was shut off.

"Well, Kuipers? The names?"

Kuipers shook his head mutely, no longer trusting himself to speak, convinced that if he did, it would be to betray Schelhaas and the others. It was no good. He couldn't withstand another jolt of current scything through him. If Kreissner turned it on again, he'd talk; he knew that, with an utter certainty. He'd have to; he just couldn't take any more.

Kreissner looked at the watch. It was 7.15 now and he was meeting Marika at eight. Kuipers could wait until tomorrow;Kreissner wanted to touch her smooth flesh again, to run his hand over her body. . .

"Take him back to his cell," he said curtly. He spun on his heel and walked briskly out. Back to his quarters by 7.30, bath, shave and be ready for her arrival at eight. Excellent.

Kuipers was only vaguely aware of being carried back to his cell and of being thrown onto his bunk; it was several minutes before he fully regained consciousness but he did not open his eyes. Instead, he reached carefully under the straw-filled pillow, supressing a momentary panic as he failed to find the capsule. Supposing the bastards had found it, and removed it? And then his fingers found it, closed over it; he almost cried out in relief.

He brought his hand up to his face and opened his eyes; he stared at the tiny pill. Funny, he thought, it looks so harmless. . . He placed it on his tongue; all he had to do now was to bite through it and swallow. It was a quick death, so he had been told.

But it was death all the same. . .

He was suddenly overwhelmed by the finality of it all;he didn't want to die, for God's sake! He was only twenty–four and there were so many things he hadn't done, so many places he had never seen! It wasn't fair! All his hopes, all his dreams, had come to this, a broken wreck of a body dying alone in an underground cell. . . Was it all worth it? How had it all happened?

A tear ran slowly down his face; he could feel his body trembling in stark terror. What would happen when he bit through the capsule? The undiscovered country. . . Kuipers did not believe in God or an afterlife; any last vestiges of faith had been swept away by the conviction that if God existed, He would not permit the Nazis to go on. No; this was final extinction. He would cease to exist, would become nothing, would never know or feel, anything ever again.

And there was a simple way out, of course. Tell Kreissner what he wanted to know. Tell Kreissner everything—and betray Schelhaas and Marika and the others. Tell Kreissner—and kill them.

That was worse than dying. . .

Postpone his own suicide, then? Grab another day, give himself another twenty–four hours? He had already held out four days since Marika had left the capsule in his cell; longer than he had originally intended, so why not another day?

That was not to be risked. He recalled his feeling of utter despair in the interrogation cell, how he had been on the point of breaking; he could not possibly hold out for another session with the electrodes. It would have to be now; he did not dare wait any longer.

And he hadn't talked. Not one word. When he bit through the capsule, it would be a kind of triumph, a victory over that bastard Kreissner.

Do it now, and beat Kreissner! Do it!

Kuipers bit through the capsule and swallowed.

He screamed.

He had time for one last thought before the cyanide took effect: Why hadn't anyone told him how much it would hurt?

# CHAPTER 9

**LUFTWAFFE SECURITY H.Q., LEIDEN**

Behrens looked up as Ziegler came in and then went back to reading the document that he had been trying unsuccessfully to digest for the last twenty minutes. It was only when Ziegler closed the door behind him and approached the desk with an undeniably furtive air that Behrens began to pay attention to him.

"You asked me to keep you informed about Kuipers, Herr Major."

"Yes, I did. I gather Kreissner isn't getting very far."

"Worse than that, Herr Major. Kuipers is dead. Apparently, he committed suicide last night. He took a cyanide pill."

"He did what?" asked Behrens incredulously. "Where the devil did he get it from?"

"Someone smuggled it in to him, so they think—the Gestapo, that is, Herr Major."

"But who, for God's sake? And how?"

"Well, I don't have many details, Herr Major, but it seems they're interrogating one of their own men, an Unterscharführer named Hauser. He's suspected of stealing secret documents and they think he's implicated in Kuipers' suicide as well. He had plenty of opportunity to get the pill to Kuipers, of course."

"But why would he do it?"

"Money, so Kreissner thinks. They found a thousand Reichmarks in Hauser's locker that he couldn't account for. Or maybe Kuipers could have revealed that Hauser was working for the Resistance and he had to be silenced."

"So Hauser was their source," said Behrens, half to

himself. Yes, it made sense. Hauser could easily have furnished the Dutch with the correct identification codes so that they could make that phone call to Schramm. "Very well. Keep me informed."

"As you wish, Herr Major."

Behrens took a brief sip from his wine and smiled across the table at Trudi Neuberger. "You were right," he said. "The wine is excellent. I'd love to know how they manage to get it." Although, he thought to himself, the answer to that was fairly obvious; the restaurant catered, virtually exclusively, for the occupying forces. The only Dutch customers, he suspected, were the young, attractive women sitting with German officers or Nazi Party functionaries. But the food and service were good, as she had said they would be.

He had been mildly embarrassed when he had picked her up at her home; it had occured to him that he knew nothing about Leiden restaurants. Ziegler had made some suggestions but it had been Trudi, recognising his dilemma, who had decided on the Ambassador.

"I'm glad you like it," she said, smiling. Behrens decided that he liked her smile; it was natural and unforced. He was also aware that his first impression of her had been wrong; he was finding her very easy to like and was enjoying her company.

He put his thought into words. "I am having a marvellous time."

She smiled again. "I'm glad, Major."

"Please—call me Anton."

"Only if you call me Trudi."

"It's a deal, as the Americans say." He looked around the restaurant. "Have you been here often?" And that, he thought, could have been phrased more subtly.

"To be perfectly honest, I've never been here before. I heard about it from my father. I'm as impressed as you are by the service."

He grinned. "It sounds as though we're both in the same boat."

"Well, I haven't been in Leiden long, either. And, until now, I haven't done much socialising. In fact," she grinned, "I haven't done any."

"How long are you staying with your parents?"

A shadow crossed her face. "I don't really know. It depends."

"I'm sorry, Fräu—Trudi. I was prying. It's none of my business."

"It's all right. It was a natural enough question, under the circumstances. It's just that I came here from Berlin for personal reasons." She grinned mischievously at him."Don't worry, Anton. There won't be any irate husbands bursting through the door to challenge you to a duel or anything."

"Thank God for that," he said in mock relief.

"I can't say I'm sorry to be away from Berlin, though," she continued. "It all seems so false, somehow." She pointed to the Knight's Cross at his throat. "There seem to be so many men wearing medals who do nothing but go to dinners and receptions and use their decorations to try and impress women."

"Like me?" asked Behrens gently.

"Possibly," she replied, "But I don't think so. Normally, they're only too willing to bore me with all the gory details as to how they won their medals, which is something you haven't done yet. If they're trying to impress me, they don't succeed. I always wonder what they're doing getting drunk and chasing women instead of getting on with the war."

"Like me?" said Behrens, again, his voice expressionless.

"No. Not like you. I mean—you're been wounded, for one thing. And I know from Father what you did to earn your medal—and what happened to you."

"I only did my job," Behrens objected. "I just happened to be good at it," he added unselfconsciously. "It was a case of either shooting them down or being blown out of the sky myself. Nothing heroic about it at all—most of the time I was up there, I was scared stiff."

"But you still shot down—what? A hundred and seventy aircraft? That's pretty impressive."

"Pure and simple survival. I was in a better aircraft, most of the time, and I'd had more experience after the first six months. Given all that, I was bound to shoot a few down, wasn't I?"

She looked at him a thoughful smile on her face. "So. A

reluctant hero."

"Just a pilot who was doing his job. If I'd been shot down in the first six months or so, which is when it's much more likely to happen, nobody would ever have heard of me. After that, anyone who's still flying starts running up impressive totals on the Russian Front. Bound to, really. Until recently, the Russian planes have been more or less sitting ducks, although the newer ones, like the LA–5 and the Yak–9 are damned good—" He broke off and grinned sheepishly. "Sorry. Talking shop."

"No, it's all right. It's the first time I've actually got you to talk about your exploits."

He shrugged. "It's all over, now. I don't imagine they'll let me near a 109 now."

"Because you upset someone in Berlin?"

He glanced at her, sharply. "Where did you find that out?"

"I didn't. I guessed. When a wounded holder of the Knight's Cross, a fighter ace to boot, turns up in a backwater like Leiden to take over a job as Luftwaffe Area Security Officer—" She broke off and smiled apologetically. "That wasn't exactly tactful, was it?"

"Possibly not, but it's absolutely true."

"What happened? She asked. "You don't have to tell me if you don't want to."

Behrens hesitated and then said, "I simply told the truth. I told a Luftwaffe General a few facts of life about the medal system, the war and the extravagant reception I was getting drunk at. Then I went and upset his daughter—I never did do anything by halves."

"And what were these facts of life?"

"Oh, it was the whole set-up. There are thousands of men dying in Russia, some of them from starvation, and they sit there in Berlin drinking bloody champagne and awarding each other pointless medals—" He took a deep breath. "There I go again. My hobby horse."

"No need to apologise," she replied softy. "I'm impressed. I wish there were more men like you who are not afraid to speak their mind." She was silent for several seconds as though she were about to say more, but evidently she decided against it. Instead, she smiled ruefully. "And to think that when I saw you at my father's reception, I thought you were just another bragging hero, showing off his medal! Just shows how wrong you can be. I'm afraid I misjudged you, Anton."

"I'm guilty of the same thing, Trudi. I regret to say that I catalogued you along with the Klara Hallers of this world."

"Klara Haller?"

"General Haller's daughter. The one I upset back in Berlin. You'd know her by the look in her eyes; it's the same one that a female praying mantis has after mating. I think she was after my medal, really."

"And you thought I was like her?"

"I'm afraid so," he confessed.

She chuckled. "Looks like we're both appallingly bad judges of character, doesn't it?"

"Looks that way. Still, at least we found out our mistakes."

"I'm glad we did."

"Me too. Otherwise I would have missed this evening." He looked at her hesitantly. "Maybe we could do it again, sometime?"

"I'd like that, Anton."

They smiled at each other; and then Behrens' attention was distracted as the restaurant door opened. Kreissner stood in the doorway in full SS uniform, his arm linked with an attactive young woman. As at the reception, their eyes met and Kreissner bowed ironically. He ushered his companion across the floor to a vacant table; the girl, Behrens noticed, seemed curiously ill at ease as if she were terrified of being recognised.

As well she might, Behrens thought idly, if she were Dutch.

"A penny for them, Anton?"

"What? Oh—er—sorry. Just someone I know."

Trudi followed his gaze. "She's very beautiful," she said archly.

"It's not her I know," he protested. "It's the man she's with."

"The Gestapo," she said quietly and seemed to give an involuntary shudder. "Let's forget them, Anton. Please?"

"Forget who?" said Behrens, grinning. Their conversation moved onto another subject, but a corner of Behrens' mind kept returning the question: Who was she?

"Her name's Marika Schuurmann. She's Kreissner's mistress," said Ziegler. "The gossip's all over Gestapo HQ. He's been—ah—consorting with her for the last week or so. All the men there are pretty jealous, so I gather."

"So she's Dutch?" said Behrens thoughtfully.

"Oh yes, Herr Major. Been working at Gestapo HQ for over a year now. She's Kreissner's secretary."

"Is she?"

"Among other things," Ziegler said, grinning.

"And it's only been going a week? No longer than that?"

"No. It's common knowledge when it started. He dragged her down to the cells to see what they'd done to Kuipers. He probably threatened her with some of the same treatment if she didn't co-operate. Typical Gestapo," Ziegler added disgustedly.

"So she was in Kuipers' cell?"

"Apparently, yes."

"So she could have smuggled the poison in?"

Ziegler thought for a moment. "Well, yes, I suppose she could have, Herr Major. Only—she was dragged down there, by all accounts. It wasn't her idea."

"Yes, but the fact remains that she's Dutch and she was in that cell. I'd say that makes her at least a potential suspect."

Ziegler stared dubiously at him. "But they reckon Hauser did it, Herr Major."

"And if he didn't? Put it this way, Ziegler. The senior Gestapo officer in Leiden is having an affair with a Dutch girl. Wouldn't you say that might constitute a possible security hazard?"

"Well—yes, I suppose it does, Herr Major."

"And this girl is just as handily placed as Hauser for passing on information; in fact, she'd be a better bet for the Resistance—she's Dutch and therefore less likely to betray them."

"We've no evidence, though, Herr Major."

"Agreed. So this is what I want you do do, Ziegler. First, find out exactly what they've got out of Hauser and what evidence they have that he actually did smuggle the pill in to Kuipers. At best, what I've heard so far sounds pretty circumstantial."

"Finding money in his locker is rather more than circumstantial, Herr Major."

"I agree. But it somehow seems—what? Rather obvious? If you wanted to 'frame' Hauser, as the Americans put it, what would you do?"

"Put money in his locker," said Ziegler reluctantly. "But you don't know that's what happened, Herr Major."

"I know I don't. But it's a possibility. Anyway, find out everything you can.

"Secondly, I want you to put this Marika Schuurmann under discreet surveillance. Round the clock. I want to know where she goes, who she meets, everything. Is that clear?"

"Perfectly, Herr Major."

"And make damned certain it is discreet. I don't want her or the Gestapo spotting it. Understood?"

Ziegler grinned conspiratorially. "Perfectly, Herr Major."

**LONDON**

If nothing else, Cormack was punctual, Cathcart reflected, when the knock on his door came at exactly ten o'clock. "Come in," he called, nodding significantly at Guthrie, who had already arrived and was sitting in front of the desk.

Cormack looked more refreshed now than he had done two days before, but his eyes still had an undeniable hint of strain. He placed the folder they had given him on the desk. "It's not on," he said as he sat down.

"Perhaps you'd care to explain, Captain?" suggested Cathcart.

"Firstly, there's the problem of Kuipers. Now, I know they're trying to smuggle cyanide in to him but until he actually takes it, he remains a potential threat. No operation could be mounted until—well—the threat has been removed. Until the poor sod kills himself, in other words." These last words were spoken with a vehement bitterness that took Cathcart and Guthrie by surprise. Cormack continued, "Even if that problem is removed, there still remains the fact that the Jerries are going to be on their guard over there, both at Verwijk and all round Leiden. I'd say it'd be next to impossible to get into the airfield and then out again with the photos. If we wait for a few weeks until their vigilance dies away, then it might be feasible."

"I'm afraid we don't have that time," said Cathcart.

Cormack stared intently at him, as if to see whether Cathcart would elaborate on that statement, but when it was obvious that no further information would be forthcoming, he went on, "Right. Let's look at alternative plans if we're in such a tearing hurry.

"I imagine you've investigated the possibility of a full–scale commando assault?"

Cathcart and Guthrie exchanged glances again. Was this all Cormack had to offer? "We considered it, yes, but we felt that it would have very little chance of success."

"So I should think. It'd be all right if the base were on the coast, like the Bruneval raid, but it isn't. Three miles there, three miles back. Suicidal."

"Guthrie cleared his throat. "Are you telling us it can't be done, Captain?

Cormack hesitated a long time before replying. "No, I'm not saying that. There is one more alternative, one that hasn't been mentioned by anyone yet. It'd be extremely hazardous, but it would stand a better chance of success that any other approach.

"You see, the greatest problem will be in getting out of the base with the information. Gaining entrance will be difficult, of course, but, given luck and good on-the-spot planning, it could be done. It's getting out afterwards that will be next to impossible. The raiding party would have to remain undetected all the while they were inside and would then have to break out again, still without being spotted. Then they'd have to make their way to the rendezvous point on the coast, again without being detected. I'd say their chances of doing all that would be non–existent. It only needs one German to see them and the whole thing falls apart. And there's nothing they can do to ensure that they're not spotted."

"So what do you suggest?" asked Cathcart with an impatient edge to his voice.

"As I said, I think I could get the party inside the base. If we had an aircraft available to take them out almost immediately, then it'd make life a lot simpler." There was a very faint, but infuriating, grin on Cormack's face as though he were deliberately taunting the other two men.

"You're not suggesting that we land an RAF plane on a Luftwaffe airfield?" protested Guthrie."

"No, I'm not," said Cormack, still with that maddening grin. "Tell me," he continued, apparently apropos of nothing, "wouldn't the boffins rather have an actual radar set to study than a photograph?"

Realisation struck Cathcart and Guthrie at the same instant; they stared at Cormack in awed amazement. "You're joking," said Guthrie eventually.

"Anything but," said Cormack. "The quickest way to get out of that airfield is to steal a JU88 and fly it back to England with the bloody radar aboard."

There were several seconds of dumbfounded silence before Cathcart spoke. "This is utter insanity, Cormack."

"I agree," said Cormack levelly. "But do either of you have any better ideas?"

**LEIDEN**

Kreissner replaced the telephone receiver and took a deep breath to calm himself. Standartenführer von Krug, his superior, had been scathing in his criticisms; as far as he was concerned, Kuipers' suicide had been the result of gross negligence on Kreissner's part. Von Krug had not even been mollified by the information that they had Hauser under interrogation; he had wanted concrete results and, thus far, Hauser had revealed nothing whatsoever. Indeed, he still maintained his innocence, despite the intensive questioning he had undergone.

Kuipers had also not given away anything of any significance at all and so, for the moment, Kreissner was at a dead end. Kuipers' known associates were still being investigated and interrogated, but with no success so far; his home had been almost torn apart in a fruitless search. Pressure was being brought to bear on Dutch collaborators and informers but, again, with no results.

Which left the phone call that had so conveniently distracted Schramm so that Kuipers had been left alone with the aircraft. There was no doubt that it had been a deliberate decoy move; the call had not originated from any Gestapo station. Only two people had actually heard the caller's voice; Schramm had said it had been that of a middle–aged woman, but the operator had thought she sounded younger. Both agreed that she had spoken German like a native—Schramm had even asserted that she had been a Rhinelander—but neither felt they would recognise the voice again if they heard it. This was hardly surprising when one considered that neither had spoken to her for longer than about fifteen seconds.

Here, again, Kreissner was aware that he had been remiss, in that he had not yet tried to follow up this lead; with Kuipers under arrest, he had not seen any great need to do so. Now, however, he would have to initiate a thorough investigation, if only to cover himself with von Krug. The woman would have to be traced. Every single German–speaking woman would have to be checked, not only in Leiden itself, but also in Haarlem, Delft, The Hague and Rotterdam; a mammoth undertaking that would tie up a good deal of manpower.

It was a long list, running to over five hundred names. These were only the ones that were known to the Gestapo; there could be dozens more. Still, the attempt had to be made. Idly, Kreissner picked up the list that related to Leiden and scanned through it. There were a hundred and seven names printed on the sheets; he noted, with no more than momentary curiousity, that the eighty–ninth name was that of Marika Schuurmann, but then dropped the list onto the desk. The matter was dismissed from his mind as Opitz came in with yet another negative report.

**GUNNERY RANGE, BISLEY**

Cormack reeled in the target and nodded in approval: six shots, six bulls. He turned and nodded to the man who had fired the shots. "Not bad," he said in a grudging tone. "Where did you learn to shoot like that?"

The other man smiled deprecatingly. "My father's always been mad keen on guns. I was more or less brought up on them." The voice matched the face; aristocratic, refined, cultured, in marked contrast to Cormack's own accent, which had more than a trace of his East End upbringing.

Cormack regarded the other man thoughtfully. "So you can handle a rifle as well?"

"Oh yes."

Cormack went over to the table behind them, on which was piled an assortment of guns: pistols, rifles, shotguns and even a Sten. Selecting one of the rifles, a standard Army issue Lee Enfield, he tossed it over to his companion. "Try this one." He signalled to the observation post fifty yards away; they immediately began to set up a man–sized target.

"I've never used one of these before." For the first time, the voice was hesitant, uncertain.

No, I don't suppose you have, Flight Lieutenant Woodward, thought Cormack bitterly. I should imagine Father's guns were more in the Purdey shotgun bracket, used for shooting hell out of the wildlife on the jolly old estate, don't you know, what? "Give it a go, anyway."

Woodward raised the rifle to his shoulder, operated the bolt action, took aim and fired.

Cormack had his field glasses to his eyes, focussing on the target. "Low and to the left," he reported.

Woodward adjusted the sight and then fired again.

"Outer ring. Right height, but out to the right."

This time, Woodward did not bother to adjust the sight, but merely corrected his aim before firing.

"A bull," said Cormack, impressed despite himself. To score a bull on the third shot with an unfamiliar weapon was no mean feat; Woodward was a marksman, no two ways about it.

The problem was that he was only a good target shooter; he took his time lining up the barrel before squeezing the trigger. As Cormack knew only too well, in the field you just did not have that time.

"Right," he said, taking the rifle back. "Let's see how you do with the rapid targets." He signalled again to the Observation Post and then directed Woodward's attention to the left of where they had been shooting. "Now, what you'll get in a moment will be man–sized targets popping up over there, range thirty yards. You'll have exactly two seconds in which to aim and fire, then it'll disappear. Got that?"

Woodward nodded dubiously.

"Right. Load your gun up. You'll have six targets, one shot at each. Ready?"

Woodward finished loading his pistol and nodded. Cormack signalled to the Observation Post.

The targets were nothing more than cardboard silhouettes that lay flat in a trench. When a spring mechanism was activated, one of them would shoot up into a vertical position into view of the marksman; two seconds later, it fell back again. There were twelve of them, three feet apart, but only six would actually pop up in a random pattern. The marksman's reactions had to be fast even to get a shot in before they disappeared again.

Woodward did not fire his first shot until after the target had fallen back; after than, he speeded up, but did not need to be told that he had failed to register a single hit. "Not very good, was it?"

"No, it wasn't," Cormack agreed bluntly. "That's the sort of shooting you'll have to learn to do if you're going to operate behind enemy lines, though."

"It'll take some doing."

Cormack stared at him for several seconds and then shouted out, "Sergeant! Set those targets for one second only, will you?"

"Will do, sir," answered the voice from the Observation Post.

Flight Lieutenant Tony Woodward was then treated to an exhibition of rapid pistol shooting the like of which he had never seen before. Cormack seemed to aim and fire in one motion, the Browning pistol held two-handed as he turned his whole body to left and right, in a slight crouch, ripping off six shots in rapid succession.

They waited in silence for the results to be called out: Cormack had registered five hits, missing only with his first shot. In fact, Cormack was slightly disappointed; the last time he had been here, four months before, he was hitting six out of six every time. But to say anything along these lines would be rubbing salt in Woodward's wounds; the tall, dark–haired pilot was looking chastened enough as it was.

"Point taken," said Woodward quietly.

Cormack walked over to the table and then turned to face Woodward. "I gather you volunteered for this operation, Woodward."

"Well—not exactly. I was approached and asked if I was interested."

"And what were you told about the mission?"

"That I would have to go undercover behind enemy lines and that I'd probably have to fly an enemy aircraft out—a Ju88."

"So you said you were interested?"

"Naturally." Woodward's voice held a note of surprise.

"Why?"

"Well, I could hardly say no, could I?" asked Woodward, the bewilderment only too evident in his voice. "It's a matter of duty, isn't it?"

Cormack could only stare at him dumbfounded. Did Woodward honestly mean that? A matter of duty? Could he really be that gullible, that naïve, that he could volunteer for a suicidal mission like this simply because he felt duty–bound to do so?

Gradually, it dawned on Cormack that this was precisely what Woodward meant. He came from a family that had probably been lords of the manor back in the Middle Ages, a family steeped in tradition, where duty and honour were constantly being re-affirmed and reinforced to the extent that they were a way of life. Woodward's upbringing had been completely different to Cormack's own; Woodward came from a world of wealth and privilege, a world that Cormack had despised.

Until now.

Because whichever way you look at it, there was something to be said for a way of life that produced men like Woodward, who would unhesitatingly risk their lives, would go to their deaths out of a sense of duty. Call them gullible, naive, foolhardy even: it was probably that sort of attitude that led to the Charge of the Light Brigade, but it was not to be decried. It might be a very simplistic code: Woodward had felt he ought to volunteer because it was the 'decent' thing to do, but he had volunteered all the same.

And for that Woodward deserved his respect.

Even if he was a bloody fool. . .

"No second thoughts, then?" asked Cormack, knowing what the answer would be.

"Of course not."

"Right. I want you to practise on those targets until you start hitting them. Clear?"

"Perfectly."

As Woodward began to fire at the targets, Cormack saw a car approaching; he walked down the track to meet it. He was not at all surprised to see Guthrie in the back; indeed, he had been expecting him.

"How's he doing?" Guthrie asked, once they were out of earshot of the driver.

"Woodward? Bit green, but willing to learn. Good shot,but I don't know how he'd do shooting at a live target. It's all very different then."

Guthrie nodded. "I know. But we're not exactly spoilt for choice. Woodward's a brilliant pilot; he's flown practically everything from Spitfires to Lancasters. He's completed over forty bombing missions to Germany; we couldn't really ask for a better pilot. The pistol shooting is no more than an unexpected bonus, after all."

"True," Cormack conceded. Guthrie had the right of it;they were looking for a top–class pilot, primarily, and Woodward's credentials in that respect were impeccable. "But he's still got a hell of a lot to learn about undercover work."

"That's hardly critical, though, is it?" asked Guthrie. "I mean, your plan calls for him to be kept hidden away—if he has to use any of your tradecraft, then it'll be because something's gone wrong, won't it?"

"I suppose so," said Cormack reluctantly. "But he'll need looking after."

"Precisely. However, we've found a baby-sitter for him. You know him, actually. Poortvliet."

"Really?"

"Really. He'll complete your little team. I gather you've worked together?"

"Yes, we have," Cormack and Henrik Poortvliet had been

parachuted into Belgium five months before and Cormack had gained a healthy respect for the Dutchman's abilities. Poortvliet was not only highly resourceful and capable; he was also utterly ruthless. His wife and two children had been killed by SS troops in 1940; his sole purpose in life was revenge and he killed Germans cold–bloodedly, single-mindedly, without remorse. His motives were irrelevant to Cormack; all that concerned him were the little Dutchman's skills as an undercover agent, which were considerable. "He'll do," he said at length.

"And Woodward?"

Cormack looked back at the tall figure still squeezing off shots at the elusive targets, face set in a frown of concentration. Perhaps Woodward was a bloody fool, but. . . "He'll do as well," he said, nodding. "Provided the bloody thing goes ahead at all, that is."

Guthrie, perhaps intentionally, had been saving the most significant item of news until last. "We've heard from 'Voltimand'."

"And?" prompted Cormack.

"They got the poison to Kuipers. He killed himself four days ago, without saying one word. A brave man."

"Poor bastard," murmured Cormack, his face bleak.

Guthrie didn't hear him and continued, "So 'Voltimand' is safe. There's no security leak. Your mission can go ahead."

"Sod your mission, Guthrie! A man's just killed himself to protect his friends and all you're concerned about is your bloody mission! Is that all you damn well care about? Is it?"

Involuntarily, Guthrie took a step backwards in the face of Cormack's naked fury. "Of course it isn't, Cormack," he snapped. "But the man's dead. He died bravely, which is all we can ask of anyone. And one of the reasons he died was so that this mission could go ahead."

Cormack stared at Guthrie for several seconds and then turned away. "Right," he said, almost to himself. "Right. So the mission goes ahead. When?"

"As soon as you're ready."

Cormack did not answer for almost a minute and then he said:

"Four days' time. Tell Cathcart we'll be ready in four

days' time." Then, without another word, he walked away from Guthrie, back towards Woodward.

Guthrie watched him go, his face thoughtful.

# CHAPTER 10

## LEIDEN

Marika spotted her shadower as soon as she left the building; it was the shorter one this time. She was relieved; the other one would have been more difficult to shake off, but this one looked as though he would not be able to move very rapidly.

She had first detected the surveillance three days before, but had no idea how long they had been following her before then. There were just the two of them; one of them was always waiting outside her home when she left in the morning and the other would follow her back in the evening. If she went out for a walk at lunchtime, she was followed; the surveillance was constant.

She did not know either of them, which meant that they were unlikely to be Gestapo, unless Kreissner had drafted them in from elsewhere; she doubted that. If he suspected her of any subversive activity, he would have had her arrested by now. So, if not the Gestapo, then who?

She would have to talk to Schelhaas; but she dared not contact him while she was still under surveillance. Therefore, she had to shake off her shadower, but in such a way that it would appear quite accidental so as not to attract suspicion.

Easier said than done, of course.

She joined the queue at the Town Hall as she always did at this time; her shadower idled along, further down the street, until another three people had joined the line and then he came up to take his place. He, or his colleague, had watched her board the tram and go home every evening since they had begun the surveillance; she wanted him to be convinced that tonight would be no different.

Eventually, the tram appeared and the line began to shuffle forward. Marika took out her handbag and began to rummage inside it as if looking for her purse. Evidently, she could not find it; her face took on a look of puzzled concern. She stood to one side to allow those behind her in the queue to pass as she continued to search through her bag.

The short, stocky man hesitated and then went past her; he had no alternative, if he wished to remain inconspicuous. He paused with one foot on the platform and looked back at her; everyone else had now boarded. She took two or three steps forward, still intent on hunting for her elusive purse.

"Come on there," called the conductor impatiently. "Move on inside, meinheer," he said to the stocky man. "And you too, love," he added to Marika.

She looked up and smiled, her face confused, evidently trying to remember what she had done with her purse. Her eyes met those of the stocky man, who immediately ducked inside the tram, not wishing to attract her attention.

"You coming, love?" asked the conductor.

"Er—yes. Sorry." Marika stepped up on to the platform and the tram moved off. Glancing into the interior, she saw that the stocky man was just sitting down.

"Of course!" she cried suddenly. "That's what I did with it!" She turned and jumped off the platform: the tram was only travelling slowly and she landed safely enough. Briskly, she began to walk back the way she had come.

Within seconds, she had turned a corner and was out of sight of the tram. She ducked into a newsagent's and wandered along the rack of magazines, watching the street to see if the stocky man would appear.

A full five minutes passed before she emerged; she then headed in the oposite direction to the tram stop, checking the street behind her very carefully. She could not afford to be tailed to her intended destination, not now; but the street was bare of anybody following her.

Ten minutes later, she had reached the park and walked rapidly to the bandstand. She saw Schelhaas immediately and walked towards him, her steps now unhurried. Schelhaas had placed his newspaper on the bench beside him; a signal that all was clear and that it was safe to approach.

Marika sat down and they exchanged pleasantries, in the now unlikely event that they were being observed, before Schelhaas said quietly. "What's the problem? Pieter said you wanted to see me, urgently."

"Yes, I did. I'm being followed, Vim. Oh, don't worry,I've shaken them off for the moment, but they've been following me for the last three days."

"How many of them?"

"Two." Briefly, she described them.

"And you don't know them?"

She shook her head. "No. They're not any of Kreissner's men."

"They could have been brought in from outside, I suppose," mused Schelhaas. "They're just watching you? No more than that?"

"No, that's all."

"And only two of them?"

"Yes."

"They're probably not the Gestapo, then. They've got enough manpower to use several men so that you wouldn't spot them so easily."

"So who is it then? she asked.

"Behrens?" suggested Schelhaas.

"Could be," said Marika. "But if it is, what do we do about it?"

"Simple," said Schelhaas, grinning. "We tell Kreissner about it. Or, rather, you do."

Kreissner looked at Marika as she stripped; he was already naked, lying on the bed, waiting for her to join him. To his irritation, he found that he was not especially aroused; although Marika had a superb body, he knew that it would be little more than a slab of cold meat when he came to possess it in a few minutes. She would lie back on the sheets, eyes closed, and she would . . . submit . . . to whatever he wanted to do to her. It was scarcely better than masturbating; she did not participate at all. Kreissner was beginning to wonder if she had been worth the effort . . .

She came and sat on the bed next to him, naked. "Herr Sturmbannführer?"

"Yes, Marika?"

“May I ask you something?” she said hesitantly.

He nodded assent.

“Are you—have you. . . ” She hesitated.

“Have I what?” Idly, he reached out and stroked her breast; it was cold, like the rest of her.

“Are you having me followed, Herr Sturmbannführer?” she said, almost inaudibly.

He froze. “What are you talking about?”

“Those two men. They’re following me. They have been for days now. Everywhere I go.” Her voice was tearful. “They frighten me, Herr Sturmbannführer. They’re always there.”

Kreissner barely heard her. Behrens! It had to be! That bloody cripple was poking his nose in again! Unless . . . Supposing von Krug already knew about his affair with Marika and had sent down his own men to spy on her? No. It wasn’t von Krug’s style, to be honest; if he suspected anything like that,he’d have confronted Kreissner with it already. No, it had to be Behrens. . .

“Don’t worry, Marika. I’ll see to it. You won’t be bothered again, I promise you.” He gave what he hoped was a reassuring smile.

“Are you sure, Herr Sturmbannführer?” Her voice was tremulous.

“Absolutely certain, Marika. You will not have to worry about it any more, believe me.”

She let out her breath in a great sigh. “Thank you, Herr Sturmbannführer. I’m ever so grateful to you.”

Kreissner reached out again and touched her breast, cupping it in his palm. “Then why don’t you show me your gratitude, Marika? After all, I do a lot for you. Clothes, stockings, expensive dinners . . .”

“I know, Herr Sturmbannführer. If I’ve appeared ungrateful, it’s because I’ve been so worried the last few days. Those men . . .”

“But there is no need to worry any longer, my dear. So relax . . . Come and lie beside me. Show me how much you appreciate what I’ve done for you.”

She took a deep breath as she lay down; she had always known it would come to this eventually, but she was not at all certain she could go through with it. Having to submit to sex was bad enough, but to have to pretend to enjoy it . . . her whole body recoiled at the thought.

But it had to be done; if he were to grow bored with her and discard her, then he might well start wondering about her part in Kuipers' death. And if she could continue to wheedle favours out of him by using her body, then she would do so. Kreissner was a prize catch, from Voltimand's point of view; she had to exploit the situation to the utmost, regardless of her own feelings. Jan Kuipers had been obliged to pay a far greater price than mere sexual degradation and he had not hesitated; she had to put her own qualms to one side. This was war.

But it would not be easy.

Turning towards him, she pressed herself close to him, putting her arms around him. She pressed her lips to his, her tongue probing into his mouth in a long, sensual kiss; he began to respond immediately. As their lips parted, she whispered huskily, "I'll try to show my gratitude, Herr Sturmbannführer."

This time, she was everything a man could possibly desire. . .

The door of Behrens' office was hurled open, crashing back on its hinges as Kreissner stormed in. "I would like a word, Herr Major." He glared meaningfully at Ludwig, standing in front of Behrens' desk. "In private, if you please."

Behrens bit back an angry retort; he was damned if he was going to lose his temper in front of Ludwig. "Very well, Ludwig, we'll finish this off later."

"As the Herr Major wishes." Ludwig gave Kreissner a brief salute and then left, closing the door behind him.

"Well, Sturmbannführer, what brings you here? asked Behrens with exaggerated courtesy.

"Have you put my secretary under surveillance, Behrens? If so, then call your men off."

Behrens stared calmly back at Kreissner. "If you'll explain precisely who and what you're talking about—"

"You know damned well what I'm talking about, Behrens. Marika Schuurmann. She's been under surveillance for several days now. What I want to know is whether they are your men who are following her."

"Yes, they are," Behrens admitted.

"And the reason?"

Behrens took a deep breath. "I have reason to believe that she may be implicated in Kuipers' death, that she may have smuggled the cyanide in to him."

"That's ridiculous!"

"Is it? She was in Kuipers' cell, after all. She had the opportunity. She could also have made the phone call to Schramm. She's a Gestapo employee with access to important files and documents. Add to that the fact that she is also your mistress and I'd say that she would be ideally placed—from the Resistance's viewpoint."

"You seem remarkably well informed. Just how did you acquire all this knowledge, Behrens?"

"That is hardly relevant just now, is it? We were discussing the Schuurmann woman."

"No—you were expounding some outrageous theory. You're overlooking several facts, Behrens. Firstly, you have no evidence to support this ludicrous hypothesis. Secondly, I fail to see how the girl could have arranged to smuggle the pill to Kuipers. She did not plan her presence there in the cell; she was dragged there against her will."

"So I heard," said Behrens. "You're disgusting, Kreissner."

"I am entirely uninterested in your opinion of me, Behrens," Kreissner replied curtly. "To continue. We know who smuggled the cyanide in to Kuipers and he is under interrogation at this very moment."

"Hauser, you mean?" Kreissner showed no reaction at the extend of Behrens' knowledge. "I've been wondering about that. Doesn't it all seem just a little too tidy, Kreissner?"

"I presume you are going to explain that inane remark."

"Of course," said Behrens, a burr of irritation in his voice. "A damning piece of evidence is found in Hauser's locker the very day after a document is stolen. In his locker, dammit, the most obvious hiding place. Why steal it? Why not just copy it? And why does Jongbloed disappear the same day as the theft? Surely that's another dead giveaway? And then Kuipers kills himself and, lo and behold, you have a ready made suspect for that as well. Isn't it rather strange that Hauser should be exposed at just that particular moment?

"A very ingenious theory, Behrens, but, as I have said, entirely lacking in substance. A mere flight of fancy. Take my advice and stay out of this investigation. Leave it to the experts, the ones who know what they're doing and who don't go round concocting preposterous theories. Just stay out of it, Behrens." He turned and strode towards the door, but Behrens' quiet voice halted him.

"One moment, Herr Sturmbannführer. Just answer me one question, please. The telephone call to Schramm was made by someone with access to the Gestapo identification codes for that day. Now, you're assuming Hauser passed on that information. I think Schuurmann could have done it and might even have made the call herself. I ask you this. Which of them would have found it easier to obtain the codes? Hauser, who was only an Unterscharführer, or the girl, who worked in the offices? Well, Kreissner?"

Kreissner turned back to face Behrens. "As I said before, Herr Major, forget it. Leave it to the experts." He spun on his heel and stalked out, slamming the door behind him.

Several seconds elapsed and then Ludwig nervously poked his head around the door. Behrens was certain he had overheard the entire conversation; probably the whole damned building had, he thought ruefully. "Any instructions, Herr Major?"

Behrens resisted an impulse to tell Ludwig to go to hell; instead, he merely said, "Find Unteroffizier Ziegler and tell him I want a word."

"At once, Herr Major."

Ziegler appeared in less than a minute; Behrens motioned him into a seat. A stray thought struck him; he always invited Ziegler to sit down, but never Ludwig. Favouritism, pure and simple; he would have to watch out for that in future.

"We'll have to call off the surveillance on Marika Schurrmann, Ziegler."

"Was that what Sturmbannführer Kreissner came to see you about, Herr Major?"

"It certainly was," said Behrens sourly. "It's pointless keeping it up, anyway, now that they know about it."

"I wonder how they got on to it?" mused Ziegler.

"I don't know." Behrens shrugged. "Maybe the girl spotted the surveillance. Or the Gestapo did. It doesn't really matter, does it?"

"It's funny though, Herr Major," said Ziegler, frowning. "Last night, Vogts was following her, but lost her soon after she left work. He went on to her home and picked her up again when she got back. Later on, he followed her to Sturmbannführer Kreissner's quarters."

"Again," said Behrens acidly.

"Again," Ziegler agreed. "Only this time she stayed the night. She's never done that before. Kreissner took her in to Gestapo headquarters."

"And this morning, Kreissner comes in here breathing fire and brimstone," said Behrens thoughtfully.

"Might be coincidence, Herr Major."

"And there again, it might not. She might have told Kreissner about the surveillance last night."

"It's possible, Herr Major," agreed Ziegler.

"And Vogts lost her earlier on? How long for?"

"He lost her at about five-thirty. She got home at about a quarter to seven."

"So there's an hour and a quarter unaccounted for. How did she lose Vogts?"

Ziegler gave him a précis of the incident; Vogts had not thought she had intentionally shaken him off.

"But it could have been deliberate on her part?" mused Behrens.

Ziegler shrugged. "If it was, then it would have to be very well done to fool Vogts. He's no amateur."

"That's exactly what worries me. On the one hand, we have a perfectly innocent explanation. The girl is unaware of the surveillance, loses Vogts entirely by accident and spends the night with Kreissner. Vogts has been spotted by the Gestapo themselves and it's pure coincidence that Kreissner comes in here the next morning. The girl's in the clear.

"Or we have the opposite theory. Marika Schuurmann spots Vogts tailing her, succeeds in losing him, disappears for seventy–five minutes, tells Kreissner all about it, while giving him a memorable night in bed and then he comes in here screaming blue murder. You take your pick.

"Only, if she spotted Vogts, then she must have been on the lookout for anyone following her. If she deliberately lost him, then she's got considerable expertise, especially if she did it well enough to make it look like an accident. It also argues that she was going somewhere in that hour and a quarter that she didn't want Vogts to know about. If it was all intentional on her part, then she's had training."

Ziegler nodded. "I see what you mean, Herr Major."

"And what was she doing after she lost him? Where did she go? Who did she meet? I don't like it, Ziegler. The more I find out about her, the more I'm convinced she's with the Resistance."

"It's certainly worth keeping an eye on her, Herr Major. But we've been warned off."

"That wouldn't bother me, Ziegler. If I thought it would do any good, I'd keep up the surveillance, never mind what Kreissner said. But if she's spotted it, then she won't lead us anywhere important. It's not worth keeping a tail on her now."

"So what do you have in mind, Herr Major?"

"She has a brother, named Pieter. They share the flat;both parents are dead, apparently. If she is with the Resistance, then he must know about it. It might be worth putting a tail on him for the next few weeks just to see if we turn anything up. They might be using him as a courier if nothing else; you never know your luck.

"It's worth a try, anyway."

Kreissner glanced up as Marika came in, carrying a pile of folders which she set on the desk. He smiled up at her; her response seemed half–hearted, as if her mind were on other things. "You won't forget tonight, Marika?" Kreissner said silkily. "Eight o'clock?"

"Of course I hadn't forgotten, Herr Sturmbannführer." Again, the smile was forced, but now he could see the expression in her eyes. It was fear; she was still terrified of him, even now. He watched her go out, admiring her hips thoughtfully.

Was Behrens right, damn him? Had he fallen for one of the oldest espionage tricks in the book? Despite his opinion of Behrens, it had to be considered as a possibility. It would indeed be a major coup for any Resistance group if one of its members could succeed in gaining the confidence of a senior Gestapo officer. By becoming his mistress, for instance . . .

But she hadn't behaved like one; not at first, anyway.One would have thought that if she were involved in such a plan, she would have been far more compliant, more wanton in bed. But that first night, she had been totally unresponsive, lying like a statue, cold, lifeless. Admittedly, after he had agreed to deal with the men who had been following her, she had been more uninhibited, deliciously so, but even now there were still moments of restraint that tended to contradict any Mata Hari theory. It was as if she had decided to make the best of an unavoidable predicament, but had not yet succeeded in overcoming all of her moral objections. . .

He shook his head. She had to be innocent. True, she had been in Kuipers' cell, but he refused to believe that he had been manipulated into taking her down to see the Dutchman. She could not possibly have predicted his reaction; indeed, he had only thought of it himself on the spur of the moment. No, she could not have planned it . . . On the other hand, she might have taken advantage of the situation once it had arisen.

And Behrens had hit upon a telling point when he had asked who would have found it easier to obtain the identification codes. It would not have been impossible for Hauser, by any means, but it would not have been very easy, either, while Marika would have had little difficulty. On any objective assessment, he knew that she had to be considered a possible suspect. Perhaps Behrens had been right; maybe the evidence implicating Hauser was all too pat. Certainly, Hauser was still protesting his innocence, despite days of sharpened interrogation. Could he be telling the truth? Had be been the victim in a move designed to draw attention away from the real Resistance agent?

Marika could certainly have stolen the documents. She had been working late the night the theft had occurred and would have known that there would be files on Opitz's desk only two doors away. It would have been easy for her to plant the money in Hauser's locker. And it had been her going to see Opitz the following morning that caused the theft to be discovered so rapidly. Pure coincidence or had she been ensuring that the missing file would be noticed as soon as possible?

Kreissner cursed under his breath. He knew what he should do; drag her down to the interrogation cell and beat the truth out of her. The thought of losing the luscious body was almost unendurable, but if she knew anything at all they would soon prise it out of her.

Unfortunately, there was more to his quandary than that. He had to consider his own standing with his superiors. Von Krug had left him in no doubt as to what would happen if he made any further mistakes in this investigation; if it ever came out that he, Kreissner, had taken a Dutch girl as his mistress who had proved to be a member of the Resistance, von Krug would crucify him. Kreissner's career would lie in tatters; worse, he might well end up on the Russian Front, commanding one of the SS Punishment Units. It has happened before to Gestapo officers who had fallen foul of their superiors. . .

So the bitter irony of Kreissner's predicament was that, even if Marika were a member of the Resistance, he could not afford to denounce her publicly, could not arrest her; it would bring about his own downfall. What was he to do with her,then? Both his own personal inclinations and the sheer practical need for survival decreed that he do nothing about her for the present. After all, he told himself, she might be totally innocent. All this might be for nothing. . .

Kreissner made his decision. He would keep her under observation; he was in a unique position to do so. Indeed, he told himself, by adopting a low–key approach, she might well be lulled into making some error that would lead him to her accomplices. If he could arrest all of them and make it appear that he had deliberately gone along with her schemes, he would be vindicated. Von Krug would not be able to touch him.

Kreissner smiled to himself. The perfect solution, one that would allow him the best of both worlds, given luck. He could continue to enjoy her body, would preserve his own standing with von Krug and, if he was patient and devious enough, he might well gain the personal kudos of rounding up a highly dangerous Resistance group. A softly softly approach, with Marika Schuurmann the unwitting centre of attention, the fly trapped in his web. . .

**LONDON**

"What time is it, darling?"

Woodward lifted up his arm and peered at the luminous

hands of his watch. "Just after midnight. Why?"

"Just wondering how much longer I can have you, Tony. You'll have to be gone by six, I'm afraid. That's when Miles gets back from the Ministry."

"Don't you worry, Sarah. I have no wish to confront Miles at six o'clock in the morning."

"Do you have a cigarette, darling? I'm absolutely dying for one."

Woodward grinned to himself in the darkness: Sarah always wanted a cigarette after making love. "Certainly." He reached over and flicked on the bedside light. He found the packet and passed it over to Sarah, who was sitting up beside him, her full breasts revealed; he lit the cigarette for her but did not take one himself.

"Thanks, darling. Ooh, that's better."

"That's what you said five minutes ago."

"Don't remind me of my more lascivious tendencies, darling. Remember I'm a respectable married woman."

"Whose husband is conveniently at work."

"I know." She looked at Woodward. "So you're off tomorrow?"

"Today, to be perfectly accurate."

"And when will you be back?"

"Within a week, if it all goes well."

"Take care of yourself, Tony. I'd hate anything to happen to you. Who would keep my bed warm at nights?"

"Don't worry, Sarah. We'll be back with that Jerry plane in no time."

"Careful, Tony. Don't say so much about it. You shouldn't be telling me anything at all about it."

"What, all this 'Walls have ears' rubbish? That's all childish propaganda and you know it."

"All the same, Tony, it is a secret mission and you've gone and told me all about it. You shouldn't have, really."

"Oh, don't be silly, Sarah. We've known each other for years, haven't we? I'm quite sure you're not a German spy. Unthinkable. The Lady Sarah, daughter of a belted earl, no less, working for the Nazis?" He held out his arm in a Nazi salute, placing a finger of his left hand under his nose in a parody of a Hitler moustache. "Sieg Heil, mein Führer!" he barked in schoolboy German.

She didn't laugh; indeed, she looked somewhat irritated. "I'm being serious, Tony. To you, it's all a big game, isn't it? A wizard prang, what? Like when you fly those reconnaissance ops in the Mosquito, just a joyride, as you call it? I suppose the idea of stealing a German plane appeals to your sense of romance, doesn't it? Well, this one isn't a joyride, Tony. It's about time you started taking this seriously. From what you've told me, it sounds damned dangerous and I wish you'd realise that and not treat it as a game. You could be killed, Tony."

There was no mistaking the genuine concern in her voice; Woodward was taken by surprise. He had never thought that he might mean more to her than a mere bed partner. "I'll take care, Sarah. Don't worry."

"Make sure you do, Tony." She put her hand on his arm;anxiety was written all over her face. What did she really think of him? Woodward wondered. She had only married for money and prestige, he knew that; Miles Winstanley was a good twenty years older than her, but what did she think of her lover?

"Anyway, I've got good protection. I don't think Cormack will let me do anything irresponsible."

"Cormack? What's he like?"

"Well, put it this way. I don't think they'd ever accept him for membership at the club. He's from the East End; one can hear the accent, but—well—he knows what he's doing. I can't pretend to like the man but he's the best marksman I've ever seen."

"A professional, you mean?"

"Exactly."

"Good. With any luck, he'll keep you in line." She looked at him. "I know you're not really as wild as you make yourself out to be, Tony. I know you take your flying very seriously, even though you might joke about it when you're down on the ground. It's just that you're getting into something that isn't in your field and I'm worried for you." She rolled over on top of him and kissed him. "Promise me you'll come back, Tony."

"I promise, Sarah." Her lips pressed hungrily against his and he felt an unmistakeable stirring in his groin as she moved voluptuously against him, her dark hair covering his face. She was fascinating; so coldly regal, so aristocratically aloof in public, but a wanton harlot in bed, totally uninhibited. And she was ready for him again, her legs already parting to receive him. The thought came once more: what does she really think of me? And then he felt her enclosing, moist warmth and he stopped wondering.

# CHAPTER 11

**NIGHT OF 6/7 MAY: NORTH SEA**

"Captain Cormack, wake up, will you, sir? The skipper'd like a word with you."

It took Cormack several seconds to awaken, even with the insistent hand that was shaking his shoulder, and it then needed three or four more seconds for him to realise that he was lying on a bunk in the tiny, cramped wardroom of a submarine. Of course. HMS *Strenuous*. S–class sub, with Lieutenant–Commander Wickham as Commanding Officer. He looked at his watch: 23.07. They weren't due off the Dutch coast for another two hours yet; what was going on?

"Right, I'm coming. Where is he?"

"Control Room, sir."

"Cormack swung his legs off the bunk, wearily. Christ,he was tired; he had stretched out on the bunk only an hour before.

Wickham was peering intently into the periscope lens; he glanced briefly across at Cormack as he arrived. "Ah, there you are, Captain. Bit of a problem, I'm afraid."

Cormack had already noted Wickham's tendency to speak in terse, clipped sentences, with a pronounced upper–class drawl that made him sound like the proverbial silly–ass; on the other hand, he issued his orders crisply and had an air of relaxed capability. "Problem?"

"Take a look," Wickham offered, stepping back from the eyepieces.

Cormack peered through the lens. At first, he could see nothing and then, suddenly, the scene leapt into focus. A ship, dead ahead of them, with the low, raked silhouette of a fighting vessel.

"Wolf class escort destroyer," he heard Wickham say. "Probably on anti–submarine patrol."

"Has it detected us?"

"Not bloody likely. Wouldn't be buggering about here if it had. Right in our way, though."

"What are you going to do, then?"

"Have to detour round it. Probably make us late, though."

"Fair enough. Can't be helped. We've a couple of hours leeway, anyway."

Cormack went back to the wardroom, where Woodward and Poortvliet were waiting, both seated on bunks. Woodward looked dreadful, Cormack thought. His eyes were darting everywhere like a caged animal's. Probably claustrophobic, Cormack realised, although he hadn't said anything when he had been told about the approach by submarine. Still, he wasn't having hysterics; he was keeping it under control.

"What's up?" asked Woodward in a voice that was too casual.

"Jerry destroyer. We're having to detour round it."

"I see." Woodward lapsed into silence.

Briefly, Cormack wondered if they should have gone in by parachute, but then dismissed the thought. He had made the decision and it was too late to go back on it now. The submarine approach offered a better chance of going in undetected; any aircraft would be almost certain to be picked up by one of the numerous German radar stations on the Dutch coast. In addition, Woodward had been given no parachute training beyond the basic advice given to aircrew; as Cormack had once heard, it was little more than "Jump, pull the rip–cord, close your eyes and pray. Not necessarily in that order, either." No, this approach was better, but would he have decided otherwise if he had known about Woodward's claustrophobia?

Somehow, he doubted it.

There was a sudden hubbub of voices from the Control Room, instantly quelled. Almost before he realised what he was doing, Cormack was sprinting out of the wardroom.

Wickham was by the periscope, issuing orders rapidly, calmly. "Flood main tank. Fifty feet. Group up. Steer O–

eight–three. Five knots." He glanced over at Cormack, almost apologetically. "Two R–boats turned up. They've got us on their detection gear. Going to be a bit rough, I expect."

"Listen!" said Woodward tensely; Cormack had not even been aware that the pilot had followed him out of the wardroom.

Cormack heard it then, a metallic pinging sound, running through the submarine's hull every three or four seconds. It was eerie, as though some alien, supernatural force had them in their power.

"What the hell is it?" Woodward whispered.

"Asdic," said Wickham quietly. "Means we're on their screens. It'll go away in a minute." He smiled faintly. "That's when you start worrying. Means they're about to attack."

Cheerful sod, thought Cormack. There was another sound now, a continuous 'shushing' noise that was growing steadily louder. He could guess what that was: the attacking ship's propellers.

Coming straight at them, for God's sake . . .

Abruptly, the pinging ceased; simultaneously, Cormack heard the voice of the hydrophone operator:

"Lost contact, sir." And then the operator did a curious thing; he removed his earphones. Cormack observed this little by–play; he was fastening onto such trivial details with a desperate intensity.

"Hard a–port. Full power. Steer double–O–five," said Wickham impassively.

The sound of the propellers above reached a crescendo and then began to fade away as the ship passed overhead.

"Here we go," said Barnett, the First Lieutenant, who was standing next to Cormack. "Hold on tight, gentlemen."

Cormack barely had time to take hold of a thick length of tubing before the submarine lurched, first one way, then the other. The noise of the exploding depth charges was deafening; Cormack could feel his ears popping under the concussions and suddenly realised why the hydrophone operator had removed his headphones. If he'd kept them on, his eardrums would have been ruptured when that lot went off.

It seemed incredible to Cormack that the submarine could

possibly have survived such a battering, but Wickham and the rest of the control room personnel looked distinctly unimpressed.

"Little way off, sir," commented Barnett, as if he were discussing the weather.

"Ye–es," drawled Wickham nonchalantly. "Where are they, Spinks?"

Spinks, the hydrophone operator, had now replaced his headphones. "Bearing one–nine–three, sir. They're not in contact."

"Good. Ahead slow." Wickham looked at Cormack and then explained,"Keeps our revs down. Less likely to hear us."

I take it all back, thought Cormack fervently. There was no way that Lieutenant– Commander Wickham could ever be described as a silly–ass.

There was absolute silence for the next five minutes as *Strenuous* crept stealthily northwards. Gradually, there was a lessening of tension in the control room as the distance between the submarine and the patrolling ships increased. Perhaps they would get away without further problems. They might not be too late arriving off the coast . . .

"They're coming back," said Spinks suddenly.

"Bugger," muttered Barnett; Wickham glared at him.

"In contact," reported Spinks.

Cormack heard nothing for several seconds, then the pinging sound was only too audible as the electronics pulses struck the pressure hull.

"Maintain present course and speed." Wickham glanced at his watch.

Cormack did the same: 23.45, he saw, with a shock; he felt as though he had been standing there for hours.

"Lost contact, sir."

"Starboard twenty. Full power. Steer O–nine–O."

The deck tilted as *Strenuous* came round onto the new course. O–nine–O; that was due east. Wickham was trying to move closer inshore, evidently. Trying to out–guess the pursuing ships, perhaps; they would expect him to head out to sea, to deeper water.

Once again, the propeller noise grew to a climax and then

began to fade. Cormack flicked a brief glance at Woodward;the pilot's eyes were screwed tightly shut and his lips were moving, forming soundless words. He was deathly pale, but perspiration was running down his face in rivulets.

Poor sod, thought Cormack. Maybe . . .

And then all hell broke loose. Cormack was hurled to one side, slamming into the bulkhead before falling to the crazily tilting deckplates, deafened by the shattering concussion.

And blinded too, he suddenly realised, choking back a scream of stark terror: everything had gone black. He couldn't see!

He almost sobbed in relief as he was bathed in a dim red glow; the emergency lighting had come on. Incredulously, he saw that Wickham was still on his feet, clinging on to his handhold as the deck remained slanted at a drunken angle.

"Full astern. Blow ballast tanks."

"Fifty–five feet. Sixty. Sixty–five feet."

"Blow Q tank." For the first time, Cormack detected the merest hint of strain in Wickham's voice and the wild thought came to him that things must really be serious . . .

The submarine was bow down and diving, out of control. How deep was the bloody sea round here, anyway?

"Eighty. Eighty–five. Ninety."

They were still going down and fast; if they didn't stop the dive, they'd plunge straight into the sea bottom, bow first. If they were lucky, the hull would split wide open and they'd die quickly. If not, they'd stay on the seabed and suffocate, slowly.

"Oh, sweet Jesus, no, no!" Woodward's voice was growing in volume; he was lying on the deck next to Cormack, trembling uncontrollably, on the verge of hysteria. Cormack leapt to his feet and grabbed Woodward by his jacket front, hauling him upright. He slammed Woodward up against the bulkhead and slapped him across the face, hard.

Woodward's eyes opened, dazed, shocked; but he had stopped shaking.

"You do that again, Woodward, and I'll use my fist next time. Savvy?" hissed Cormack.

Dumbly, Woodward nodded. He swallowed, nervously. "I—I'm all right now."

"You'd better be, sunshine."

"One twenty-five . . . One thirty . . . We're slowing down, sir. One thirty-five . . . One forty . . . Steady on one forty feet, sir."

"Good show," drawled Wickham and it was then that Cormack saw through the façade; it was all an act on Wickham's part, all this nonchalant suavity. It was a front to cover his true feelings. "Flood rear tank."

Slowly, *Strenuous* came back onto an even keel. "Where are they, Spinks?" asked Wickham.

"Circling, sir. They've lost us."

Wickham was silent for almost thirty seconds; then he looked at his watch and came to a decision. "Right. Slow ahead.Steer O–nine–O." He grinned across at Cormack. "Have to drop you off, don't we?"

Cormack looked around at the shattered instrument gauges, at the Chief Petty Officer whose head was being bandaged. The control room looked as if a bomb had hit it; indeed, in effect, this was not so far from the truth. Yet Wickham looked as though he had just emerged from a shower, so spruce and alert did he look. Beyond him, a seaman was busily sweeping up the debris that littered the deck plating. All in a night's work . . .

Cormack made himself a silent promise. Never, ever, would he say anything against the Royal Navy again.

**LEIDEN**

Trudi was aware of a feeling of nervous anticipation as Behrens held the door open for her. This was the first time she had accompanied him back to his quarters, although they had been in each other's company a good deal over the last few weeks. Whatever happened tonight, their relationship had moved at least one step forward; if his behaviour were to turn out to be less than gentlemanly, then she had only herself to blame, as it had been she who had suggested that they come here. She shuddered to think what he might think of her after such a blatant suggestion, but she found that she was less worried by this than by wondering whether he would take her up on her implied offer.

His quarters were immaculately kept; the furnishings were fairly basic, Spartan even, but everything was meticulously tidy. She smiled. "So this is where you live, Anton. From the way you'd described it, I thought it would be an unholy mess."

"It was, when I went out," Behrens replied, smiling. "All this is entirely due to Weidlinger, my batman. I have to admit that."

As he spoke, Behrens had been heading towards the kitchen door; for the first time, Trudi heard a low–pitched whining coming from beyond it. Behrens opened the door and a glossy black Labrador leapt out at him, tail wagging furiously, licking his face in frantic joy as he bent forward to stroke its ears. He reached down to caress the dog's stomach. "This is Lotti," he explained to Trudi. "She likes a fuss."

Lotti came trotting over to Trudi and sat down, gazing appealingly up at her. Trudi ruffled her ears; the dog's tail began to beat, frantically. "She's beautiful, Anton.How old is she?"

"I don't know exactly. About three, I'd say. She turned up at my quarters one afternoon two years ago and I made the mistake of giving her some of my dinner. I haven't been able to get rid of her since." Lotti padded back to him as he crouched down; she jumped up, placing one paw on each of his shoulders as he petted her, his expression giving the lie to his words. He was as devoted to the dog as she was to him, that much was evident.

And, seeing the tender way that Behrens treated the dog, Trudi, to her astonishment, realised that she was actually jealous—of a dog! It was his display of affection that moved her; she was suddenly aware that she very much wanted to see that look in his eyes when he looked at her.

"All right, all right, Lotti. Yes, I have got a present for you being a good girl." He went into the kitchen, opened a cupboard and took out a bone, which he gave to Lotti. The dog retired to a corner of the kitchen to gnaw at it.

"Do sit down, Trudi. Can I offer you a drink?"

"No, thanks, Anton. I'm fine."

"Coffee?"

"Again, no thanks."

"Fair enough." He came and sat next to her on the sofa.

"You've never mentioned having a dog before now."

"Oh, I try to forget her whenever I can."

"Rubbish!" she laughed. "You dote on that dog, and you know it!"

"Yes, I suppose I do," he admitted. "Maybe it's because she's never let me down. Dogs never do, not if you're kind to them."

"Unlike human beings? she said, probing gently.

He smiled wryly. "That transparent, am I? Yes, unlike some human beings."

"Who was she?" she asked, greatly daring.

Behrens hesitated. "Anneliese. My fiancée. Ex–fiancée, rather."

"What happened, or would you rather not tell me?"

"She didn't like the idea of marrying a man in my condition—after the crash, I mean."

"I see."

"Oh, I know that she couldn't really have cared and all that. It must have been a devil of a shock for her when you think about it. I can't really blame her. Maybe some women could have come to terms with my—appearance—but not Anneliese. So she said goodbye."

Bitch, thought Trudi, with sudden vehemence, but she made no comment. "Seems like we're both in the same boat, Anton."

"Really?" He looked at her.

"Oh, I wasn't engaged, but I was—no, I thought I was—in love. And I thought he loved me. Obviously, though, he didn't. He went off with someone else, just like that."

"I'm sorry."

"Don't be. I'm not, now. Not any more. It would have been a mistake if it had gone on." She shrugged. "So that's why I had to get away from Berlin for a while. There's something about the whole atmosphere there . . . it's decadent. All of a sudden, I couldn't stand the place or the people any longer. Too many memories." She broke off suddenly, aghast at how much she had told him; yet she found it so easy to talk to him, even about things she had never discussed with anyone before. Be careful, Trudi . . . you might be getting in over your head with Major Behrens.

He did not seem to notice her sudden silence; Lotti had come back in from the kitchen and had placed her forepaws in his lap; he was apparently engrossed in petting her. "Yes, I know what you mean," he said absently. "There's a sort of desperation in the air. Everyone seems intent on grabbing whatever's going, before it all blows up in their faces. And, sometimes, what they're trying to grab is—well—sick."

"Are you talking about this—what was her name? The other general's daughter?"

"Klara Haller."

"She was exactly the opposite to your fiancée?"

Behrens nodded. "Anneliese was repelled by my injuries so I suppose you could say her reaction was fairly normal, but Fräulein Haller . . . I think she found the idea of a maimed hero rather erotic."

"Was she attractive?"

"Very."

"Were you not tempted?"

"Oh, I was tempted all right. But the price she wanted was too high."

Trudi raised her eyebrows at this cryptic remark but let it pass; she had asked too many personal questions already tonight. Indeed, she had found out more about him in the last half hour than in their entire acquaintanceship up till then. So much had been explained, especially his diffidence. She knew the reason for his constraint now, but how to deal with it? Because, she realised suddenly, she very much wanted to go to bed with him.

"Anton?"

"Yes?"

"Do they worry you? Your injuries?"

"In what way?"

"You said this Klara Haller was only after an erotic thrill. You also said Anneliese couldn't come to terms with your injuries. Do you think that women—normal women, that is—would not find you attractive?"

He grinned, wryly. "Well, I'm not exactly a pretty sight, what with all the scars and burns."

She looked into his eyes. "Why not let me be the judge of that?"

And then, somehow, they were in each other's arms, kissing, his tongue probing into her mouth, her own responding in kind. She felt him relax against her and smiled to herself.

Yet he was still, clearly, self–conscious about his wounds, turning them away from her as they undressed in the bedroom. She went over to him and put her arms round him. "You mustn't worry about it, Anton. I want you to make love to me. Not Major Behrens, the Luftwaffe flying ace, with the Knight's Cross, but plain Anton Behrens, who's all soft–hearted and silly about his dog and one of the nicest men I've ever met. That's who I want, Anton. You. And I couldn't care less about this." She placed her hand gently on his scarred flesh. "It just doesn't matter. Understand?"

He nodded gratefully and smiled. She moved away from him and continued to undress until she was absolutely naked and then she pressed herself to him, holding him tightly in her arms, feeling a sudden surge of emotion, a mixture of desire and tenderness. The scars were not just on his body, they were in his mind as well. I'll help you, Anton, she said to herself. And you can help me as well. Because I need this, perhaps even more than you. I have to know that I can be wanted, needed . . .

They sank down onto the bed, and slowly, gently, they began to make love.

**DUTCH COAST, NORTH OF NOORDWIJK**

Cormack was the first out of the rubber dinghy and splashed ashore, Sten at the ready. He looked carefully around and then beckoned; within seconds, first Woodward and then Poortvliet had joined him and the submarine's dinghy was disappearing into the darkness, on its way back to *Strenuous*.

They headed into the sand dunes, moving inland, Cormack leading the way. After some fifteen minutes, he called a halt.

"Right. You two stay here. I'll go on ahead, and make contact with Voltimand. Just stay put, right? I'll be back in under an hour."

"And if not?" asked Poortvliet in heavily accented English.

"Head back to the beach. Wickham will wait offshore until five-thirty, so you'll have plenty of time to signal him."

Poortvliet nodded; he was man of few words at the best of times, Cormack knew.

"Right. An hour, no more than that. Be seeing you." Cormack moved further into the dunes and, within seconds, was lost to sight.

Poortvliet looked around and then gestured up at a nearby dune. "I go up. You stay put. Yes?"

"Yes," said Woodward moodily and watched Poortvliet go. He was fed up with being treated like a kid by these two. Fair enough, they were professionals and he wasn't, but they didn't have to be quite so condescending, did they?

He reached inside his tunic for the bar of chocolate he had opened shortly after they had left the beach; he couldn't find it. Irritably, he tried the other pockets without success. Where the hell was it? Slowly, methodically, he went through his pockets again; no, it definitely wasn't there. He must have dropped it on the way . . .

Oh, bloody hell, he thought. That would be a dead give–away if the Jerries found it. Cormack would explode when he found out . . .

Only he wasn't going to find out, Woodward decided. He wasn't going to admit to Cormack that he had dropped a chocolate bar; he could imagine Cormack's scathing comments only too well, especially after the scene in the submarine. Woodward was still smarting from the memory of how he had broken down and how Cormack had treated him; he wasn't going to face anything like that again.

So the alternatives were to say nothing and hope that the Jerries wouldn't find it or go and look for it. He couldn't run the risk of leaving it, so . . .

Woodward began to retrace his steps. He had always had a good sense of direction and visibility was good under a moonlit sky. It wouldn't be far from their route: it must simply have fallen out of his pocket.

Within twenty minutes, Woodward was back at the beach.There was no sign of the chocolate. He headed back, attempting to recall his exact actions. Let's see, he thought. I took it out around here. Yes, along here. Broke a piece off, folded the wrapper back over the rest, put it back in the pocket, about here, walked on, chewing it . . .

"Halt!" a voice barked from behind him.

A German voice.

"Hands up!" Heavily accented, guttural English; Woodward obeyed instantly.

"Turn around."

Woodward did so. The German soldier was standing about five yards away, a carbine aimed at Woodward's stomach. Woodward felt icy fear knotting his insides. This was a nightmare, it couldn't really be happening . . .

"Who are you? What are you doing here?"

Woodward opened his mouth but no sound came out.

"Answer!"

Woodward was never quite sure what happened next. The German soldier was standing alone, in total command of the situation; then a shadow seemed to materialise out of the darkness behind him, moving swiftly towards him.

And in utter silence.

Cormack . . .

Woodward saw Cormack's left hand clamp itself over the German's mouth, wrenching the soldier's head back and then the right hand moved rapidly across the offered neck.

It was only when Woodward saw the blood gushing from the six inch rent under the man's chin that he realised that Cormack had been holding a knife; he had slit the German's throat almost from ear to ear.

Cormack released the dying soldier and stepped back as the German fell forward, frantically gasping for air that would not come, could not come, as the knife had sliced cleanly through the windpipe . . . He made horrible, bubbling noises as he died, rolling over so that his heels drummed briefly on the sand before they were still.

Woodward stared horror–struck at the corpse and then turned away, his stomach heaving. Cormack came over to him.

"I told you to stay put. What the hell were you doing?"

Woodward had to wait until the urge to retch had subsided before he could answer. "I—I dropped a chocolate bar. I came back here to look for it."

"You came back here to look for it," said Cormack hollowly. He shook his head slowly and sighed. Raging at

Woodward would not serve any useful purpose, not now. "Then we'd better damn well find it, hadn't we?" he said mildly.

Woodward found that he could not stop himself looking at the dead German. Cormack had killed him—no, worse than that—had murdered him, without any display of emotion at all. What sort of man was he, for heaven's sake? A ruthless killer . . .

Cormack came up beside him. "Not very pretty, is it? But death never is, Woodward. And remember this: if you hadn't dropped that bar of chocolate, he'd still be alive. Now get looking for it." He turned away.

"Don't try and put the blame on me, Cormack! You killed him! That was cold–blooded murder!"

Cormack spun round. "And dropping high explosives on defenceless civilians isn't, I take it? How many bombing missions have you flown, Woodward? Forty–odd, isn't it? How many bombs have you dropped? How many people have you killed? A hundred? A thousand? And how many of them were women and children? Well?" His eyes were boring into Woodward's stricken face. "They're just as dead as he is, Woodward, only you don't ever get to see them, do you? And how many nights' sleep have you lost over them? Well, Woodward?" He paused in his onslaught, as if waiting for Woodward to reply; but Woodward said nothing.

"Right," said Cormack eventually in a curiously subdued voice. Let's look for this bloody chocolate, shall we?" He turned away again.

Woodward watched him as he moved away. Still he said nothing; he could find no words with which to counter Cormack's bitter attack.

No words, because Cormack was undeniably, incontrovertibly, right.

Cormack left Woodward to search on his own after about fifteen minutes and went to collect Poortvliet and the man who had identified himself as De Vriess; he was their contact with Voltimand. He brought them back with him to join in the hunt for the missing chocolate; Woodward was left in no doubt by their expressions what they thought of him.

At five-thirty, Cormack called the search off; they had to reach their hide–out before dawn and could not afford to delay any further. "We'll just have to hope that the Jerries don't find it," Cormack said gloomily. "Still, if we can't find it, then, with any luck, neither will they. Especially as they won't be looking for it in the first place."

They trooped off into the dunes, leaving the dead soldier buried in a shallow grave of sand. He would still be found, of course, but his death might well be attributed to the Resistance. It would be the chocolate bar that would tell the Germans that there had been a landing by British agents.

If they found it; on balance, Cormack reckoned that the odds of that happening were probably seventy–thirty against. Reasonable odds, if you were a gambling man . . .

Unfortunately, nobody had thought to search the dead soldier's pockets; he would have had nothing that would be of any interest or use. They had no way of knowing that he had, in fact, discovered the chocolate bar some ten minutes before Woodward had come back; he had put it in his tunic pocket.

It was still there . . .

# CHAPTER 12

**LEIDEN: MORNING, FRIDAY 7TH MAY**

They came diving out of the sun, straight at him; he spotted the first one perhaps four seconds before the Russian opened fire and he was already wheeling away from the onslaught, standing the Bf109G on its wingtip, as the tracers scythed past, only metres away. Behrens swore; he must have been half- asleep, letting himself be jumped like that. Too many sorties, dead on his feet, but no excuse for negligence . . .

And the Russian was following him round, matching the Messerschmidt's turn; Behrens glanced behind him and felt a cold chill grip him. There wasn't just one of them, there were four! And there wasn't a single bloody German plane in sight . . .

Behrens wrenched the stick to starboard and hauled back on it; the 'Gustav' staggered in mid-air, almost stalling, before he pushed the column forward, still turning. He saw the leading Russian hurtle past to port, guns firing, completely thrown off by his manoeuvre. Behrens came round after the Russian, a part of his mind absently identifying the enemy aircraft: one of the new La–5s. Fast and manoeuvrable, they were the very planes he did not wish to see at this moment.

The Russian twisted to one side and Behrens followed him round, remorselessly, knowing that the second La–5 would be behind him, but that his only hope of escape was to shoot down the Russians, one by one. He couldn't out–run them; the La–5s were believed to be capable of 650 k.p.h. while the Gustav's maximum was some 75 k.p.h. less than that.

The Russian twisted and turned, frantically; it was all Behrens could do to keep on his tail. They'd been right, Behrens thought, abstractedly; these La–5s were damned handy in the air. Mind you, the 109G, the Gustav, handled like a pregnant cow compared with its predecessor, the 109F, but they'd taken the F out of production, now. Stupid bastards.

And then, at last, he had the La–5 in his sights. He pressed the firing button and the 109 shuddered as the cannons fired, the tracers stitching a pattern across the Russian's fuselage and tail assembly. Behrens followed his victim round and then banked violently away as the second Russian opened up.

He wasn't quite fast enough; he could feel the impacts as shells ripped through the Messerschmidt's body and wings. Behrens hauled the stick round, but the Gustav was slow to respond; the shells continued to slam into the fighter.

Behrens throttled back, breaking all the unwritten rules of aerial combat, and dropped the flaps right down. The Gustav seemed to fly into an invisible brick wall and reared up like a startled horse in a manoeuvre that ought to have ripped the wings off, according to the book.

Only it didn't. The Russian swung violently to one side to avoid running full tilt into the Messerschmidt; instantly, Behrens brought the flaps up, pushed the throttle wide open and banked round in pursuit.

The Gustav was sluggish; he could feel the mushiness in the controls. And the last two Russians were after him, side by side . . .

Behrens yanked the stick over again, but the 109 seemed to take an eternity to respond; the shells tore into the Messerschmidt, raking it along its entire length. Something exploded into his left ankle, sending a white–hot shaft of agony searing up his leg.

The Gustav was dropping away now, out of control; through the cockpit perspex, he could see that the port wing was on fire. The fighter was doomed, the dive already steepening; she was beginning to roll over. Behrens knew he had only seconds left in which to bale out, before the roll became a lethal spin that would pin him into his seat.

He dragged the column to starboard and towards him, ignoring the pain in his ankle; somehow, the Gustav stopped rolling, began flying on an even keel—but it was still diving. Behrens braced both feet and hauled back on the stick with every ounce of strength he could muster; for long seconds, nothing happened and then, slowly, slowly, the nose came up.

He glanced at the altimeter; it was smashed, but the ground was suddenly very close beneath. Too close . . . The only way he could fly the aircraft was like this, with the stick over to starboard and pulled right back. The instant he let go of the column to clamber out of the cockpit, the plane would go of into a vertical spin and would hit the ground long before he could bale out, especially with his ankle slowing him up . . .

So, like it or not, he was going to have to make a crash–landing. And, he realised, as he saw a line of trees flash past seemingly only just below the wings, he would have to do it pretty damned fast. A belly–landing, then, without undercarriage or flaps; he dared not let go of the stick, even for an instant, to reach out for the controls. All he could do was to keep the crippled aircraft flying straight and level until the ground came up to meet him . . .

The 109 hurtled through a gap between two trees and then slammed into the earth with a bone–wrenching impact. It rebounded into the air and then smashed back down, careering across the grass as Behrens finally let go of the column, reaching up for the hatch release with one hand, finding it and operating it as the port wing dug into the ground, spinning the aircraft round and round. He had a momentary glimpse of a tree coming straight at him and then the wrecked aircraft ploughed into its trunk, the impact throwing Behrens to one side.

And now the ice–cold, almost inhuman control that had enabled him to land the plane at all was replaced by a panic–stricken urgency: the aircraft was on fire—he had to get out of it! He slammed back the cockpit cover as the instrument panel burst into flames and released his seatbelt. Behrens reached up and began to climb out, yelling in agony as his wounded ankle took his full weight for an instant.

He screamed as a tongue of flame licked out at him; his flying gear was on fire. Desperately, he fought to escape from the blazing cockpit, his almost pathological dread of fire giving him the strength he needed to scramble out. He fell to the ground and rolled over, beating frantically at himself to put out the flames, still screaming hysterically, even after they had been extinguished.

Behrens began to crawl away from the wreckage and saw men running towards him, soldiers in field–grey uniforms: Germans, thank God. He was on his feet now, lurching and stumbling forwards on his good leg, yelling at them to get back, get down, the fuel tanks would go up any moment . . .

The aircraft exploded behind him in a gushing fireball that enveloped him and he fell to the ground, his body ablaze, his hands, his feet, his hair burning, twisting and writhing on the ground in unspeakable agony, all the torments of Hell in his last few seconds of life . . .

"Anton! Anton! Wake up, darling! Please! Anton!"

His eyes came open then and he was suddenly aware that his body was trembling violently, was drenched in perspiration. And he was being held by a naked woman, his head pressed to her breasts. So there was an afterlife, after all: was this Heaven or Hell?

And then he remembered; he was in his own quarters and he was with Trudi. He held on to her for several seconds as if to reassure himself that she was there and that he was still alive, before lying back on the pillow. He let out his breath in a great gasp.

"Jesus," he whispered hoarsely. "That was a bad one."

Trudi said nothing; she could still picture the expression of unreasoning terror on his face. Just what had he been through, for heaven's sake?

"Thanks, Trudi. For waking me up."

"That's all right, darling." She hesitated and then asked softly, "Was it the crash?"

He nodded slowly. "I dream about it a lot, unfortunately. It's always the same." The same dream, yes, he thought, but it didn't actually happen like that. Not quite. The dream had been a completely accurate record of the incident, right up to the last sequence: yes, he had staggered away from the burning aircraft, he screamed at the others to get clear and, yes, the fuel tanks had exploded, but the rest, the fireball engulfing him, had not happened. It had been there in his mind at the time, a vivid mental image that had given him the impetus, the overwhelming urge that had driven him away from the blaze, crippled as he was. The explosion had been bad enough; it had hurled him to the ground and a flying shard of metal had neatly severed his left hand at the wrist, but not as bad as the dream, where fact and his terrified imaginings had become inextricably entwined in his nightmares.

He realised that Trudi was pressing herself against him,

that her lips were on his throat, soothing him. He put his hand under her chin, gently, and lifted her face to his. They kissed, tenderly at first, then with increasing fervour. She was trying to make him forget his dream in the most effective way possible; Behrens understood and was grateful. He was a lucky man . . .

He began to caress her back, lightly. Their lips parted and she smiled at him. "Feeling better, now, Anton?"

"Much better, thank you, Trudi." He grinned at her.

The telephone began to ring; Behrens cursed softly and looked at the alarm clock. It was not yet 7.30; who the devil could that be? He reached out for the receiver; Trudi rolled over on top of him, blocking his arm. "Leave it, Anton," she whispered playfully.

He smiled at her and grabbed the receiver. "Behrens here."

"It's Ziegler, Herr Major. Sorry if I woke you up."

"What is it, Ziegler?"

"A soldier has been murdered, Herr Major, in the sand dunes. Probably by the Resistance. His throat was cut."

"Good God," exclaimed Behrens; Trudi saw his expression change and sat up, her face troubled.

"One of our tracker dogs found him," Ziegler was saying. "The victim was an Army private on patrol on the coast north of Noordwijk. He failed to report in at 0400 so they instituted a search for him. They contacted Oberleutnant Halldorf at Verwijk and borrowed one of our dogs. They found the body at just after six o'clock; it had been covered over with sand."

"I see," said Behrens. "Has the Gestapo been informed?"

"Yes, Herr Major. Do you wish to go to the scene?"

"Yes, I'd better." He looked apologetically at Trudi. "I'll be at the office inside half an hour; have a car ready." He put the phone down, looking thoughtful.

"Business, I take it," said Trudi regretfully.

"I'm afraid so. I'm sorry about that."

"It's all right. There'll be other times."

"Is that a promise?"

Her eyes met his. "It certainly is, Anton," she said softly.

Behrens looked down at the body, amazed that he could be so

unmoved. He had seen corpses before, of course; far too many, in fact, on the Eastern Front, but none as horrifically mutilated as this one, with his neck sliced open from ear to ear. He looked up at Kreissner, who had already been on the scene when he had arrived. Kreissner had not exactly looked pleased at Behrens' presence, but he had made no comment.

"A professional killing," Kreissner observed, in the neutral tones of a detached investigator. "The killer must have come up from behind, grabbed him, probably a hand on the chin or mouth, pulled the head back and then slit his throat. You said the wound was from left to right?" he asked the corpulent Gestapo doctor who was neatly packing his equipment away.

"Yes, Herr Sturmbannführer."

"So, a right-handed man, who knew what he was doing."

"Why kill him, though?" asked Behrens.

"He probably saw too much."

"Resistance?"

"It certainly looks like it," said Kreissner reluctantly.

"So what were they doing here?"

Kreissner shrugged. "Checking minefields or on their way to take a look at the radar station over there—" he gestured vaguely to the north. "Or anything, really. Your guess is as good as mine."

Behrens looked out to sea. "Might they have been rendezvousing with a boat?"

"Quite possibly."

One of Kreissner's assistants was carefully searching the dead soldier's pockets, turning out a pitiful array of personal effects: keys, identification documents, a letter in a tattered envelope. He reached into the breast pocket, hesitated and then took out a bar of chocolate. "Herr Sturmbannführer?"

"Yes, Brandt?"

Brandt handed the chocolate up to Kreissner, who examined it carefully. "British Army issue," he said flatly.

"Yes, Herr Sturmbannführer."

"That explains a lot," said Behrens.

Kreissner looked sharply at him and then nodded. "It would indeed appear that someone came ashore from a boat," Kreissner said heavily.

Behrens could reconstruct the scene with little difficulty; someone had come ashore and dropped the chocolate, which had been found by the soldier, who had put it into his pocket. The soldier had then been killed, but the killer had not known about the chocolate or he would not have left it on the body.

Which still left many unanswered questions, however. What had the soldier seen that had been so important that he had been killed to ensure his silence? Had someone come ashore, or had it been a pick–up, an agent going out to a waiting submarine or MTB? How many people had been involved? And where were they at this moment?

"I think," he said slowly to Kreissner, "that we may have a problem on our hands."

Kreissner's eyes glinted in surprise at Behrens' statement, at its hint of co–operation, and then he nodded. "You could well be right, Major."

Behrens was in a thoughtful mood as he returned to his office and even thinking about Trudi failed to dispel his gloomy preoccupation. That private had been no more than eighteen; he had hardly even begun to live his life and now he was dead. His killers were quite possibly on the loose somewhere not far from here. But what exactly had happened in those desolate sand dunes last night?

The more he thought about the incident, the more puzzled he became. Kreissner had said that the killer had been a professional, a highly trained killer, and he had to take the Gestapo man's word for it. But dropping a chocolate bar so that it could be found by the first German soldier that came along was anything but professional. It was this mixture of expertise and amateurism that baffled him; it implied that there was more than one man involved, one a trained undercover agent, the other a tyro, at least as regarded espionage. So what was the tyro doing here?

Two possibilities, thought Behrens, aware that he was building his hypothesis on very flimsy evidence, but giving his imagination full rein. One: the amateur might have been a sailor, if one assumed that a boat had come ashore. If that was the case, then he would be back on his own ship or submarine and was of no further interest to anyone. Or, two: he was a specialist in some other field than espionage, brought into Holland for a specific purpose. A scientist or an engineer, come to examine something of interest to the Allies.

Behrens sat up suddenly. The Liechtenstein radar? Why not? The Allies were certainly interested in it, as Kuipers' mission had proved; they might well be preparing to try again. What was there to stop them from trying to penetrate the airfield at Verwijk a second time? It would be the last place anyone would expect them to make a second attempt, which might be precisely what they were counting on.

He relaxed slowly back into his chair, smiling to himself. Talk about letting your imagination run away with you, he thought ruefully. There was absolutely no evidence to support any of this; he could imagine how Kreissner would react if he mentioned any of this to him. A pure flight of fancy . . .

All the same, it would do no harm to tighten up the security at Verwijk still further.

Cormack hesitated at the doorway of the restaurant and took a deep breath before going in. He looked around the interior; it was only half-full and every pair of eyes seemed to swivel accusingly in his direction as if to say, you are an outsider, you are not one of us.

He saw a man rising to his feet at the corner table, beckoning to him; Schelhaas, unless De Vriess' description had been totally incorrect. Cormack grinned broadly, a man seeing a friend, and raised his hand in acknowledgement. He began to make his way over; he was halfway there when he noticed that Schelhaas had a companion, a dark–haired girl in her mid–twenties.

"Sit down, sit down," said Schelhaas heartily. "And how is Groningen these days?" he asked, apparently casually: it was the code introduction.

"Much the same, Vim," Cormack replied, equally off–hand. "Piet sends his regards." He sat down next to the girl.

"I don't think you've met Lena before, have you?" said Schelhaas. "Lena, this is Henrik Boersma."

"Oh yes, you've mentioned him several times," she replied. She had a low, husky voice, Cormack observed.

"And this is Lena Maas." Cormack recognised the name; she was one of the Voltimand group.

Schelhaas leaned forward. "Everything all right, then?I gather there was some trouble."

"Yes. They might well know we're here by now."

"I see." Schelhaas nodded gravely. "But your mission?"

"Is still on."

"Good. Your colleagues are at the farm?"

Cormack nodded: he had left Woodward and Poortvliet at a farm belonging to a man called Mulder and he had walked into Leiden with De Vriess. They had parted company some thirty minutes before; evidently, De Vriess had already reported to Schelhaas. Cormack was impressed by their rapid communications.

"They should be safe enough for now," said Schelhaas. "But it's becoming increasingly dangerous to move around. The Gestapo have instituted many more spot searches since Jan was arrested. So, unless you had something else in mind, I suggest that they stay where they are for the time being, especially as I gather one of them does not speak Dutch?"

"That's true," said Cormack. "That would suit us fine." He ignored Schelhaas' implied question.

"And what about you? What do you require from us?"

"I'll have to reconnoitre the airfield as soon as possible. Until I do that, I can't really start making plans."

"Tonight soon enough?"

"Of course."

"Right. I'll take you out there. Failing that, I'll send De Vriess with you. Satisfactory?"

"Perfectly."

"You also said in your message that you wished, if possible, to be hidden here in Leiden?"

"Yes," Cormack nodded. "Various reasons. I want to be near a telephone so I can contact you rapidly. Also, I want to be centrally placed so I can meet you or any of your cell at short notice. The farm is too far outside town."

Schelhaas nodded agreement. "You can stay at Lena's house, if that's all right. It has a telephone as well as a back gate that opens into a secluded alley. You should be able to enter and leave unobserved."

Cormack glanced at Lena. "You're sure?" he asked her; it never occurred to him to question Schelhaas' choice, so favourably impressed was he by the Dutchman.

She nodded. "Of course. I live with my uncle and he's in Amsterdam for the next five days."

"Her uncle is a collaborator," Schelhaas explained. "Above suspicion, as far as the Nazis are concerned."

"As much as any of us are," Lena said contemptuously. "But, yes, my uncle is so co–operative that it provides a useful cover for me."

Which says a lot about her relationship with her uncle, thought Cormack; she was probably tougher than she looked. "Fine," he said. "Then it's settled, if you're sure you don't mind?"

"Of course not," she said and added lightly, "I could do with the company."

"Good," said Schelhaas. "We'd better get you under cover, then, Captain. I'll telephone you before nine o'clock tonight to make the arrangements; Lena will understand the references I make. So, before Lena takes you home, is there anything further you want from me?"

"Yes. I'd like to talk to your agent inside Gestapo HQ, if that's at all possible. I'd like to know more about Kuipers' interrogation. And about Kreissner. Also, any information you've got on this Behrens. I don't think we know enough about him."

Schelhaas nodded. "Yes. I know what you mean. At least we know where we are with Kreissner, but Behrens—he's an unknown quantity. He's already done more in a month than his predecessor did in two years; he could be our main danger. As for your other request, I'll arrange a meeting with Marika. Probably tomorrow; she's working today. All right?"

"Certainly."

"Very well. Until tonight, then, Captain."

Lena's home was only a few minutes' walk from the restaurant and so they strolled along the street, taking advantage of the Spring sunshine. As soon as they left the café, she linked her arm with his, smiling impishly at him.

"Makes us less conspicuous," she explained.

Cormack stared at her noncommitally. Lena Maas was not his type, he decided: she was too slim, for one thing, and her face was unremarkable, although her blue eyes were, he suspected, very expressive. All of which was totally irrelevant, of course . . . "Who am I, if anybody asks?"

"My boyfriend, of course. Visiting me from Groningen and we haven't seen each other for ages."

"Fair enough." It would pass muster, if anyone checked his papers; the address on them was in Groningen and he had a travel permit covering the next five days. All forgeries, of course, but what struck Cormack was the thoroughness with which Schelhaas had briefed her; he had no doubt that she would even know his fictitious landlady's name, if she were to be asked. "Have you known Vim long?" The question just slipped out; he had not meant to ask it at all. He was more tired than he had thought . . .

"He taught me at school." She smiled, faintly embarrassed. "I had a terrible crush on him, as did most of the girls in his class. I lost touch with him when I left, of course, and I didn't meet him again until after my parents died. That was in 1940—they were both killed in a car crash. He came to the funeral—I hadn't realised he knew my father quite well. I met him several times after that when I went to live with my uncle.

"Anyway, one evening, I found some papers on Uncle Johann's desk. They were Nazi travel documents. I'd known he was a Nazi sympathiser, but hadn't realised he was actually working for them. I told Vim about it—I knew he didn't like the Nazis—or my uncle, come to that—and that was how I joined the Resistance. Vim got me to photograph any documents I found and before long I was a fully-fledged member of the cell."

Cormack was faintly disturbed: he hadn't asked for her life story and if she was usually this garrulous, she could be a serious security risk. But she was talking to a British agent; it was one of the few occasions that she could relax, drop her guard, even if only for a while.

She tensed and Cormack immediately saw why; two uniformed Gestapo men had set up a checkpoint in the street, some thirty yards ahead, and were questioning passers–by at random. There was now no question of turning round and beating a retreat; they would be seen and pursued. They would have to bluff it out.

He smiled at her as though they were exchanging pleasantries. "On our way from the station where you met me on the train. Right?"

"Right. It arrived at 11.35. It was twenty minutes late."

"Good girl."

She glared at him and he was instantly aware of two things: firstly, that it had been an extremely patronising remark on his part and, secondly, that she did, in fact, have very expressive eyes indeed. That look had gone right through him and had made him feel about six inches tall.

They walked on, not hurrying, and, as they moved into earshot of the Gestapo men, Cormack said in a normal voice, "And how is Dirck these days, then?"

"Dirck? Oh, the same as usual. Still chasing the girls."

"He'll still be chasing them when he's in his bath-chair. Is he still going out with—what was her name?"

"Greta? No, that finished almost a year ago. He's going round with Erika Vandemeer now."

"Don't think I know her."

"Yes, you do. Tall, very blonde. Used to go out with Rolf De Haan."

"Oh, yes, of course. How long have she and Dirck been together?"

"About three months."

"Sounds serious, then."

No, it was no good; the nearest Gestapo man was stepping out in front of them. There hadn't really been much of a chance that he wouldn't; Lena was a presentable young woman and they'd stop the two of them just to get a chance to talk to her. Cormack sized up the German in rather less than a second; he was wearing the uniform of an SS–Rottenführer, but his Schmeisser machine pistol was slung over his shoulder, with the safety catch on. The German was clearly not anticipating trouble.

"Papers, please." His Dutch was poor; he would be unlikely to detect Cormack's own accent. Cormack and Lena obediently handed over their documents; the Rottenführer spent some time on Lena's, comparing her face with the photograph on the pass. Then, reluctantly, he turned his attention to Cormack and his whole manner changed.

"Name?"

"Henrik Boersma."

"Age?"

"Twenty–eight."

"Occupation?"

"Railway clerk at Groningen."

"When was your travel permit signed?"

"Yesterday."

"Purpose of visit to Leiden?"

"To visit Fräulein Maas." He nodded in Lena's direction.

"Is she a relative of yours?"

"No—" Cormack feigned embarrassment, "—she's my girlfriend."

"I see." The Rottenführer's tone left no doubt as to his opinion of Lena's taste. Cormack saw the danger signs; the Geman was clearly attracted to Lena and might become awkward out of sheer jealousy. "Where are you staying?"

Cormack gave the address that would be on the document, praying that they were heading in the right direction for it, but the Rottenführer's next words shattered that hope.

"But that is on the other side of town. Where are you going at the moment?"

"To visit Fräulein Maas' uncle."

"And his address?"

Cormack gave it, aware of the rising knot of tension in his stomach; this was all taking too long. The German was showing far too much interest in them for his liking.

The Rottenführer checked the address on Lena's papers and then nodded reluctantly. "Very well," he said surlily and handed their documents back. "You may go." He smiled at Lena. "Good day, Fräulein."

"Thank you," said Lena as they turned away.

Then the Rottenführer called out in English, "I hope you enjoy your stay in Leiden."

Cormack turned back slowly, his face set in a frown of puzzlement. "I beg your pardon?" he said in Dutch.

"Nothing," said the Rottenführer, disgusted, and turned away to choose another victim.

Cormack walked unhurriedly away from the scene, his arm once more linked with Lena's, his face showing only the amount of relief that would be normal for anyone emerging from such a spot-check unscathed. "Are they always that thorough?" he asked her.

"No. They're generally very cursory. Did they suspect you, do you think?"

"I don't think so. They'd never have let us go if they did. He's probably tried that English trick on everyone so far—it's a bit bloody obvious, though." Mind you, he thought, Woodward would probably have fallen for it. They knew,or suspected, that British agents had landed last night; that accounted for the increased security presence and the childish attempt to catch him out. Damn Woodward and his bloody chocolate!

"Still, we got past them," she said, a subdued note of triumph in her voice.

"We certainly did." He had managed to carry off the bluff; his training had taken over, enabling him to convince the German that he was who he claimed to be. Big deal, he told himself, cynically. So he had managed to fool one not very bright Rottenführer, so what? Hardly the mark of a top–calibre agent, when all was said and done.

"We're almost there," said Lena suddenly.

Kreissner looked up as Brandt came in. "Herr Hauptsturmführer Opitz has just reported in, Herr Sturmbannführer. They've just finished searching the Krol farm. Nothing."

"Very well," said Kreissner irritably. "Carry on."

Another blank, thought Kreissner. He had almost a hundred men combing the countryside inland of Noordwijk, hunting for those agents who might or might not have landed last night. Extra men had been drafted in from Haarlem and Delft, but so far nothing had turned up. By now, of course, they could be in Amsterdam—or Antwerp. But the gesture had to be made, if only to keep von Krug happy. One never knew; they might strike lucky.

He could do with some luck,he thought. The investigations into the list of German–speaking Dutch women had proved fruitless so far. There had been two possible suspects, but both had been cleared. The reports from other stations were equally discouraging.

He took the list from his desk drawer and checked down it until he found Marika Schuurmann's name. Neatly, he drew a line through it and scrawled an illegible initial beside the entry. Now, his officers would simply assume that she had already been questioned and cleared; she would not be approached. He replaced the list in the drawer.

There were now fewer than thirty names left on it; they would be able to check them out within the next forty–eight hours, given luck.

The eighteenth name on the list was that of Lena Maas.

# CHAPTER 13

**EVENING, FRIDAY 7TH MAY**

Cormack emerged from the bathroom, feeling almost human after his shave; that, and the few hours of sleep he had snatched during the afternoon and evening had helped to restore him to nearly–optimum condition. He went through into the back bedroom and smiled at Lena as she brought in a tray of food: four rolls and cheese with a coffee jar and cups.

"It's only ersatz coffee," she apologised. "It's all we can get, now."

"It's not exactly freely available in England these days," said Cormack. "This'll do fine. Thanks." He took a mouthful of roll and cheese. "Any news?"

She shook her head. "Vim hasn't called yet."

Cormack looked at his watch: it was just after eight. It was already growing dark outside and it would soon be time to move. If Schelhaas did not phone by nine o'clock, then the reconnaissance of the airfield would have to be put back by at least twenty–four hours.

He ate, but without appetite; he was too tense, waiting for the telephone to ring and yet, at the same time, wanting it to remain silent. The thought of staying here in comparative comfort and safety for another day was suddenly very attractive; with the realisation came a feeling of sneering self–contempt, that he was chickening out, going yellow. . . He shouldn't have come. His nerves were shot to pieces; he was liable to crack at any moment. For perhaps the hundredth time, he wondered just what he was doing here. What was he trying to prove, and to whom?

And for the hundredth time, there was still no answer.

"Is it that bad?" asked Lena, smiling. "The food, I mean."

"No, no. Not at all. It's just that I've got a lot to think about.

I find it difficult to eat and think at the same time."

She looked at him thoughtfully and seemed about to say something; she opened her mouth and then evidently changed her mind. Eventually, she asked, "Where did you learn to speak Dutch?"

"Three years ago, when I transferred to SOE. They were intending to send me in then, so I was given three months' intensive instruction. I suppose I've always had a fairly good ear for languages—I seem to pick them up pretty quickly."

"Is this your first time in Holland?"

"Yes. Typical SOE—they trained me in Dutch and then sent me to France. Probably just as well, actually."

"You don't seem to think much of them."

"No, I don't. They're mostly amateurs."

She smiled. "Vim doesn't think much of them, either. He's eternally relieved he's working with SIS and not them."

Cormack looked intently at her. "You're pretty close to him, aren't you?"

She nodded. "I suppose I am, yes, although not in any—well—personal way. I respect him as a leader, but—I don't know. There's something—cold—about him. It's not that he doesn't care about us. He'd do his damnedest for all of us if we were in trouble, but he seems to keep himself uninvolved. Detached. He can be a little frightening, sometimes."

Cormack nodded to himself; he had seen that already in Schelhaas. A dedicated man, he would keep his feelings to himself and would be capable of ruthless measures if necessary;Kuipers' suicide, for example. A man to respect, yes, but difficult to like or know. An ideal Resistance leader.

And what of Lena Maas? he wondered. How did she shape up as a member of the underground? She had certainly kept her head that afternoon at the checkpoint: she seemed acute, observant and intelligent.

"In fact," Lena added at length, "he's a little like you, really. You don't give much away, do you, Mynheer Boersma?"

"Don't I?" Cormack said noncommitally.

"No, you don't. Not even—"

She broke off at a knock on the front door downstairs.They exchanged brief glances and then, without a word, she went out of the room, closing the door behind her. Cormack took the tray and placed it under the bed, out of sight. Then he crossed to the window and opened it, silently lifting the sash frame before moving soundlessly back to the door. His shoulder holster was hanging from a peg in the door; he took out his Browning Hi–Power automatic pistol and began to screw on the silencer.

To his surprise, he felt utterly calm.

Lena took her time answering the door; she knew exactly the preparations the Englishman would be making upstairs and she wanted to give him the necessary time. Just in case.

She opened the door and her heart sank. A tall SS–Obersturmführer stood in the porch with three troopers behind him. The officer flashed a pass at her before striding arrogantly into the hall. Lena stood to one side as the troopers followed him; she knew better than to demand an explanation.

Cormack heard the commotion and flattened himself against the wall behind the door, but some four feet away from it so that he would not be hit by it when the door was flung open; it seemed ludicrous, a not very funny clip from a comedy film, but he had seen it happen and the man had paid for his lack of foresight with his life.

He could hear footsteps coming up the stairs and he flicked the safety catch off. The door of the front bedroom was hurled open with a crash and he heard the soldier moving about, opening up the wardrobe and then going back to the door. Any second now. . .

The door was thrown open, abruptly, crashing back into the wall beside him and rebounding back to an angle of about forty degrees to the wall; he would still be obscured behind it.

The incoming trooper had a direct view of the open window from the doorway and jumped to the obvious conclusion. He came into the room at a run, heading straight for the window, his only thought being to see if there was anyone in view outside.

Perhaps he caught sight of Cormack out of the corner of his eye or maybe it was some sixth sense of danger; whatever the reason, he spun round towards Cormack, who now had the Browning raised in a classic pistol-shooting stance, feet spaced apart, facing the target, his left hand holding his right wrist steady as he squeezed the trigger.

The 9mm Parabellum bullet slammed into the trooper's chest, hurling him back against the wall before he slumped forward, a growing red stain on the front of his tunic. Cormack sprang forward to wrench the Schmeisser machine pistol from the trooper's lifeless fingers.

A voice was calling up from downstairs, evidently disturbed by the sound of the falling body. "Everything all right up there, Ebert?"

"Yes. I had to break open a wardrobe," Cormack called out in fluent German.

He waited for what seemed an eternity: what if the other man realised that it was not Ebert's voice? If he had, then it was all over. . .

"Right. Carry on."

Cormack let out a long, slow breath and then moved silently to the door, out onto the landing. He went to the top of the stairs and descended them, slowly, carefully, the Schmeisser cradled in his arms, ready for instant use. There was one man in the kitchen, probably checking the large fireplace and another in the living room, presumably with Lena. He hoped she had remembered her instructions: keep out of the firing line, if at all possible.

The door to the front room was slightly ajar; Cormack paused outside, listening intently. The man in the kitchen was still opening cupboards and drawers, but there was no sign of any other activity in the house. As it should be.

Cormack took a deep breath and then kicked the living room door open. He leaped through it and landed on both feet, locating everyone in the room with a single glance. The Schmeisser stuttered as he squeezed the trigger, cutting down the trooper by the window. Lena dived flat for the floor; he swung round, the gun still firing. The SS–Obersturmführer spun round under the impact of the bullets, his legs buckling.

Cormack pivoted round and took three swift steps back into the hall, facing the kitchen as the last trooper came pelting out. The Schmeisser clattered again and the trooper reeled back, arms outflung, sprawling in an untidy heap against the wall.

Letting out his breath in a long sigh, Cormack turned to see Lena picking herself up off the floor, obviously unharmed. She bent over the dead officer and picked up his machine–

pistol before coming quickly over to him, her face white, tense, but forcing a smile.

"All right?" he asked her.

She nodded. "Yes."

Cormack turned out the light and went to the window. The Germans' vehicle, a Kubelwagen, was parked outside the gate: there was no–one in it, nor was there any sign of any more troopers. A Kubelwagen would normally only carry four men, he knew; they had all been accounted for. "We're all right for the time being," he said and turned to her. "Get your things together. We're going to have to get out of here."

She nodded wordlessly and went upstairs, still holding the Schmeisser.

They were ready in less than two minutes; Cormack only had to collect his jacket and suitcase from upstairs and Lena took only a small satchel that she slung over her shoulder. Evidently, it was permanently packed, ready for just such an eventuality.

"We'll go the back way," he said. Nodding in agreement, she followed him out into the kitchen but stood for several seconds at the rear door, looking back inside the house. Cormack understood her feelings; she could never come back, not until the war was over. And, ultimately, he was responsible; if he had not been there, she would have been absolutely safe.

"Come on, Lena" he said gently.

She turned, then, and went past him, still without a word. He followed her, his thoughts racing. There was nothing else he could have done; they could not possibly have bluffed it out, not when his papers had said he should be elsewhere after the curfew. There would have been a search and that would have been it. Perhaps he could, in fact, have escaped through the window, taking his suitcase with him before the trooper had come into the bedroom, but the search would have revealed the meal for two on the tray; Lena would have been instantly arrested and interrogated. No, there had been no alternative but to shoot his way out.

What was also worrying him was why the Gestapo had arrived at the house at that particular moment. Was there a leak in the operation? Was one of the Voltimand group a traitor? But only Schelhaas had known he would be there, apart from Lena herself. Lena could have betrayed him while he was hiding upstairs, but she hadn't; she was in the clear. Schelhaas? Unthinkable. He could have had Cormack picked up that morning at the restaurant or soon after, if he'd wanted. So why had the house been searched?

Lena had reached the gate, a six-foot high affair. She unlocked it and turned towards him as if about to say something, but, instead, she shouted, "Look out!"

He spun round and hurled himself to one side, dropping the suitcase as he saw the German trooper silhouetted in the kitchen doorway, machine pistol aimed at him. Cormack still had his own Schmeisser slung over his shoulder and, with a numbing chill of despair, knew with utter certainty that this was it, that he'd never unsling it in time. He was a dead man . . .

Lena's Schmeisser stuttered as she crouched to one side of the gate, finger on the trigger, her slender figure shaking to the recoil. The trooper threw up both arms and then fell backwards, out of sight.

Cormack rolled over, freeing his machine pistol and lined it up on the doorway. He heard a crash of breaking glass as the kitchen window was shattered and then he rolled away again as he saw the flashes of gunfire, the bullets slamming into the earth where he had been.

Lena fired again, a three-second burst that raked the window as Cormack's hand stretched out for his suitcase. Flicking it open, he reached inside and took out a grenade. He pulled the pin out and then lobbed it through the doorway in a high, curving arc.

The explosion was deafening; Cormack saw one of the troopers hurled bodily through the window by the blast, cartwheeling through the air and then rolling around the ground in a disjointed, boneless fashion.

A silence fell on the scene. Cormack rose to his feet,cautiously, and approached the doorway, Schmeisser at the ready. One glance into the wrecked kitchen was enough; one man was lying slumped in the corner, half his chest torn away by the detonating grenade, while another motionless form was draped over the table. Cormack could see a slow trickle of blood from this second body, dripping onto the floor; he spun on his heel and walked back down the path.

Lena was waiting for him; she looked interrogatively at

him. He nodded at her and she sighed wearily. She went out through the gate, followed by Cormack. They set off down the alley at a brisk trot; this time, Lena did not look back at all.

Behrens picked his way gingerly over the debris in the kitchen to where Kreissner was standing. "What caused this?" he asked, indicating the wreckage; the bodies had been removed, but what was left of the kitchen was still a scene of utter devastation.

"Grenade. Lobbed in from outside."

Behrens whistled softly. "How many of them were there?"

"Just two," Kreissner replied disgustedly. "A man and a woman. The woman was almost certainly a Lena Maas, but we have no clues as to the man's identity as yet. He is obviously very dangerous, although, according to the only man who survived in here, the girl was using a machine pistol very effectively as well."

"What exactly happened?"

Kreissner hesitated momentarily before answering. "It started off as a routine enquiry. Four of my men came here to search the premises and were ambushed inside the house; all of them were killed, one of them upstairs with a pistol, the other three with a Schmeisser, which, by the look of it, the killer took from the first victim. We have to assume that he was using a silencer on the pistol or the alarm would have been raised earlier; he seems to have taken the other three entirely by surprise. Which indicates that he is very highly skilled."

Behrens nodded. "And in here?" He gestured vaguely around the kitchen.

"The gunfire was reported and a back–up squad was sent. They were nearby and arrived just as the two agents were leaving by the back gate. There was a gun battle in which three of our men were killed, two by a grenade and one by the girl. The fourth trooper was severely injured by the blast, but was able to make a statement. The killers have disappeared. We've put out extra patrols, but there's been no sign of them so far."

Behrens looked thoughtfully at Kreissner; his account of the incident had sounded stilted, artificial, almost as if he were preparing his office report aloud. Perhaps he was; he certainly seemed to have been rattled by the affair, which was not surprising, when one considered that he had lost seven men in less than ten minutes.

Which was probably why he had been informed, Behrens realised. He had received a telephone call from Kreissner about forty–five minutes earlier, requesting his assistance; Behrens' first reaction had been that Kreissner must be getting really concerned, actually to ask for help, or, more likely, he wanted a possible scapegoat if it all blew up in his face.

"You say that this was originally a routine search?" asked Behrens.

Kreissner nodded. "They were following up a line of enquiry," he said evasively.

"So they weren't expecting trouble?"

"No."

"So. We have a highly trained man—the same one who killed the soldier on the coast?"

"It seems entirely possible, yes. Also—" Kreissner hesitated and then went on, "Also, it seems likely that Lena Maas was the woman who spoke to Schramm on the telephone."

"I see," said Behrens. "So he could be a British agent? The killer?"

"It certainly looks that way. Which is why I notified you. There seems to be very little in this area that would be of sufficient interest to the British for them to send in such a man except for the various Luftwaffe installations—which are your responsibility, Behrens."

"There's no guarantee that he's after anything round here, though."

"He's stayed in this area, if we assume that it's the same man, and I think we must. We haven't had any physical assaults on German personnel in Leiden for the last two years or more and then, suddenly, we have eight deaths in less than twenty-four hours. It has to be the same man and he's had about eighteen hours to get clear of the area—but he's still here. So he's after something in Leiden, or nearby."

"I see what you mean. Very well, I'll put my men on full alert."

"And I'll be having a word with the girl's uncle," said Kreissner, almost to himself: the man had been considered a reliable collaborator until now. He would be having some very pertinent words with Maas indeed.

Behrens took one more look around the kitchen and shook his head incredulously. Who was this man they were hunting, for God's sake?

Kreissner was back at Gestapo HQ by eleven o'clock; he was not in a good mood. He had not liked bringing Behrens in on the incident, but there had been little choice; Kreissner now needed all the help he could get, just to survive. Once the news of the killings reached The Hague, all hell would break loose. The only chance Kreissner now had was to show that no effort had been spared to track down the killers.

It was now entirely possible that von Krug would decide to take over the investigation personally, after what he would see, or choose to see, as the latest in a series of débâcles; Kreissner estimated that he only had the weekend before that happened.

Forty–eight hours then, with precious little to go on. He thought again of Marika; she was still a suspect, whichever way one looked at it. Perhaps it was time to bring her in for interrogation; his back was to the wall now and he could not afford sentiment. If he could break her, get her to confess, he might yet retrieve the situation. . .

There was a knock on his door; it was Brandt. "We have a lead on Lena Maas, Herr Sturmbannführer."

"The devil you say, Brandt."

"Apparently Rottenführer Dietrich stopped her in a routine check earlier on today. He remembered her; she was with a man."

"Excellent! Does he remember the man's name?"

"Yes, Herr Sturmbannführer. His papers identified him as Henrik Boersma from Groningen; he had a travel permit. I've checked with Groningen and they have no record of any Henrik Boersma being issued with such a permit."

"It's him. It must be," murmured Kreissner. "Why the hell didn't Dietrich detain him?"

"His papers seemed to be in order, Herr Sturmbannführer. There was no reason to do so."

"Can Dietrich give a description of him?"

"He has already done so, Herr Sturmbannführer. It's quite detailed."

"Excellent, Brandt. Excellent." This was it; the break he had needed. Not only did they now know what the killer looked like, they also knew what name he was using; if he tried to pass through any checkpoints, they would have him.

It was only a matter of time. . .

**NIGHT OF 7/8 MAY**

The barn was about three miles outside Leiden and Lena and Cormack reached it shortly after 10.30. Lena had telephoned Schelhaas from a public call box, giving him the code message for an emergency. Thirty minutes later they had met Schelhaas on the outskirts of town and had told him exactly what had happened. He had directed them to this barn; it had apparently been thoroughly searched earlier that day and was therefore highly unlikely to be visited by the Germans again in the foreseeable future.

They had exchanged very few words on the way; Lena had been quiet and subdued. Presumably, thought Cormack, she was beginning to realise her predicament; she would eventually have to be smuggled out of Holland altogether, probably for the remainder of the war unless she volunteered for SOE. She'd be a bloody fool if she did, thought Cormack, grimly; she would be signing her own death warrant if she let them send her back into the Netherlands. He would have to warn her.

But then, what business was it of his? It was up to her, after all; she was an intelligent, resourceful young woman, who had already shown she could look after herself. Even so, he felt responsible for her; if it had not been for him, she would not be in this situation.

Cormack sat gratefully on a bale of hay after he had checked the barn and its surroundings. Lena sat down, her face a mere shadow in the darkness. "What time is it?" she asked quietly.

"10.40," he replied. Schelhaas had said he would come out to see them at about six; seven hours' time. Seven hours, in which he had to decide what to do. The temptation to call it all off was overwhelming; all he had to do was to send a one-word signal to London and they would be picked up, either by a boat on the coast or by a Lysander from the Moon Squadron. Nobody would think any the worse of him; with the Gestapo hot on his heels, it would be the prudent thing to do.

On the other hand, though, he had shaken them off. At this particular moment, they had no idea where he or his team were. Admittedly, they would be combing the countryside, looking for him, but he was still at large, with considerable freedom of action. In addition, the Germans would not be expecting him to continue with the mission; they would be anticipating a run for it. And, when you thought about it, the quickest way out was still in a German aircraft.

Cormack knew he was wasting time, but he could not come to any decision. He had to, however, if only for the sake of Woodward and Poortvliet. To be honest, the mission was not completely dead yet. There was still a chance they could pull it off, in spite of their setbacks to date; and if there was still a chance, then it had to be tried. . . Even if it meant the deaths of all of them. And that was precisely why he did not want to have to be the one to decide; the deaths would be on his head. Why me, for Christ's sake? he asked himself; I never asked for the responsibility. . .

Gradually, he became aware that Lena was sobbing quietly, her face buried in her hands. Almost before he realised what he was doing, he went over to her, sat down beside her and put his arm around her shoulders. She turned to him, instantly, nestling her head against his chest. "It's all right," he said gently. "Everything's all right, Lena. We're safe here." He stroked her hair, soothingly, amazed at how protective he felt towards her, at how much her weeping was affecting him; after a minute or so, she sat back and looked at him.

"I'm sorry," she whispered. "I shouldn't have done that."

"It's all right," he said, while an inner part of him envied her; if only he could express his own doubts and fears like that.

"It's just that I feel so afraid. And alone. I can't believe what's happened to me. This morning was just the same as every other morning, but now . . . Nothing's the same. Everything's changed and I don't know where I am or what I'm going to do."

"I know, Lena. And I'm sorry. It's all my fault for getting you involved in all this."

"I'm not blaming you. You're doing what you have to do. We're fighting a war and we just have to get on with it. But I feel so lost, somehow. . ."

Cormack could hear the unspoken plea in her voice; he pulled her gently towards him again, sensing her need for warmth and understanding. And perhaps he needed someone to hold on to as well. . .

Presently, Lena felt herself beginning to relax. She hardly knew the man who was holding her, yet already she felt safe with him, trusted him. And she liked the feel of his arms around her, holding her. There was a gentleness about him that was in stark contrast to the ruthless way he had killed those Nazis. A very enigmatic, fascinating man, this Britisher. . .

She lifted her head and saw that he was staring at her with an expression of surprising tenderness. Then, very gently, hesitantly, he pulled her towards him and kissed her. She sensed his desire for her. And, as she returned his kiss, she could feel her own body responding. Suddenly, nothing else mattered but the need to forget the horror and fear of the last two hours; they clung desperately to each other.

She stared intently at his face. "What is your real name?"

He did not seem at all surprised by her question. "Alan Cormack," he replied quietly.

"We hardly know each other," she whispered tremulously.

Cormack said nothing; there was an almost palpable tension in the air.

She stood up suddenly, her mind made up, and turned her back to him; she unbuttoned her dress and let it fall to the ground. Quickly, before she could have second thoughts, she removed her underclothes until she was naked. Still keeping her back to him, she unrolled the blankets that Schelhaas had brought for them, putting one on the ground. She held the other one between her and Cormack and lay down on the first blanket, pulling the second one over her.

Only then did she look at Cormack; she said nothing, but simply patted the space next to her in silent invitation.

Cormack had caught only the barest glimpse of her slender body, but it had sent a surge of pure desire through him that could not be denied. Rapidly, he undressed, telling himself that this was all madness, that a German patrol could come along at any moment, that it could get them both killed; but he couldn't give a damn. He wanted, very much, to make love to Lena, but there was more to it than that; he needed her, with an urgency that both surprised and delighted him.

He slipped under the blanket; she had her back to him. Gently, he stroked her hair, until she turned onto her back. She stared intently at him, her eyes searching his face.

"Alan," she whispered.

# CHAPTER 14

**MORNING, SATURDAY 8TH MAY**

Schelhaas had the uncomfortable feeling that he was being watched as he walked up the track towards the barn. Cormack was waiting for him at the door, but the Dutchman was certain that Cormack had been observing his approach, probably from the small copse; the Englishman was not one to take chances.

Lena was brushing her hair in a compact mirror; for an instant, Schelhaas was struck by the domesticity of the scene. The moment passed and he turned to speak to Cormack. "No trouble during the night?"

He was looking at Cormack and so did not see Lena's smile, instantly suppressed. Cormack merely shook his head, his features impassive. "No. Anything happening in Leiden?"

"All hell's broken loose. House to house searches and anybody remotely suspicious is being taken in for questioning." He looked uncomfortable. "There are also rumours that they're going to take hostages and kill them if we don't give ourselves up."

"Will they do it?" Cormack asked sharply.

Schelhaas shrugged. "They might. Kreissner is a big enough bastard to do anything."

"What about your group?"

"We're all right, for the moment. I've put out the alert. Everything's hidden away, radios, guns, the lot. They won't find anything incriminating in any of our houses."

"How safely are they hidden? We may need them in a hurry."

Schelhaas looked sharply at Cormack. "Nowhere's foolproof. If they search hard enough, they'll find the equipment eventually but I doubt if that will happen for several days at least and, in the meantime, we can see about moving it to somewhere they've already searched."

"Good enough," said Cormack thoughtfully.

"And you, Captain? What are your plans?"

Cormack made no response for almost half a minute; then, he looked briefly at Lena before speaking. "We go ahead," he said quietly, amazed that his voice could sound so calm, so unconcerned. "We just put the reconnaissance back twenty–four hours."

Schelhaas stared at Cormack in reluctant admiration. "You certainly don't give up easily, I'll say that for you. Very well, Captain, you're in command."

"Can you get a message to the other two?" asked Cormack. "Let them know it's being put back by a day."

"Yes. That shouldn't be too much of a problem. I'll make sure they're notified." He consulted his watch. "Now, I'll have to be getting back." He opened the knapsack he had been carrying. "There's some food here and a flask of coffee. I'll be back here this evening at 8.30 and I'll take you to the airfield." He turned to Lena. "I'm afraid you'll have to lie low for a few days, Lena, until all this blows over. It's impossible to contact the Lifeline organisation at the moment."

Lena nodded. "All right, Vim." She glanced at Cormack and then added. "I wasn't really expecting anything else. I'll be all right here with Captain Cormack."

"Fine." Schelhaas turned back to Cormack. "In that case, unless there's anything else?" Cormack shook his head. "Until 8.30, then."

It was only a quarter of an hour later that Schelhaas, by now pedalling his bicycle back to Leiden, realised that Lena knew Cormack's real name. It surprised him; Cormack had not struck him as being the sort to reveal information unnecessarily and there had been no reason for Lena to know his real identity. But, clearly, he had told her; she could not have found it out any other way.

And then he remembered the way they had looked at each other, almost as if secret, non–verbal messages were being exchanged; a shared knowledge, intimacy, even. Surely not? They had spent the night together, certainly, but . . . No. He was imagining things. He could not conceive of the idea of Cormack behaving like that and Lena . . . No.

The whole notion was ridiculous. Preposterous.

Wasn't it?

Behrens felt as though he had drunk too much the night before; his tongue was furry, his eyes bloodshot and he had a dull, nagging headache. But it was not the result of wild debauchery; far from it. He had not actually returned to his quarters until 2.30, following the incident at the Maas house and he had managed barely four hours' sleep before he had been awakened by a phone call from Ziegler, who had something he wished to report, but which he'd rather not discuss over the telephone. And so, here he was, lurching blearily into his office at just after eight o'clock on a Saturday morning. He must need his head examined . . .

Ziegler was waiting outside the office. Behrens nodded vaguely at him and went inside.

"Right, Ziegler, this had better be good."

"It is, Herr Major. Uhlmann has reported in. One of the men we've got watching Pieter Schuurmann," he explained.

"Go on."

"There was a visitor to the Schuurmann house at seven o'clock this morning; 7.03, to be precise."

"Curious time of day to be visiting someone," observed Behrens. "Go on."

"The visitor stayed for about ten minutes and then left; Uhlmann didn't really get a good look at him, apparently. Anyway, at 7.30, Uhlmann phoned in again; Pieter Schuurmann had just left the house and Uhlmann was intending to follow him."

Behrens waited for Ziegler to say more, but it was evident that this was all the Unteroffizier had to report. "Is that all, Ziegler?"

"Forgive me, Herr Major. I know it doesn't sound much, but—I have a feeling about it. It seems too much like a message being passed. The odd hour, the very shortness of the visit and then Schuurmann's almost immediate departure: I don't like the smell of it. I think Schuurmann is delivering a message to somebody."

Behrens nodded slowly to himself. He had already acquired a healthy respect for Ziegler's instincts as regards anything remotely extra–legal. Take a thief to catch a thief . . . "But we don't yet know where Schuurmann is going?"

"Not yet, Herr Major. Uhlmann hasn't reported in yet."

"So what do you suggest we do, assuming Uhlmann is able to tail Schuurmann to wherever he's going?"

"It might be an idea to have a squad of men ready, Herr Major," said Ziegler.

"Very well, Ziegler. See to it, will you? And let me know as soon as Uhlmann reports in, will you?"

Left by himself, Behrens reached for the telephone, intending to call Trudi; it was only when he remembered that it was still an unearthly hour of the morning that he decided against it. He had arranged to meet her the previous evening and had been obliged to cancel the rendezvous, because of the Maas incident. Trudi had been understanding enough on the telephone and she had agreed to meet him tonight instead; he had a strange premonition that this, too, would have to be postponed. He had a feeling about this saboteur, spy, or whatever he was; he had struck twice now with savage, violent effectiveness and he could do so again. Indeed, thought Behrens, the killer, whoever he was, must know that the Gestapo would be scouring the countryside looking for him; either he would run for it or he would act. If he chose the latter course, he would have to do it quickly, before he was tracked down.

Tonight . . .

The telephone rang; he picked it up, looking at his watch: 8.30. "Hallo, Major Behrens speaking."

"Anton? It's Trudi."

"Trudi? What are you—I mean, how are you?"

"What am I doing telephoning you at this dreadful hour of the morning? Was that what you were going to ask? I tried your office first, you see. I thought, well, if he's awake, he'll be at his office. If not, then I wasn't going to disturb you. I hope you don't mind."

"Of course not, Trudi."

"I just wanted to check whether tonight was still on, actually."

Behrens remembered his earlier foreboding. "As far as I know, yes, Trudi."

"You don't sound very certain."

"I'm not," he confessed. "But if I can possibly manage it, I'll be there."

"I see. Or I think I see." Her voice sounded unconvinced.

"Look, Trudi, I want to see you tonight. Really I do. But—I can't guarantee it. I'm afraid I can't say anything more than that, not over the telephone. Do you understand?"

"Yes, I do," she said slowly. "Anton?"

"Yes?"

"Take care, will you?"

He grinned, relieved. "I will, don't worry."

As he put the phone down, he realised that he had an expression on his face not dissimilar to that of a Cheshire Cat. He was like some love–struck teenager on his first date . . . But he had been only too pleased to hear her voice. Trudi Neuberger had become very important to him . . .

The door opened and Ziegler came in; if he noticed Behrens' beatific expression, he made no comment. "Uhlmann's just phoned in, Herr Major."

The smile vanished as if it had never been. "Go on."

"Schuurmann went to a farm about five kilometres outside Leiden. He's in there at the moment; Uhlmann's telephoning from a village shop while still keeping the farm under observation."

"Where is this farm?" Behrens went over to the large road map of the Leiden area pinned to the wall. Ziegler pointed out a location north-east of the town. "Here. It's the Mulder farm."

Behrens stared intently at the map for several seconds. A farm. An excellent possible hiding place for the killer, of course. And one that had not yet been searched by the Gestapo; they were still concentrating their efforts on the area to the west of Leiden. "You've gathered together a squad, Ziegler?"

"Yes, Herr Major. A search party. Six men, plus myself. Seven in all."

"Eight," said Behrens curtly. "I shall be in command."

Ziegler nodded. "As the Herr Major wishes."

Behrens could see Ziegler's hurt at the implication that his superior did not trust him with a simple search operation, but this was not the case at all. Whatever the outcome of this search, Kreissner would be furious at what he would see as yet another infringement of his jurisdiction; if that were to be the case, then Behrens could not delegate the responsibility to anyone else. Especially if it were to prove a wild goose chase . . .

He looked at the map again. They could be there in less than an hour; in ninety minutes he would know whether or not he had made an utter fool of himself.

Or, he thought, grimly, he could be dead, if the killer was indeed hiding at Mulder's farm . . .

Woodward stood in the barn doorway, staring moodily out across the yard. The farmhouse was to the right, some thirty or forty yards away; ahead and to the left was a flat expanse of polder land, stretching away as far as the eye could see, unbroken but for a church steeple and some rooftops some five or six miles away. Idly, he wondered which town it might be: Woodward had a photographic memory where maps were concerned. Alphen, he decided, judging by the bearing; he had probably flown over it on bombing missions to the Ruhr.

All of which was totally irrelevant, of course, but it helped to pass the time. He checked his watch: almost nine-thirty. Half an hour yet before he could wake Poortvliet for his spell as lookout; then, perhaps, he could grab some shut–eye himself. Some hopes, he thought gloomily.

He looked back into the barn's interior, to where Poortvliet was stretched out, dead to the world. How the Dutchman could sleep so easily, so readily was beyond Woodward; he simply closed his eyes and was asleep in seconds.

Woodward tensed as he heard the sound of approaching vehicle engines, steadily increasing in volume; he was about to call Poortvliet when the Dutchman rose swiftly to his feet, roused by what was still only a faint noise.

"Germans?" Woodward asked nervously.

Poortvliet nodded. "Probably."

Woodward felt a soft explosion of pure fear in his gut, but tried to keep his features under control. "A search?"

The Dutchman nodded again. "I would think so." He spun on his heel and went over to his equipment. "Come. Our only chance is to get out before they see us." He gestured impatiently at Woodward, still standing motionless at the door. "Move, damn you!"

Woodward was suddenly galvanised into action. He snatched up his knapsack and, without conscious thought, took out his revolver, spinning the chambers to check that it was fully loaded. Poortvliet nodded in approval as he scooped up his own Sten and returned to the doorway.

He muttered something under this breath and then ducked back, flattening himself against the corrugated iron wall next to the door. He motioned urgently to Woodward, who joined him.

"What is it?" Woodward whispered.

"Trouble. Take a look."

Woodward peered cautiously round the door jamb and immediately jerked his head back. A car was pulling up in the yard and the German troops were already piling out. He did not need Poortvliet to tell him what was happening; one car had stopped in front of the house, while the second had gone round the rear to cut off anyone trying to escape.

And to search the barn, of course.

"You stay here," said Poortvliet suddenly. "I'll draw them off. Stay here and hide yourself."

"But—" Woodward began, but then Poortvliet had gone, sprinting across the yard in a low crouching run. He threw himself full length behind a pile of hay bales and slithered to a halt. Cautiously, he peered round the bales at the Kubelwagen.

He muttered an oath.

Two of them were heading for the barn.

There was very little time. He glanced around and then dashed across the ten metre gap to the next available cover, a two-wheel cart. Poortvliet looked at the scene again, a half second glance; the two soldiers were nearly halfway to the barn. A third was walking slowly away from the car, towards the house's rear entrance, his eyes fixed on the door, while the fourth was still in the Kubelwagen, seated behind the mounted machine gun with his back to Poortvliet; perhaps twenty metres away, now.

Again, Poortvliet flitted silently across the yard, pausing

behind the well. A second time, he checked the position of the two Germans heading for the barn—ten metres to go—then reaching down into his boot, took out his commando knife.

One last check. Two Germans nearly in the barn—he hoped that Woodward had hidden himself—the third still watching the house, the machine–gunner still with his back to Poortvliet, idly traversing the gun's barrel across the yard.

Poortvliet silently rehearsed his next moves. A stealthy approach, covered by the noise of the engine, arm round the gunner's neck, hand over the mouth, pull back the head, then one quick slash across the throat. A clean, silent kill.

Still all clear.

Go.

Poortvliet never knew why the gunner suddenly chose that moment to look around just as he was starting his run: had he heard something or was it instinct? Or simply bad luck? Irrelevant; all that mattered was that he had been seen and that the damned Nazi was opening his mouth to shout a warning.

Poortvliet's right arm whipped forwards in a blur of motion; the knife embedded itself in the gunner's chest, piercing his heart. The breath the German had taken into his lungs to give the alarm was now expelled in an inarticulate scream, abruptly cut off as he toppled backwards, reeling out of the car to sprawl untidily in the mud.

By this time, Poortvliet had unslung his Sten and was already lining it up on the third soldier, who had spun round in shocked surprise. The German had not even begun to react when he was cut down, the impact of the bullets hurling him several metres across the yard.

Poortvliet pivoted round, aiming at the two soldiers by the barn; one pirouetted on one leg, a grotesque parody of a ballet dancer, as the bullets tore into him, but the other was diving for cover as the fusillade screamed past him, inches too high.

The Dutchman leapt into the Kubelwagen's driving seat, slammed the gear lever into first and released the handbrake. He spun the wheel savagely as the tyres gained traction; the car slewed around until it was pointing the way it had come. Poortvliet straightened up and put his foot to the floor; the Kubelwagen began to pick up speed.

There was a burst of fire from the barn as he changed up into second, but then he was turning the corner round the side of the house and was out of sight. He unclipped a grenade from his belt and yanked the wheel to the right, following the muddy track around the front of the house. The rear of the car swung out, but he corrected the steering, straightening the Kubelwagen up, almost absently; he was already assessing the situation that greeted him.

The other Kubelwagen was parked in front of the main door; its gunner was swinging the machine gun towards him. Using his teeth, Poortvliet pulled the pin out of the grenade and lobbed it in a gently curving arc at the other car.

He ducked down at a burst of fire from the front door;he heard the bullets clatter into the bodywork and then the grenade detonated.

It had landed just short of the Kubelwagen, but had rolled under it before exploding. The entire car was lifted upwards by the blast and then, a split second later, was engulfed in a mushrooming gout of flame as the petrol tank went up. The gunner was hurled through the air, blazing from head to foot; mercifully, he was already dead, killed instantly by shrapnel from the grenade's initial detonation.

Poortvliet's face was impassive as he changed up into third, pointing the car at the main gate. Once through that, he would be concealed by the stone walls on each side. Just four or five seconds and he'd be clear . . .

He was concentrating so intently that he did not see the German to his right, a Schmeisser cradled in his arms. The first warning he had was when the bullets started spraying into the Kubelwagen; he was only ten yards from the gate when the front right-hand tyre blew out.

The car slewed to one side; desperately, Poortvliet fought the wheel that had almost been torn from his grasp, trying to correct the slide, even though he knew that it was too late, an eternity too late . . .

The Kubelwagen smashed into the solid brick wall at about thirty miles an hour. Poortvliet was thrown forwards, his chest slamming into the steering wheel, which buckled under the impact so that the column speared through his lung at the same instant that his head went through the windscreen, the glass severing the carotid artery. The remnants of the windshield were suddenly stained red as the blood gushed from the savage rent in his neck.

He was dead long before anyone could reach him.

# CHAPTER 15

**THE MULDERS' FARM**

Woodward lay absolutely still under the pile of hay that he had thrown over himself. If anything, the silence was even worse than the pandemonium of shots and explosions that had been abruptly sheered off only minutes ago. Now, the utter quietness was disturbing, ominous. Had Poortvliet escaped? Woodward doubted it; there had been no gradual lessening of the gunfire as if Poortvliet were being pursued away from the farm. So he hadn't drawn them off.

The sound of voices made him tense suddenly. He had clambered up onto the upper level in an instinctive attempt to be as far as possible from the entrance. Utterly futile, of course; if they were going to search the barn, they would still find him . . .

Slowly, carefully, he took out the revolver from his jacket. He flicked off the safety catch and cocked it; with any luck, he could take out two, maybe three of them before they killed him . . . He wasn't afraid to die.

Woodward paused, considering. What would Cormack do in this situation? Somehow, Woodward could not believe that Cormack would choose to die a hero's death. He'd try bluff, deception, anything that offered even the slightest chance of escape. Not for him the glorious, futile gesture . . .

Woodward hesitated a moment longer and then uncocked the gun. Replacing the safety catch, he slid the gun out of sight, deeper into the straw. He took a deep breath, nerving himself, and then rose to his feet, hands held high in the air.

"Je me rends!" he cried in a voice of sheer terror. "Je me rends!"

The soldiers below him spun round, startled; instantly, two machine pistols were being trained on him. Slowly, careful not to move suddenly, Woodward climbed down the ladder and walked towards his captors.

Behrens' first thought was that his prisoner cut a less than imposing figure; he was dishevelled, to say the least, dressed in peasant's clothes that, to Behrens, looked ridiculously incongruous on this man. Even dirty and bedraggled as he was, the prisoner looked as though he would be more at home in an officer's uniform.

An officer . . .

"Who are you?" he asked in English.

Woodward's face registered momentary surprise, but he said nothing, merely shaking his head in evident incomprehension.

Behrens tried again. "Who are you?"

"I'm sorry," Woodward replied in French. "I do not understand German."

Behrens shook his head, exasperated. "Search him," he said irritably.

The captive's papers identified him as a François Tanvier, an agricultural worker from Rouen, who had been brought into the area by the Todt Organisation. So what was he doing hiding in the barn?

"I was frightened by the shooting," Woodward replied, trying to sound as feeble–minded as he could.

"Who do you work for?"

Woodward hesitated. "I don't know his name. Somebody over there." He gestured vaguely to the east.

Behrens sighed; he did not believe a word of it, but he was puzzled by the implausibility of the cover. He had no doubt that the prisoner was not, and never had been, a farm worker; his hands were too clean and well–kept, for one thing. Also, the eyes were too alert, too shrewd to be that of a simple-minded peasant. So why was he given so flimsy a cover, one that could be so easily checked and discredited?

He ignored the question; all that concerned him now was to get the prisoner back to Leiden. 'Tanvier', or whatever his real name was, would have to be handed over to Kreissner, along with the Mulders; there was no way around that issue, unfortunately.

"Telephone Gestapo Headquarters," he said to Ziegler, seeing the captive's reaction to 'Gestapo'; he knew what that meant, all right. "Tell them to come and pick him up."

Woodward heard the words with a despairing sense of defeat; he could not speak German with any fluency, but he could understand it well enough. So the gamble had failed; it had been foolish to expect otherwise. Perhaps Cormack might just have pulled it off, with his training and experience, but . . . It had only been intended as a last-ditch cover story, devised in an attempt to explain his ignorance of Dutch, but it would only have stood up to the most superficial examination. But then, the whole idea had been that he would be hidden away throughout the mission, that he would never be exposed to questioning, let alone found in a situation like this . . . For an instant, Woodward thought longingly of the revolver he had left behind in the hay loft. That would have been the easy way out.

But it was now denied to him; he had let the opportunity slip by.

He doubted if the Gestapo would give him any further chances . . .

Marika stood under the shower, eyes closed, trying to forget the last hour and a half, to let the water cleanse not only her body, but also her thoughts; but it was useless. It was always the same, this feeling of somehow being stained, defiled, after she had been in bed with Kreissner. No matter how much she bathed herself afterwards, she still felt soiled, unclean.

She had spent the night in his quarters, although he had been summoned away by a telephone call at about nine-thirty the evening before and had not returned until almost dawn. He had awoken her then and had taken her with no effort at all to arouse her. After she had brought him breakfast, she had been obliged to pleasure him again. She had hoped that, in time, having to sleep with Kreissner would become less onerous, that she would become inured to it, but she had been wrong. If anything, it was worse, now; he was more demanding, not only in frequency, but also in the things he was asking—no, telling her—to do. It was as if he were gloating in his power over her and was trying to see just how far he could make her go; she knew it would not be much further now.

She heard the telephone ring over the sound of the water. Hesitating for an instant, she slipped out of the shower and padded quietly over to the bathroom door, which was slightly ajar; Kreissner insisted on her leaving it open when she showered so that he could come in and watch her if he so desired.

Kreissner's voice was faint, but perfectly audible; she smiled at the thought of how his insistence was now rebounding on him. Then the smile faded; what she heard made her blood run cold.

"Yes . . . When was this? . . . I see . . . Just a moment . . . Right, go ahead . . . Two men, one dead, one in custody, yes . . . French papers . . . Radio equipment found in the barn? . . . Excellent, excellent . . . What about the farmer? . . . Mulder, was it? What about them? . . . You've got them, too. Excellent, Major Behrens. My congratulations . . . Yes, certainly . . . Yes, in about half an hour. Goodbye."

Hastily, Marika returned to the shower and had just reached it when Kreissner came into the bathroom. She turned to face him, hoping that he would direct his eyes to her body rather than to her face; she was not at all certain that she had her features sufficiently under control.

He looked her up and down slowly, almost insultingly, before speaking. "I'm afraid I have to go again, my dear," he said silkily. "Business before pleasure, I'm afraid."

"Do you want me to stay here and wait for you?"

He considered the idea for a moment and then shook his head regretfully. "I shall be at headquarters for some time. I shall be able to contact you at home if I need you, of course?" It was a statement, not a question. "See yourself out, will you?"

Fifteen minutes later, Marika was knocking frantically on Schelhaas' front door. It was a serious breach of security, she knew, but, judging by what she had heard Kreissner saying, it was an emergency of the first magnitude.

Schelhaas opened the door; his surprise was only too evident. "Marika! Why—?"

"Mulder's been arrested," she said abruptly, pushing past him into the house. Schelhaas stared at her and then closed the door, hurriedly.

"Mulder arrested? How?"

"Kreissner's just had a phone call from Behrens. They arrested someone in Mulder's farm—I don't know who. It sounded as if there were two of them, but one's dead. They've got the other one and they've arrested Henning Mulder and his wife."

Schelhaas muttered an oath. Marika knew nothing of Cormack or his party and so did not appreciate the full significance of her news. But she did know that Mulder and his wife could betray the other members of the cell to the Gestapo; Voltimand was in grave danger of being completely blown unless they did something, fast.

But how in hell had the Nazis found the two British agents? They weren't searching in that area at all yet; they weren't due at the farm for another forty–eight hours, at least. And what the hell had Behrens been doing there?

Pieter. It had to be Pieter; they must have followed him to the farm that morning. Something had aroused Behrens' suspicions and he'd decided to raid the farm. Schelhaas cursed himself; he should never have entrusted the message to the boy. He was too young, too inexperienced by far. And, beyond this, Schelhaas also knew that he had been guilty of seriously underestimating Behrens . . . Damn him!

But all this was academic now, was wasting time. How it had happened was irrelevant; what he had to consider now was how to deal with the situation. "You'll have to contact Pieter and De Vriess," he said crisply. "Tell them to make for the emergency rendezvous. You go there as well."

"What about Lena?"

"She's already there."

Marika raised her eyebrows, and started to say something; one look at Schelhaas' face changed her mind. "Right," she said "What will you do, Vim?"

"I have to go to the Gestapo Headquarters."

Schelhaas arrived outside the Gestapo Headquarters with only about five minutes to spare, as it turned out. He sat himself down in a window seat in the café opposite; his coffee had only just arrived when two black Mercedes cars came roaring to a halt outside the Gestapo's main entrance.

He stirred his coffee, displaying only mild interest as the

prisoners were hustled out under armed guard. The middle-aged couple that emerged from the second car were immediately recognisable; Henning and Marta Mulder. Marta was protesting volubly, as usual, Schelhaas thought, with a trace of sadness; Henning's head was bowed, resigned.

But it was the solitary prisoner being escorted out of the first car that held Schelhaas' interest. He had never seen him before, but he memorised his appearance carefully, so that he could describe him to Cormack later.

Not that it would make a great deal of difference now, he thought bitterly.

## AFTERNOON, SATURDAY 8TH MAY

"Someone's coming," Cormack said and rose to his feet, cat-like. He was at the barn entrance almost before Lena had registered his words. "It's Schelhaas," he said, relaxing. "He's got three others with him." Then he added, "One of them looks like De Vriess."

Lena joined him and peered intently at the three approaching figures. "It is De Vriess. There must be trouble," she said agitatedly. "That's Marika and Pieter with them. If they're here, then something's happened. Vim would never bring us all together at once unless—" She broke off.

"Only in an emergency?" Cormack said flatly. He forced himself to remain calm. "We'll find out soon enough."

Schelhaas waited until they were all inside the barn before speaking. "The Gestapo have got the Mulders," he said succinctly. He looked at Cormack. "And one of your men."

"Damn . . . Do you know which one?"

"He's tall, slim, with dark-brown hair. Does that identify him?"

"Yes. Woodward. What about the other one?"

"Dead." The single word was delivered with a blunt finality. "The cell is blown. The Mulders know all of us and, unfortunately, they'll talk. Henning won't be able to hold out for long if they start torturing Marta. He's devoted to her."

"What the hell happened?"

"I don't know the details, but the farm was apparently searched by the Luftwaffe, not the Gestapo. I'm afraid that

Pieter must have been followed there. Your man—Woodward?—was taken, but the other man was killed. Trying to escape, I presume."

Cormack shook his head. "Not Poortvliet. More likely he was attempting to draw the Germans off so that Woodward could get clear."

"It doesn't really matter, does it? said Schelhaas testily. "What matters is that your mission is blown and we have to get the hell out of here."

"It isn't that simple, I'm afraid," said Cormack slowly. "You see, Woodward is a pilot in the RAF. He knows how to contact the Lifeline Organisation; all aircrew do, in case they're shot down. And Woodward was given more detailed briefing before this mission in the event of anything happening to Poortvliet and me."

"So he could tell the Gestapo," said Schelhaas woodenly. "We could find the Nazis waiting for us. What the hell is an RAF pilot doing on this mission? You never said anything about this, Cormack." Schelhaas' voice was bitter, accusing.

"Why the blazes should I? There was no need for you to know that at all and you know it, Schelhaas," Cormack retorted angrily. "In any case, it doesn't matter a damn now, does it?"

Schelhaas glared at him. "It will if he blows Lifeline."

"Well, if your man hadn't led the Nazis straight to the farm, then we wouldn't be in this bloody mess, would we? But we are, so let's forget about whose fault it is and start thinking about what the hell we're going to do."

Schelhaas seemed about to make some angry retort, but then, visibly,he controlled himself and then nodded. "You're right, of course. So what do we do? Walk to Spain?"

Cormack did not answer. Instead, he walked to the doorway, his back to the others. He stared out into the night, but he saw nothing; his thoughts were racing. It was obvious what they should do; make a run for it. If Schelhaas had a radio hidden away, as he said, then they could contact London and arrange for an emergency pick up on the coast. They could be safe in England inside twenty–four hours. Simple. And perfectly feasible. Nothing to it . . .

"You can do what you like," he said softly. "But I'm going to get Woodward out."

The others stared at him in stunned silence. It was Schelhaas who spoke, eventually. "You're mad!" he breathed. "Absolutely mad!"

Cormack shrugged, as if the matter was of no consequence. "I'm still going to try. I came here to do a job, to carry out a mission I put together myself and I'm not going to give up now."

"Mission? It's over, Cormack!" Schelhaas protested. "Woodward is as good as dead and we will be as well if we don't move soon."

"But that's precisely the point," said Cormack. "Woodward is our way out of here. Look, the reason he was included in this operation was because he's a pilot. One of the best. He can fly anything; including a Junkers Ju88 night fighter."

Schelhaas' face registered utter amazement. "You were going to steal an aircraft!" he whispered incredulously. "From right under their noses!" He shook his head slowly. "They're right. The British really are crazy." He looked at Cormack, steadily. "So you're saying if we rescue Woodward, then he can fly us out of here in a stolen plane."

"Why not? It'll be the last thing they'll be expecting, won't it?"

"You're right there," said Schelhaas. "Nobody in their right mind would attempt it!"

"So we'll have the advantage of surprise, won't we? A Ju88 can hold up to nine people; there's six of us here plus Woodward and the Mulders. We could all get out in the plane; and we'd pull off this bloody mission as well."

"Is it so important to you?" said Schelhaas softly. "The mission?"

For several seconds, each man's eyes held the other's and then Cormack looked away. "No," he said very quietly. "No, it isn't that. It's not the mission." He hesitated and only Schelhaas and Lena caught his next words, so low was his voice. "I'm not leaving Woodward behind. I'm not leaving anyone behind . . . Not this time."

Schelhaas nodded slowly and placed his hand on Cormack's shoulder in complete understanding. "I see, my friend." He turned and looked at the others standing silently around them. "Well?" he said softly.

"I'm going with Alan," said Lena without hesitation; Schelhaas had expected no less from her.

"And me," said Marika. "It might give me a chance at that bastard Kreissner."

"Piet?" Schelhaas asked.

De Vriess sighed. "We've fought them for two years now, Vim. I suppose it goes against the grain just to run away from them."

Schelhaas did not need to ask Pieter; the look on his face said it all. Pieter Schuurmann would welcome any chance at all to kill a German. Madness, he thought to himself. Utter madness. Rescue a prisoner from the Gestapo cells and then steal a Luftwaffe night fighter from a guarded airfield? Sheer lunacy . . .

He turned back to Cormack and clapped him on the shoulder. "What the hell," he said, grinning broadly. "Who wants to live forever, anyway?"

The rubber truncheons rose and fell, rose and fell, in a remorseless rhythm on the naked man strapped into the chair. Woodward's head and torso were a mass of bruises from where he had been kicked and clubbed, he had blood oozing from his smashed lips and one eye was almost completely closed, but he had not broken; indeed, Kreissner had not yet even managed to persuade him to utter even a single word in English. He was still claiming that he was François Tanvier from Rouen.

"Enough," said Kreissner abruptly and the beating ceased. He stepped forward and stood in front of the prisoner. "Listen to me," he said in English. "It is pointless trying to prolong this little charade. I know as well as you do that you are not French at all. Your papers are worthless forgeries. You are an Englishman and you are a spy. I have no doubt that you know full well what we do to spies. We shoot them and then we string their bodies up on meat hooks with piano wire. Sometimes we do it the other way round, especially if the spy proves to be stubborn. As you are.

"You see, Englishman, by the time we have finished with you, you will be begging us for death, but we will not let you die until you have told us what we want to know. Is all this perfectly clear?"

Woodward shook his head, slowly, wearily. "Please—I do

not understand German," he said in French, for perhaps the hundredth time.

Kreissner snorted in disgust. "You are a fool!" He nodded to the two SS troopers and the beating began anew, brutal blows to the head and groin. Kreissner watched with a cold detachment; indeed, his thoughts were elsewhere.

That bitch Marika. He had known all along, really; that bastard Behrens had been right, of course. The evidence could no longer be ignored; it had been her brother who had led Behrens to the farm. He had to act, now; his hand had been forced.

But he had delayed too long; the squad he had sent to arrest her had reported that she had disappeared, gone to ground. If there had been any vestige of doubt, that last piece of information had dispelled it. Within hours, von Krug would know that Kreissner had been keeping a mistress who had been a member of the Resistance; worse, he had allowed her to slip through his fingers. As yet, no word of the incident at Mulder's farm had reached The Hague, but he would have to notify von Krug by tomorrow morning at the latest; Behrens' own report would have been forwarded by then and there would be no hope of keeping it under wraps after that.

By the time he made his report to von Krug, Kreissner knew that he would have to produce some tangible results if he were to have any chance of saving his own career. He would have to persuade 'Tanvier' to talk by then; he had eighteen hours at most.

He signalled to the troopers and they stepped back from their victim. Kreissner looked thoughtfully at the prisoner. Who was he? And what was he doing here? He was, quite definitely, not a member of the Todt Organisation, but it puzzled Kreissner that he had been given a cover that could be so easily broken. Had it been put together in a hurry? Or was he a decoy? Kreissner felt a chill sensation grip him. Had 'Tanvier' been deliberately sacrificed so that the real operation could be carried out while they were concentrating on him? Because Tanvier was not the man who had been at the Maas house the night before; the killer had been fair-haired, while Tanvier was dark. And where was Lena Maas?

Kreissner shook his head impatiently. There was something going on, about which he knew absolutely nothing; the only way he could find out what was to break the man before him. Or so he had thought. But if 'Tanvier' were really a decoy, he would know nothing of the real mission . . .

Damn that bitch! For an instant, he had a vivid mental image of Marika strapped into the chair, naked, as they fastened the electrodes to her . . . He'd make the whore pay.

He stepped forward again and spoke in a quiet, almost bored voice, as though the entire matter were of no consequence at all. "Who are you? Why are you here? Who else is with you?"

And still the man in the chair said nothing . . .

# CHAPTER 16

**EVENING, SATURDAY 8TH MAY**

Cormack walked idly along the street, a man apparently on his way home after a day's work, his attention seemingly elsewhere, but, in fact, he missed nothing, including the man leaning against the lamp–post reading a newspaper.

Gestapo. Had to be. He was not actually opposite the block of apartments but he could observe anyone entering or leaving without any difficulty. There was also a telephone kiosk at the end of the street; he could be in contact with Gestapo HQ within minutes. There would only be the one man to keep the flats under surveillance; there was no rear entrance. Cormack turned the corner and, twenty yards further on, ducked into an alleyway. Marika was waiting there with Schelhaas and De Vriess.

"One man," said Cormack succinctly. "That's all."

"As we thought," Schelhaas replied. He nodded to Marika. "Of you go then, Marika. And good luck."

"Thanks." She walked out of the alley and then headed towards her own street. Cormack waited until she had disappeared from view and then followed her.

She crossed the road, walking unhurriedly; the Gestapo agent saw her immediately. His attention was entirely concentrated on her as she walked along the street; he did not notice Cormack at all. When Marika went into the apartment block, the German moved towards the phone kiosk twenty yards away.

Cormack glanced over his shoulder; Schelhaas and De Vriess were walking behind him about thirty yards back. The street was not busy; there were about half a dozen other people on its pavements hurrying to reach home before the curfew. None of them were paying any attention either to the

Gestapo agent or to the apartment block.

The German was inside the kiosk. He picked up the telephone and asked for a number, turning to look at the apartment once more. Cormack came to a halt about five yards away and looked impatiently at his watch, a man wishing to make an urgent call and irritated at finding the telephone already in use.

The agent spoke half a dozen sentences into the receiver, nodded emphatically and then replaced the telephone. Cormack stepped forward, his face a mixture of annoyance and relief and almost collided with the German at the kiosk door. He muttered an apology and moved to one side, his right hand emerging from his coat pocket, holding his commando knife.

Cormack's hand travelled only about a foot or so, but it had tremendous force behind it, driving the blade upwards under the ribs and into the heart. The German's eyes widened in shocked amazement and he emitted a hoarse gasp before he slumped against Cormack, who caught him, supporting him until Schelhaas and De Vriess came up. Cormack yanked the knife out.

Cormack and De Vriess put the dead man's arms around their shoulders and carried him briskly across the street. One passer–by paused to stare at them, but Schelhaas snarled at him, in a pronounced German accent, to mind his own damned business; the other man walked hastily away, carefully not looking back.

Marika was in the entrance lobby waiting for them, holding open a door to a store cupboard. Inside were mops and brushes along with other cleaning equipment; they dumped the corpse in there, unceremoniously. Schelhaas reached into the dead man's jacket pocket and took out his papers. He held out the Gestapo identification pass to Cormack. "You or me?"

The photograph on the pass was not really like either of them, Cormack realised; if anything, it looked more like De Vriess, but his German was not good enough. It had to be either himself or Schelhaas. "You, I think," he replied.

"Right," said Schelhaas in a matter of fact voice, taking the papers from Cormack and putting them inside his own jacket pocket. He took the dead man's hat and put it on, pulling the brim well down to cover his forehead. Nodding to the others, he walked briskly through the main door into the street.

Marika closed the store cupboard door and locked it; in all probability, the body would not be discovered until Monday morning, thirty–six hours from now, but by then, for good or ill, it would all be over.

They would either be in England; or they would be dead.

Without a word, she led Cormack and De Vriess up the stairs to her second-floor flat.

Woodward arched backwards as the electric current surged through his body in a white hot explosion of agony. He made no sound; the gag in his mouth saw to that. Kreissner moved his hand; the power was shut off and Woodward flopped back onto the table. The sweat was pouring off his body and Kreissner could see faint wisps of smoke curling lazily upwards as the flesh burned.

The gag was removed as Kreissner bent over Woodward. "Ready to talk yet?"

"Fuck off," Woodward groaned hoarsely.

Momentarily, Kreissner's lips were compressed in a thin line of anger. This was the only evidence of any progress in the interrogation; the prisoner was now talking in English on occasions, but the only responses he had given had been in the form of invective. "Not even your name?" said Kreissner softly. "You can surely give me your name and rank, can't you? The Geneva Convention allows you to say that much, surely?"

Woodward was silent; he was not going to give this bastard anything. If the Nazi knew he was a pilot then he might put two and two together and realise just what they had been planning to do. Not that it would make any difference to their mission now, but it would queer the pitch for any subsequent attempt . . .

Kreissner gestured to the technician again and Woodward screamed as the current was switched on again. Kreissner watched his writhing form dispassionately. He was determined, this one; Kreissner had to admit to a grudging admiration for the prisoner's defiance. It would make no difference, of course; he would break in the end.

Only Kuipers hadn't . . . He pushed the thought aside.

It was only when the power had been turned off once more

and the prisoner's shrieks of agony had subsided that he realised that the telephone on the desk was buzzing. Kreissner picked it up. "Yes?"

"Hauptsturmführer Opitz here, Herr Sturmbannführer. Wollmann has just reported in. The Schuurmann girl has just returned home."

Kreissner stared at the wall, his mind racing. What the devil was going on? If she knew the Gestapo were after her,then the last thing she'd do would be to return home. Unless she didn't know and her absence had been mere coincidence . . .Had he been wrong about her? Was she innocent, after all?

There was only one way to find out, of course; bring her in and question her.

"Herr Sturmbannführer? Are you still there?"

"Yes, Hauptsturmführer. I heard you. Wait one moment." He was tempted to go himself and deal with it personally, but Opitz could handle it. "Take an arrest squad and bring her in."

He put the telephone down and turned back to face the interrogation table. As soon as the cow was brought here, he'd have her on that table, begging for mercy. He'd make the little bitch pay. He'd make her wish she'd never been born.

Schelhaas tensed slightly as the car turned the corner into the street; it was a Mercedes and it came screeching to a halt in front of the apartment block. Three men, as he'd expected; an officer in the back, a driver and a single trooper in the front passenger seat. The officer stalked arrogantly up to Schelhaas. "Wollmann?" he snapped impatiently.

"Yes, Herr Hauptsturmführer," said Schelhaas punctiliously. He recognised the other man; it was that bastard Opitz and, apparently, Opitz did not know Wollmann personally, which was just as well . . .

Opitz held out his hand and Schelhaas passed over Woollmann's identification papers. Opitz flicked on a torch and shone it in Schelhaas' face for no more than a second before directing it onto the pass. He gave it only a perfunctory glance before returning it; there was no reason, of course, for him to suspect that there was anything amiss. "Very well. You wait here, Wollmann. Krantz, come with me." He went into the apartment block, followed by the trooper, leaving

Schelhaas alone with the driver.

Schelhaas' face betrayed no emotion, but he was quietly satisfied. It had gone even better than he'd dared hope; Opitz's insistence that he remain here had saved him the necessity of concocting an excuse to do so. Now, all he had to do was to give Opitz time to reach the second floor . . .

He wandered around to the driver's door. "Officious sod, isn't he?" he said, gesturing vaguely at the entrance.

"Opitz?" The driver spat into the road. "Right bastard, that one."

"They all are. Bloody officers," Schelhaas grumbled. "Suppose he wants all the glory, does he?"

"Probably. He's like that."

"Fancy a cigarette?" Schelhaas asked amiably, reaching inside his coat.

"Wouldn't mind one, actually." The driver's eyes widened as he saw the silenced automatic pistol aimed directly at him.

"Out!" hissed Schelhaas venomously. The driver hesitated and Schelhaas continued in a low, savage voice, "Move or I'll blow your damned head off!"

The driver came out of the car, hands held over his head. "Put your hands down," said Schelhaas. "Walk normally. Go into the building."

Meekly, the driver obeyed, acutely aware that the man posing as Wollmann seemed to know exactly how to handle a gun. Schelhaas followed him.

"In there," he said, indicating the boiler-room door. The driver opened the door and stood on the threshold looking down the flight of steps, illuminated only by the light from the lobby.

He did not hear Schelhaas moving silently up behind him, nor did he see the crisp rabbit punch that Schelhaas gave him. All the driver was aware of was a sudden, blinding pain in the back of his neck and a sensation of falling . . .

He was unconscious before he hit the first step; he tumbled raggedly down the stairs to lie sprawled on the boiler room floor. Schelhaas found the light switch and turned it on as he closed the door behind him. He descended the stairs and began to undress the driver.

Marika could feel her heart pounding as she went to the door to answer the peremptory knock. Her actions during the next few minutes would depend a good deal on who Kreissner had sent for her; she just prayed that he had not decided to come himself. Please let it be Merkel or Opitz, she breathed silently. She tightened the cord of the dressing-gown around her waist and opened the door.

Thank God. It was Opitz, with a single trooper. "Herr Hauptsturmführer!" she said in a startled voice. "What brings you here?"

"You are under arrest," snapped Opitz curtly.

Her face registered shock, surprise. "What do you mean, under arrest? Why—"

"You have precisely sixty seconds to get dressed or we'll take you as you are," said Opitz, looking her up and down insolently.

She stared at him for about three seconds, fear written all over her face, and then turned hurriedly. Opitz followed her as she went into her bedroom and stood in the doorway, watching her. She hesitated, gazing wide–eyed at him.

"Go on," he ordered, smiling, "Or, like I said, I'll take you as you are."

She delayed a moment longer and then turned away from him to take off her gown. Opitz drew in his breath sharply; she was completely naked. He took a single step forwards. "Turn around," he ordered.

Slowly, she did so, covering herself with her hands. Opitz could see the sudden hope come into her eyes, could almost read her thoughts; maybe she could make a deal with him.She removed her hands and let him see her. "Please—" she whispered pleadingly. "Couldn't you say I wasn't here when you arrived? I'll do—anything—anything you want if you let me go. Anything . . . Please . . . Please . . ."

Opitz's eyes narrowed. He had always wondered what she would be like in bed, naked; she had a gorgeous body, no doubt about that. There was no reason why he shouldn't have her before taking her in; he could always say he was starting to "soften her up" for the interrogation . . . He realised that Krantz was standing in the doorway behind him, his eyes rapt as he stared at the naked girl.

"Wait in the hall, Krantz," he ordered brusquely, his voice thick. "I'll be out in a few minutes. Out!"

Reluctantly, Krantz backed out of the door, his eyes lingering on Marika. Opitz took another step into the bedroom, pushing the door shut behind him, his eyes fixed on her breasts, rising and falling rapidly in her agitation. He could feel a stirring in his groin . . .

Cormack took two silent steps forward from where he had been waiting behind the door and flicked the garrotte over the German's head, tightening the cord viciously around Opitz's neck. Opitz thrashed frantically about, fighting for breath, both hands reaching for the cord clamped around his throat, but it was already embedded far too deeply for him to gain any sort of grip on it.

They always make that mistake, Cormack thought, with an inhuman detachment; they always try to pull the cord away from the neck. They never try to use their hands to fight back until they're too weak to do anything. Opitz was no exception; Cormack merely held on, his features cold, determined, while Opitz's face went first blue, then black as his tongue protruded obscenely from his mouth and his eyeballs bulged from their sockets. Cormack was on one knee now; Opitz was writhing desperately on the floor and then his heels began to hammer on the carpet in a last reflexive spasm before he lay still. Even so, Cormack maintained the pressure for a further minute before releasing the garrotte. He stood up.

Marika's face was averted; Cormack was not surprised. He tensed as the door opened, but it was only De Vriess. The Dutchman nodded briefly in response to Cormack's questioning look; Krantz had been dealt with.

"It's all right, Marika," Cormack said gently. "It's all over. Go and get dressed."

Dumbly, she nodded and went to the wardrobe, deliberately not looking at the motionless figure on the floor. Cormack bent down and began to unbutton Opitz's tunic.

Lena applied the brakes and then dismounted from the bicycle. Here would do as well as anywhere, she decided; she was about four kilometres outside Leiden on the main road that led north to Haarlem. It was growing dark, but she could see the road quite clearly in both directions; yes, this would suit her admirably. She bent down and pressed the tyre valve until the tyre was completely flat. Then she consulted her watch; the lorry should be due in ten minutes or so, if it was running on time. It was a daily run, bringing nothing more significant than canteen supplies: condensed milk, ersatz coffee and so on. When Cormack had given her the task of stealing some transport, she had thought of this immediately. He had clearly not been too happy about letting her go alone, but there had been no choice in the matter. Pieter had been the only other person who could have accompanied her without jeopardising the main objective of rescuing Woodward; and both Cormack and Schelhaas had agreed that he was too young, too inexperienced to be involved. Pieter had protested, but had eventually agreed to remain at the rendezvous, although it had taken a direct order from Schelhaas to achieve this. So it was down to her . . . She would not fail Cormack.

She thought about him as she waited for the lorry to appear. While he had been organising this mini–operation, he had been calm, authoritative, assured, the completely professional agent once more. Even Schelhaas had been taken aback by the crisp, efficient way that Cormack had issued his instructions; and Schelhaas was not easily impressed by anyone. And yet, for an instant, Cormack's eyes had met hers and he had winked at her while he was telling Schelhaas and De Vriess what he wanted them to do; it had been an almost imperceptible gesture, but it had been enough to tell her what she wanted to know. He cared for her; maybe even more than that.

The sound of an approaching vehicle interrupted her thoughts; it had to be the lorry. She began to walk along the road towards Leiden, pushing the bicycle. The lorry came up behind her; she turned to face it and waved her arm, signalling the driver to stop. He did so and she walked up to the cab door. Her heart sank as she saw the second man sitting in the passenger seat; it would make it more difficult, but she was committed now.

The second soldier, the passenger, jumped down and walked towards her. She smiled nervously. "I'm so glad you stopped," she said breathlessly in heavily accented German. "I've had a puncture. I've been pushing it for ages and I'm afraid I'm going to miss curfew, now. You couldn't possibly help me, could you? I'd be ever so grateful." Her eyes were wide, the picture of innocence, but she could see that the soldier had come to his own conclusions as to what form her gratitude might take; he looked at her consideringly and smiled knowingly.

"It is strictly against regulations for us to give you a lift, Fräulein. But it is possible that we might be prepared to—ah—bend the rules a little for such an attractive young woman, if you see what I mean?"

Her face registered sudden realisation and then calculation. "Well . . . If the Gestapo catch me, I shall be in serious trouble, I suppose . . ." She took a deep breath. "Very well," she said reluctantly.

"Excellent!" said the soldier, grinning. "I'll put your bicycle in the back, Fräulein." He went past her to pick it up.

Lena assessed the chances; no, not yet, not while the driver was watching. She followed the soldier around the back of the lorry. The Geman hefted the bicycle over the tailgate and then clambered up. He turned to reach out a hand to lift her up after him and then froze as he saw the silenced pistol in her hand that she had taken from inside her coat.

The gun coughed twice in rapid succession, the bullets hitting him in the chest and throwing him backwards into the lorry's interior, arms outflung. There was a deafening clatter as he crashed into a pile of cartons, sending them flying. Lena swore under her breath. Her intention had been a silent kill, with the sound of the engine drowning out the muffled shots, but now she would have to move fast.

She took half a dozen rapid steps to the left, in time to see the driver jumping out of the cab, evidently alarmed by the noise. The Walther automatic kicked in her hands as she squeezed the trigger again; the driver gave a yell of pain and was thrown back against the bonnet as the bullet tore into his right shoulder, twisting him round. He stared at her in stunned disbelief as she lined the gun up, taking careful aim. She fired a last time and the driver was flung to his right as the shot buried itself in his left side. He fell heavily against the mudguard, hung there for a moment and then rolled tiredly over, onto his back, the look of shocked surprise still on his face as he stared up at the darkening sky.

Slowly, Lena brought the gun down, feeling her limbs beginning to tremble. She forced herself to walk forwards, to ensure that the driver really was dead, that she had actually killed him, murdered him, gunned him down in cold blood, that . . .

She turned away and was suddenly, violently, sick, in heaving, convulsive spasms that racked her entire body until she was gasping, choking in agonising dry retches, the tears streaming down her face.

Now pull yourself together, girl, she told herself. Cormack and the others were relying on her; she hadn't got time for any of this! She took a deep breath and held it, closing her eyes, forcing herself to concentrate. Slowly, the spasms died away until she could stand up again, even though her legs still felt shaky.

She had not expected it to be like this, not at all. There had been no such reaction the night before when she had killed the SS trooper at her house, but this . . .

There was a difference, she realised. Last night had been in the heat of battle in self-defence, a survival reaction. But these two deaths had been pre-meditated. She had not been at all certain that she could have merely incapacitated the two men, having had very little training in unarmed combat. There had only been the one option; she had had to kill them. A necessity of war.

She shook her head; this was no time for idle thoughts. The two bodies had to be removed; she was not looking forward to it, but it had to be done.

Another necessity of war . . .

# CHAPTER 17

**GESTAPO H.Q., LEIDEN**

Cormack was aware of a tight knot of tension in his stomach as the Mercedes pulled up outside Gestapo headquarters. He was seated in the back next to Marika; Schelhaas was driving, with De Vriess next to him. All three of them were wearing SS uniforms; Cormack's was that of an SS–Hauptsturmführer, the one that had previously belonged to Opitz.

This would be the difficult part, of course; all three men would be completely unknown to the guards on duty and they would ask for identification if their security procedure was up to scratch. That was all right; Cormack had been given three forged SS identity cards before leaving London. Each had his photograph on it, but each one bore a different name and rank; Cormack was using the one that identified him as SS–Hauptsturmführer von Beitzen. He hoped fervently that the forgeries were good enough; he was about to find out. There was one thing working in his favour, of course; an SS–Hauptsturmfuhrer was equivalent in rank to an army Captain and would therefore carry a fair amount of authority.

He climbed out of the car, suppressing the moment of doubt as to whether he was right in deciding not to use it for their getaway. Almost certainly, they would come out of the doors shooting—if they came out at all—and would have only seconds in which to escape; they would have to rely on the engine starting first time. They could be caught in a hail of bullets while they were waiting for the damned thing to fire. No, they needed a separate vehicle altogether. Although, if Lena were not successful, they might have to use the Mercedes after all. . .

Impatiently, he pushed the lingering doubts to one side; he could not afford their distractions. He had enough on his plate without that. Cormack led the way up the stairs hurriedly, arrogantly. De Vriess was hustling Marika along, with Schelhaas bringing up the rear. Cormack gave a perfunctory salute to the two guards on duty and then strode on past, ignoring their hesitant attempt to stop him and ask for his identification.

He looked swiftly around the entrance lobby and picked out a blond–headed Untersturmführer standing behind the desk. "You! Come here!" he barked.

The young officer came round the desk like a scalded cat and came rigidly to attention in front of Cormack. "Your name, Untersturmführer?" Cormack asked, his voice laden with icy menace.

"Altmann, Herr Hauptsturmführer."

"Well, Altmann, I take it that you are responsible for the guards on duty at the entrance?"

"Yes, Herr Haupt—"

"Do you realise that they allowed me to pass without stopping me for my identification? What kind of security is that, Altmann, eh?" Cormack ranted. "I'll mention this—and your negligence—in my report." He reached into his pocket and took out the forged pass. "SS–Hauptsturmführer Manfred von Beitzen at your service, Untersturmführer. From The Hague," he added silkily.

Altmann barely glanced at the pass; white–faced, he handed it back to Cormack. "My apologies, Herr Hauptsturmfuhrer. The men should have stopped you. I'll make sure they're reprimanded—"

"I've brought this girl in," Cormack interrupted. "We intercepted your radio call and, as we were in the area, I decided to pick her up myself. God only knows where your Opitz got to, but never mind." This was a calculated gamble, that Opitz had been contacted while on a routine search; even if he hadn't, the young Untersturmführer would be unlikely to know that. "I gather that Sturmbannführer Kreissner wants to speak to her personally. I have orders to speak to him as well, so please be so kind as to tell me where I can find him."

"He—he's interrogating a prisoner, Herr Hauptsturm—"

Cormack spoke quietly, absently looking down as he removed his gloves. "I said I wished to speak to him immediately, Altmann. Those are the orders of

Standartenführer von Krug himself." He looked straight into Altmann's eyes; his lips smiled, but Cormack's stare was glacial. "Please be so kind as to carry out those orders."

"Certainly, Herr Hauptsturmführer. I'll take you to him."

"I'm most obliged, Untersturmführer," said Cormack, his words dripping with sarcasm. He gestured impatiently to Schelhaas and De Vriess; they followed him, pushing Marika roughly forwards. She snarled an obscenity at Schelhaas; he slapped her round the face, hard, leaving a livid red mark on her cheek. The force of the blow sent her staggering backwards but she was still held securely by De Vriess. Her head drooped in resignation and she allowed herself to be taken along the corridor.

Altmann led them to the steps leading down to the basement and then descended them, muttering something to the troopers on guard. He took a key from his pocket and unlocked the heavy steel door. They passed through and, inside, a Rottenführer shot to his feet from behind a metal desk. Altmann merely nodded at him, while Cormack totally ignored him. The door was swung shut behind them; but Cormack had been warned by Marika that this would happen. Even so, the feeling of being trapped in a metal dungeon was difficult to dispel.

Altmann took them past the cells to the door at the end of the corridor and then pressed a button beside the door. Cormack knew that knocking would be pointless; the room would be soundproofed. The button obviously activated a bell or buzzer inside.

There was a delay of several seconds, which seemed like an eternity to Cormack and then, finally, the door was opened. Altmann went in; Cormack pushed in after him.

"There's a Hauptsturmführer von Beitzen to see you, Herr Sturmbannführer," Altmann was saying as Cormack took in the situation. Woodward was strapped down on the table, with electrodes attached to his chest and groin, but Cormack barely spared him a glance; it was the Germans who were important. Kreissner was standing by the table, face turned towards the newcomers, irritated at the interruption. A second man, the technician, was seated at a control console, his right hand on a switch, while there was a third man, a trooper, by the door; it had been he who had unlocked it. Three men, then, plus Altmann and the Rottenführer by the desk, back down the corridor.

"Sturmbannführer Kreissner?" asked Cormack, stepping forward.

"What the hell do you want?" Kreissner demanded. "And who the hell are you?"

"My papers, Herr Sturmbannführer," said Cormack, reaching inside his tunic.

It was at this moment that Kreissner saw Marika behind Cormack, saw the look of triumph in her eyes and realisation struck him with the force of a sledgehammer. "No!" he screamed and then, reacting very fast, he launched himself at Cormack in a head–down rush.

Cormack had just pulled the Browning clear of his jacket when Kreissner's shoulder slammed into his chest, the impact knocking the breath out of him. The force of Kreissner's rush sent Cormack staggering backwards, to crash into the wall; the gun was knocked from his hand and fell clattering to the floor.

Kreissner was slamming punches into Cormack's stomach and groin as he leaned against him, pinning him to the wall; Cormack grimaced with pain and then, clasping both hands together, he brought them down onto the back of Kreissner's neck with murderous force.

It was a blow that would have knocked most men unconscious, might even have proved fatal in some instances; Kreissner reeled back, stumbling, but he was still on his feet, still conscious. He shook his head to clear it; in that instant, Cormack could see what was happening to the others. The trooper by the door was staggering back against the wall, clutching his testicles where Schelhaas' rifle butt had been driven into them like a piston; Schelhaas was taking out his silenced automatic to finish him off. The technician had risen to his feet, terror-stricken and reeled back as a bullet from De Vriess' pistol took him in the chest.

And then Kreissner was coming at him again, right foot lashing out at Cormack's groin with blurring speed; Cormack twisted to one side. The boot still caught him on the hip, however, knocking him sufficiently off balance to forestall any counter-move.

Once more, Kreissner came at him, his right fist scything towards Cormack's face. Cormack blocked the punch and then his right hand, fingers rigidly extended, crashed into Kreissner's solar plexus. Kreissner gasped and doubled up, fighting for breath; Cormack again bunched his fists together and swept them from right to left, smashing them into the side of Kreissner's head. Kreissner went sprawling as Cormack stepped back, taking in great gasps of breath.

But Kreissner was not finished; Cormack stared incredulously as the German rose to all fours, shaking his head like an angry bear. Despite himself, Cormack felt a surge of reluctant admiration; Kreissner was finished, but just refused to admit it. . .

There was a coughing sound and a red rose of blood blossomed on Kreissner's chest. Kreissner's eyes opened wide and he held out his hands in front of himself as if to ward off a blow; then he was thrown to one side as the second bullet tore into him. Cormack spun round; Marika had retrieved the Browning and was holding it, two–handed, staring at Kreissner with an expression of utter loathing. As Cormack watched, she squeezed the trigger a third time and a fourth, then Cormack sprang forward and wrenched the gun from her grasp. She stared at him, wild–eyed, and then, suddenly, her shoulders slumped and she nodded slowly to herself as if in satisfaction. Cormack touched her gently on the shoulder; she had earned the right to take her revenge on Kreissner.

Cormack looked around. It was all over; the entire incident had lasted fifteen seconds at the most. Schelhaas and De Vriess were both standing in the doorway, guns in hand, grim–faced; Altmann, the technician and the trooper were lying absolutely still. "The other one?" said Cormack. "The one by the desk?"

"Dead," said De Vriess stonily. Cormack nodded.

He looked down at Kreissner, at the man who had fought with such extraordinary strength and determination in the last seconds of his life; his body was absolutely motionless, his eyes sightless as a thin rivulet of blood trickled from his mouth. Cormack took a deep breath and expelled it slowly in a deliberate effort to calm himself down, to quell the surge of adrenalin.

Then, he turned away; there was no time to dwell on what had happened; the alarm could be raised at any moment. They had all been using silenced weapons and the entire basement area was soundproofed; they were probably in the clear for the time being, but all it needed was for someone to open the main door and all hell would break loose.

"See if you can find the Mulders," he said to Schelhaas and De Vriess. "And some clothing for Woodward. Marika, can you give me a hand with Woodward?" He bent over the table and had unfastened the straps binding Woodward's left wrist before he realised that Marika had not responded at all, that she was still staring mesmerised at Kreissner. "Marika!" he snapped.

With a visible start, she came out of her trance. "Yes. Of course. Sorry." She began to unfasten the bindings holding Woodward's legs.

Woodward groaned softly and muttered something; Cormack could not make it out, but it sounded French. "It's all right, Tony. It's me, Cormack. We've come to get you out of here, old son," he said in English.

Marika looked up, surprised by the gentle, soothing tone of Cormack's voice, so totally at odds with the impression she had already formed of him. Perhaps this explained the way Lena looked at him.

Woodward's eyes flickered open. "Cormack? What are you doing here? What's going on?" His voice was surprisingly alert, Cormack noted.

"You've been rescued, me old mate. We're going to get you out of here."

He helped Woodward to sit up; the pilot winced. "I feel bloody awful," he said.

"You look it," said Cormack, grinning. "But it's hardly surprising, all things considered." Woodward had been given a really thorough going-over; he must have been a bloody sight more resilient than Cormack had thought he'd be. They wouldn't have tortured him like that if he'd talked. He'd got guts, you had to give him that . . .

"No clothes," said De Vriess, coming back in. "Only blankets." He tossed one over to Cormack.

"No—they took my clothes away," said Woodward. His voice sounded hoarse; through screaming, probably, thought Cormack grimly. He draped the blanket around Woodward's shoulders.

"Can you stand?"

Woodward forced a grin. "Try anything once." Helped by

Cormack, he rose to his feet, tottered unsteadily, but clung on to the table for support. "Fit and raring to go."

Schelhaas came in with the Mulders. Henning Mulder was clutching his ribs, evidently in pain, but with a determined look on his face; Marta looked angry rather than frightened. "I think Henning has a broken rib," said Schelhaas,"but he can walk."

"Right. Let's get moving." He led the way out of the interrogation room; Schelhaas pulled the door to behind them. Cormack was followed by the Mulders, Marika and Woodward;Schelhaas and De Vriess brought up the rear, their Schmeissers covering the "prisoners".

Cormack pulled the main basement door open and strode out, his entire attitude and bearing one of utter arrogance. He barely acknowledged the salutes from the two startled troopers beyond the door, but merely continued up the steps, followed by the others; again, Schelhaas closed the door after them.

They went along a corridor—a Scharführer emerged from an office, clearly surprised, but he saluted, all the same—round a corner, still no challenge. Keep going, Cormack told himself, look as though you belong here. Return the salutes, but don't look at them, don't acknowledge their presence in any other way. One more corner and they would be in the entrance lobby; would the incredible happen? Would he be allowed to walk out of the door with the prisoners without anybody stopping him?

"Herr Hauptsturmführer?"

No, he wouldn't, evidently. Cormack stopped and turned. A burly NCO was striding towards them, purposefully. "Yes, Sturmscharführer—?"

"Kohler, Herr Hauptsturmführer. May I ask where you are taking those prisoners?"

Cormack glared at him, but without any real hope that it would have any effect. Kohler had already shown that he was not easily intimidated; it took nerve to question an SS–Hauptsturmführer. And he was no callow youth; Kohler's rank was equivalent to a Regimental Sergeant Major, and he would not have risen to the highest NCO rank without knowing what he was doing. "I'm taking them to Gestapo headquarters in The Hague, if that is all right with you, Sturmscharführer?" he added scathingly. "I shall need two cars, so if you could make the necessary arrangements?"

Kohler shook his head apologetically but firmly. "I am sorry, Herr Hauptsturmführer, but Sturmbannführer Kreissner's orders are quite explicit." There was a deliberate emphasis on the two rank titles; Kohler was making the unspoken point that Kreissner was the senior of the two. "I'm afraid I have to confirm this with Sturmbannführer Kreissner, Herr Hauptsturmführer, so if you would be kind enough to wait one moment—" He went over to the main desk and picked up a telephone. "Get me Sturmbannführer Kreissner, please," he said into the receiver, never once taking his eyes off Cormack. "He'll be in the Interrogation Room."

Cormack, his face like thunder at Kohler's impertinence, turned abruptly away, stifling an oath. He nodded almost imperceptibly at Schelhaas; the Dutchman took a step to one side, with De Vriess moving the other way. Both men unobtrusively gripped their machine pistols more firmly. Cormack reached inside his tunic and took hold of the Browning's butt.

"What do you mean, there's no answer?" demanded Kohler angrily. "He must be there!"

Cormack nodded a second time; a split second later, Schelhaas and De Vriess opened up with the Schmeissers, both men crouching low as they traversed the barrels, to and fro. Cormack spun round and sprinted towards the door, firing from the hip at a trooper in front of him; the man clutched his stomach and fell heavily forwards. Out of the corner of his eye, Cormack saw Kohler being driven backwards by a hail of gunfire; he was still on his feet, but the bullets were boring into him repeatedly in a bloody pattern across his chest and stomach.

Cormack launched himself at the door, feet first, kicking it open and then twisted round in mid air, so that he landed on his feet, facing the left, the Browning lined up on the astonished guard. The trooper reeled back as the bullet took him in the chest and then Cormack pivoted round to take out the second guard. He stepped to one side, instinctively, as he heard the guard's rifle fire, the bullet missing him by less than six inches. Again, he squeezed the trigger. The guard spun round, cannoned into the wall and then fell heavily onto his side, clutching his ribs, trying desperately to staunch the flow of blood.

Cormack never even spared him a glance; he beckoned, urgently, and the four "prisoners" came towards him in a headlong rush. He could hear the sound of a lorry approaching along the street, gathering speed; Lena, it had to be. If it wasn't, they were finished; it was only then that Cormack realised that the Mercedes they had arrived in was no longer there. So much for using it as a getaway car. . .

"Come on!" he yelled as Woodward ran unsteadily past him. Schelhaas and De Vriess were backing towards him, still raking the lobby with a murderous fire. Schelhaas unclipped one of the stick grenades from his belt, armed it and tossed it gently across the lobby; he and De Vriess spun round and sprinted for the door, reaching it just as the grenade detonated in a shattering explosion that blew out the glass in the door's windowpanes.

The lorry was already slowing to a halt. Lena had left the tailgate lowered and Marika was already scrambling into the back. Just another fifteen seconds, Cormack thought, that's all we need now and we're clear. . .

"Go on!" Schelhaas yelled at him. "Get in the cab—we can hold anyone who comes out!" He gestured to his Schmeisser. Cormack nodded and ran for the lorry, climbing in on the driver's side; Lena had already moved over.

Schelhaas and De Vriess were running for the lorry now; a second grenade exploded in the entrance, the blast almost knocking Schelhaas off his feet. He waved to Cormack as he pelted past the cab, an exultant grin on his face. "Get moving, my friend!" he bellowed. Cormack slammed the gear lever forward and let out the clutch.

There was a burst of gunfire from a first floor window; De Vriess, running full tilt towards the lorry, suddenly threw up his arms and spun round, falling and rolling, over and over, limbs flailing disjointedly. Schelhaas, at the back of the truck, turned and raked the window with a three-second burst. There was the unmistakable sound of shattering glass, a scream of agony and then silence.

Schelhaas looked down at De Vriess; a single glance was enough. If De Vriess was not already dead, he would be within seconds; no man could possibly live with half his chest torn away by bullets. Schelhaas scooped up De Vriess' Schmeisser and jumped up into the back of the moving lorry.

Cormack had his foot to the floor, but the truck was

painfully slow to pick up speed; he wrenched the wheel over to the left, feeling the lorry tilt as it took the corner, engine roaring. There was no sign of pursuit in the rearview mirror as yet, but it was only a matter of time before the Germans recovered and started taking counter–measures. He hauled the wheel over again to the right, cursing at the amount of effort it required. This was why he had taken over the driving from Lena; she did not have the brute strength needed to fling the heavy vehicle around at speed.

"Take the next right," said Lena suddenly. "That'll put us on the main road north."

Cormack nodded and laboriously turned the wheel, still picking up speed. "How far until we're out of Leiden?"

"About three kilometres."

Say two miles, then, thought Cormack. Four or five minutes; he doubted if the Germans could set up adequate road blocks in that time, but. . .

Damn! He caught a glimpse of a Kubelwagen parked in a side road as they sped past; if it was equipped with radio, as it probably would be, it could sound the alarm. Nothing he could do about it, though. He glanced at the speedometer; they were doing 50 k.p.h.; thirty miles an hour, but he doubted if he could coax much more out of the lorry.

He checked the mirror again and swore softly: the Kubelwagen had pulled out after them and was already closing up on them fast. There was a clatter of automatic fire as Schelhaas opened up with the Schmeisser; the pursuing car began to zig–zag violently and then its machine gun began to fire back, raking the rear of the truck.

Schelhaas ignored the fusillade of bullets; with the car weaving from side to side, he doubted if the German gunner could aim at all accurately. Impassively, he lined up the Schmeisser on the car's windscreen and squeezed the trigger, firing off a long burst. The Kubelwagen's windshield disintegrated into a thousand fragments and the car swerved to one side. For an instant, it seemed as though it must crash, but then, at the last moment, it straightened up, swaying drunkenly from side to side and then came on after them, although it had fallen well back now. Schelhaas swore, slammed another clip into the magazine and waited for the car to close up again.

It didn't. The driver had evidently learned his lesson, because he was maintaining a distance of some fifty metres; Schelhaas realised that the Germans had decided merely to shadow them until they could call up reinforcements. And they had the extra speed; Cormack would not be able to shake them off.

Schelhaas stared at the car for several seconds and then grinned wolfishly. He unclipped the last stick grenade from his belt. There was a five-second delay once they had been primed; he did a quick mental calculation. Estimate the speed at about fifty kilometres an hour, that meant . . . fourteen metres a second. The car was fifty metres behind, so it would take them three and a half seconds to cover that. But he wanted it to detonate in front of them; ideally, right underneath. So . . . three seconds, then. . .

He armed the grenade and leaned over the tailgate . . . and one, and two . . . He dropped the grenade and watched it bounce along the road, falling rapidly behind until it was lost to view. And three and four and five and. . .

There was a blinding flash in front of the pursuing car, although to one side. The front of the Kubelwagen was thrown violently upwards and the car slewed crazily round; in an instant, it was rolling over and over, strewing shards of metal in its wake as it broke up. Schelhaas heard a high–pitched scream of agony and then the car exploded in a sheet of flame as its petrol tank went up.

Schelhaas stared awe-struck at the blazing wreckage as it receded into the distance; then the truck rounded a corner and it was lost to view.

Ahead of them was the open countryside, but there was no sense of triumph, of achievement; De Vriess was not there to see it.

They drove on in silence, their own tribute to the dead.

# CHAPTER 18

**NIGHT OF 8/9 MAY**

Trudi smiled up at Behrens and then hugged him, her breasts still rising and falling rapidly. "I do believe we're getting rather good at this, Anton."

He kissed her gently. "Well, practice makes perfect, so they say."

"You mean this could get better? I don't think I could stand it," she chuckled.

She had arrived at his quarters two hours before; within twenty minutes, they had been in bed. There had been no reluctance on her part; indeed, her longing for him had been almost indecent. But he had prolonged her pleasure, keeping her waiting, heightening her anticipation, before making love to her, slowly, languidly.

She stroked his cheek, affectionately. He really is a wonderful lover, she thought to herself; experienced and considerate. And very skilled. But there was also a warmth, a tenderness, when they made love that had never been there with any other man. Maybe . . . maybe he would be right for her. She hoped so, with an intensity that surprised her.

The telephone rang; Behrens sighed in exasperation. "That damned phone," he muttered, as he moved away from her.

"You ought to take it off the hook," she suggested, with a mischievous grin. "I wouldn't have been very pleased if it had rung five minutes ago. It might have been rather—well, shall we say—distracting?

Behrens smiled at her and sat on the edge of the bed. He picked up the receiver. "Behrens here."

"Unteroffizier Ziegler here, Herr Major. Could you come in to the office, please, Herr Major?" Ziegler sounded subdued.

"What's happened, Ziegler?"

"I can't really tell you over the telephone, Herr Major. But—well—something's happened at Gestapo headquarters. But could you come in, please, Herr Major?" Ziegler was almost pleading with him, Behrens realised. It must be serious—and urgent.

"Very well. Forty-five minutes." He put the telephone down and looked at Trudi.

"Don't tell me," she said resignedly. "Business?"

He hesitated. "I'm afraid so, Trudi. Do you mind?"

She sat up and touched his cheek. "Of course I mind, Anton. But you must go. I know that."

He kissed her gently. "Can I drop you off on the way?"

"Certainly not. I'm going to stay here and wait for you to come back." She lay back, stretching her arms above her head, lifting her breasts upwards provocatively. "Keeping the bed warm for you, you might say." Her eyes gleamed in pure mischief.

"In that case, I shan't be long." His face became more serious. "But honestly, Trudi, I don't know when I'll be back."

"That's alright," she said softly. "I'll still be waiting, Anton."

Ziegler and Ludwig were both waiting outside the office when Behrens arrived; both men looked pale and drawn as they followed Behrens into his office.

"Well? What's the panic?" Behrens demanded brusquely. It had better be good, he thought, remembering the way Trudi had looked as he had left.

"There's been some sort of an armed assault on Gestapo headquarters, Herr Major," said Ziegler abruptly. "The prisoner—Tanvier—was rescued and so were the Mulders."

"An assault?" asked Behrens incredulously. "Slow down, both of you. Tell me exactly what's happened."

It was Ludwig who took over the story. "Three men and the Schuurmann girl got inside the building. Apparently, the men were wearing SS uniforms and appeared to be escorting the girl in as a prisoner. There was shooting—we don't have the exact details yet, Herr Major—but they all managed to escape, except for one terrorist, who was killed."

"With Tanvier and the Mulders?"

Ludwig nodded. "So it would seem, Herr Major."

"How the devil—? Never mind. How they did it doesn't matter. You say they escaped? Completely?"

"Apparently, Herr Major. They escaped in a lorry that was driven by another terrorist. They were pursued by a car for a while but the car was destroyed by a grenade and the lorry has since vanished."

"Dear God," Behrens breathed, awe–struck. Who were these terrorists? What sort of man was leading them, for Heaven's sake? Raiding a Gestapo headquarters . . . Who was Tanvier and why was he so important that they would take such appalling risks to rescue him? "Are we in contact with Gestapo HQ?"

"We have been, intermittently, Herr Major. They're in some confusion over there at the moment," said Ziegler.

"I can imagine," said Behrens. "Try and get me Sturmbannführer Kreissner on the telephone if it's possible."

Ludwig and Ziegler exchanged glances and then Ziegler spoke. "I'm afraid that will be impossible, Herr Major. Sturmbannführer Kreissner is dead. He was killed in the shooting."

Behrens shook his head slowly. "Dead," he echoed hollowly. "Get me whoever's in command over there, then."

"Yes, Herr Major," said Ludwig.

Behrens stared absently at the door as it closed after Ludwig. Why in hell had they gone to such lengths to rescue Tanvier, or whatever his real name was? Because he was important, of course: but why? Why had they just made a run for it? Again, because they needed Tanvier.

The specialist. But in what?

And if they had rescued him, it could not have been out of purely humanitarian motives; it must be because Tanvier was vital to whatever they were now intending to do. Something only he could do. . .

The radar. They were still after the radar; Behrens knew it as certainly as if they had told him. Far from calling off the mission, they were determined to carry it out, come what may. And the only thing around Leiden that would justify such suicidal risks was the Liechtenstein radar.

He turned abruptly. "Get a car ready immediately. Forget about contacting the Gestapo; we're going out to Verwijk. Tell Halldorf to expect us and to put his men on full alert."

Cormack watched Henning Mulder climb up into the lorry's cab next to his wife; he was clearly in a good deal of pain. He had protested about not being included in the assault party, but had been forced to concede that he was hardly in any condition to fight. Indeed, Cormack suspected that Mulder was a lot more seriously injured than he'd admitted.

His eyes moved to the two people standing in front of the truck: Marika and Pieter. The youth had also objected to being left behind, but he had been given a heavy burden, nevertheless; it was up to him to get the Mulders to Antwerp, where the Lifeline Organisation would smuggle the three of them to safety in Spain or Switzerland. Cormack and Schelhaas had given him his instructions: he was to take the lorry and head south, abandoning it before daybreak. After that, he and the Mulders would have to make their way across country. Pieter's initial disappointment had been partly offset by the realisation that he was actually being given a difficult and hazardous assignment.

Cormack watched brother and sister embrace and then move apart. Marika stood stock still as Pieter turned away and climbed up into the driving seat. He raised a hand in acknowledgement to Cormack and nodded to Schelhaas, who was waiting by the starting handle. Schelhaas cranked the handle and the engine spluttered into life. Pieter waved again, this time to Marika and then, with a grinding of gears, the lorry moved off down the track.

Marika stood alone watching the truck until it was lost to view and then she turned and walked slowly back towards the barn. She did not look at Cormack as she passed, but he could see the glint of tears in her eyes. It might be months, years, before she saw Pieter again.

If ever.

Cormack looked down at the ground. He was still not convinced that he had been right to include Lena and Marika in the assault party, although he knew that his doubts were purely emotional. In Resistance cells, there was no difference at all between men and women when it came to dangerous operations; everyone had to take their chances. Schelhaas, he knew, had no reservations whatsoever in the matter; as far as he was concerned, they were both experienced, resourceful members of his group, no more and no less than that. And, Cormack had to admit, Lena and Marika had more than justified Schelhaas' faith in their abilities already tonight. Equally true was the fact that had he excluded them, the assault party would have been reduced to jut three; and in terms of effective undercover abilities, Woodward would be of little use. Three men left no margin for error or mishaps; logically, the party should be larger, as Cormack well knew. Even with Lena and Marika, it was dangerously small . . . And if Lena had not been one of the two, he would not have hesitated an instant.

As it was, though. . .

He rubbed his hand across his forehead and went back into the barn. Lena and Marika were tending to Woodward, who had made a surprisingly good recovery from his ordeal and who also seemed to be enjoyed their attentions. He was now dressed in a pullover and slacks that Schelhaas had given him from his suitcase; they were a trifle large, but they would suffice. Schelhaas was busily pulling bales of hay to one side; he reached down and pulled up a trapdoor that had been concealed underneath. He lifted out a large, bulky item that Cormack instantly recognised; it was a standard British Army portable wireless. Schelhaas extended the aerial, and switched the set on, grinning at Cormack. "I told you I'd provide a radio," he said. "I try to honour my promises."

Cormack shook his head in bemused admiration and then went over to Schelhaas. He slipped on the headphones and tuned it in. He tapped out just one word: 'Fagin' and waited for a reply. It came within ten seconds: Guthrie had said they'd be listening in around the clock and he'd been as good as his word. Cormack read off the reply and then tapped out 'Twist'. There was a delay then of about half a minute before the next reply came through. Altogether, he'd been transmitting for perhaps twenty seconds, far too short a time for any direction–finding unit to obtain a 'fix' on him. Even if they did, it would make little difference; they were moving out in five minutes.

"It's on," he said to the others. "0100. Two hours' time."

That's it, he thought to himself. We're committed now.

They left the barn even more rapidly than Cormack had anticipated; they were on their way inside three minutes. Lena and Cormack were the last to go; they paused and looked back at the shadowy outline of the barn. He slipped his arm round her waist; she seemed to read his thoughts.

"I don't suppose we'll ever come back here," she said quietly. "But I'll never forget it. Never."

"Me neither," said Cormack gently. She came into his arms and they kissed. "Lena?"

"Yes?"

"When we get back to London . . ." He hesitated.

"Yes, Alan?"

"Dinner at the Savoy?" he said lightly.

"By candlelight?" she grinned.

"Of course."

"Sounds like a good idea. I'll hold you to that when we get back."

"That's what I was hoping." They kissed again, more intensely this time; both of them were breathless when their lips parted.

"Come on," she said. "We'd better be going or the others will be wondering what we're up to." She looked again at the barn for one last time and reached out for his hand. He nodded and took one last look himself. Then, hand in hand, they set off after the others.

Behrens had the door of the car open even before it came to a halt; by the time Ziegler had alighted, he was halfway to the guard–house, off–handedly saluting the sentries. Halldorf came out to greet him, saluting smartly.

"Are you on full alert?" asked Behrens, dispensing with any preliminaries.

"Yes, Herr Major. As soon as you telephoned, I—"

"Good, good. So how many men do we have on perimeter patrols at the moment?"

"Thirty, Herr Major. We have quite a few men on leave, you see, Herr Major. It is Saturday night, after all, and—"

"I'm fully aware what day it is, Oberleutnant. Have you taken any steps to have leave cancelled and to get those men back here?"

"Er—no, Herr Major. I did not realise that you wished me to do that. It was not included in your instructions," said Halldorf defensively.

"Damn it, Halldorf, I said FULL alert, did I not? What the hell did you think I meant?"

"I'm sorry, Herr Major," said Halldorf half apologetically, half defiantly. "But there has never been an established procedure for full alert. Major Gottlieb never felt there was any need for one."

No, he wouldn't, thought Behrens bitterly, but said nothing. And, in the final analysis, Behrens knew that it was his responsibility; he had never made any effort to find out exactly what procedures were in force. And so, because of that oversight, over half of the security personnel were getting drunk or chasing women in town, while Allied agents could be making off with one of the Reich's most valuable secrets. . .

"Get in touch with my office in Leiden. Talk to Unteroffizier Ludwig and tell him to take a detachment and round up as many of our missing men as possible. Drunk or sober, I want them back here as soon as possible. Understand?"

"Yes, Herr Major." Halldorf went to carry out his order, but not before Behrens caught a look of utter mystification on his face; clearly, he thought his C.O. was making a lot of fuss over nothing. Maybe he was, maybe there was nothing at all to worry about, but he was still possessed by the odd certainty that these agents were after the radar. If he was wrong, then so be it.

Behrens made his way into the guardhouse and nodded to an Unteroffizier who had shot to his feet behind the desk. "Unteroffizier Waltke, isn't it?"

"Yes, Herr Major," Waltke replied, a note of surprised pleasure in his voice.

"Right, Waltke. Can you tell me where our patrols are deployed at the moment?"

"Certainly, Herr Major." He indicated a large-scale plan of the airfield on the wall. "We have five patrols out at the moment, here, here, here, here, and here." He pointed to five widely-spaced locations. "Each patrol has five or six men."

Behrens grimaced. Thirty men to patrol over five kilometres of perimeter fence; not nearly enough. "Guard dogs?"

"Er—just three, Herr Major," said Waltke apologetically. "The other two have stomach upsets, apparently."

Behrens shook his head disbelievingly. It was as if the fates themselves had decreed that he was doomed to fail tonight. He stared at the map almost desperately; there was, quite simply, nothing else he could do at the moment. He needed more men, that was all there was to it. And until Ludwig could start rounding up men from the fleshpots of Leiden, there was only one way he could find reinforcements. . .

But that would mean sticking his neck out a long way. If he were proved wrong, if what he had done so far proved to be founded on nothing more than baseless fears, it would be embarrassing, but no more than that. But if he took it further and was shown to be over–reacting he could expect no mercy from his superiors.

Ah, to hell with it.

"Waltke, would you try and contact The Hague for me, by telephone? I would like to speak to Oberst Strassner as soon as possible."

Cormack lay full–length on the crest of a sand–dune and peered intently through his binoculars. He was fifty yards from the perimeter fence and about a quarter of a mile from where the Ju88s were parked. Slowly, he moved the glasses around the fence, noting the patrols. "Irregular intervals for the patrols, by the look of it," he observed.

"Yes," said Schelhaas beside him. "Our Major Behrens is much more efficient than his predecessor, unfortunately."

"He would be," said Cormack ironically. "Still, there's nothing much we can do about it, is there?"

"Hardly," Schelhaas agreed. "But the air–raid should distract them, surely?

"I damn well hope so," said Cormack feelingly. He glanced at his watch: 12.40. "Right, let's make a move. We'll need to get closer to the perimeter." He signalled and Lena, Marika and Woodward materialised out of the gloom behind them. Silently, they moved forward, until they were only twenty yards from the fence. Then Cormack held his hand up. "Wait here," he said in a low voice. "Keep an eye out for patrols." He took a pair of heavy wire-cutters. "Wait for my signal."

He was suddenly aware of Lena's hand in his; he squeezed it gently and then began to crawl towards the fence on his stomach. When he reached it, he checked his watch yet again; fifteen minutes to go. He found that he was straining his ears to see if he could hear the approaching aircraft, but the night was still. Far off, a dog barked and he could hear the chink of metal against metal as an aircraft mechanic carried out some repair; apart from these sounds, there was nothing.

He looked around carefully and then began to cut through the wire mesh, pausing every few seconds to listen for the sound of an approaching patrol; on this calm night, he would hear them before he saw them.

There. The sound of several men coming closer; a patrol. He flattened himself against the ground and began to edge backwards silently. There was a depression in the sand, five yards behind him; he slid down into it. Now, he would be out of sight from any patrol inside the fence; all he had to do was to keep his head down until they had passed.

Still coming closer. Unconsciously, almost, he reached inside his tunic and took out the silenced Browning; it would be utter folly to use the Sten until it was absolutely necessary. He flicked off the safety catch and waited, head pressed down against the sand.

It was Woodward, fifteen yards away, who first saw the oncoming patrol and, from his vantage point, he could see what Cormack had not yet realised; the patrol was, in fact, outside the fence and they were heading directly towards the solitary figure lying motionless in the sand. The Germans were already only about fifteen yards from Cormack; they could not fail to see him within the next ten seconds or so.

Woodward reached for his silenced Walther P38 and flicked off the catch with a practised movement. He took careful aim at the leading German and heard a sharp intake of breath from beside him; Schelhaas had seen the patrol as well. And there was no way of warning Cormack, none at all.

The gun barrel never wavered for an instant as Woodward tracked the soldier, remorselessly. The German reached the crest of the dune and then looked down; Woodward saw the look of astonishment on his face as he noticed Cormack and then the P38 coughed once as Woodward squeezed the trigger.

A scarlet hole abruptly appeared in the centre of the soldier's forehead; the German stood on the crest for a second as though transfixed and then toppled slowly to one side, rolling down the slope towards Cormack.

The rest of the patrol were in utter confusion; none of them had heard the shot and they were uncertain as to what had happened. It was only when Woodward fired a second time and the second man in the line pirouetted around, shot through the heart, that they began to react, flinging themselves to the ground.

Cormack had been taken completely by surprise; he had seen the silhouette of the German on the crest out of the corner of his eye, but, before he could even begin to react, the soldier had been tumbling down the slope towards him, shot through the head. It had to be Woodward with his target marksmanship. Had to be; Cormack realised that he probably owed his life to the young pilot.

He scrambled up the slope in time to see Woodward's second victim falling to the ground. The Germans flattened themselves against the ground, scurrying frantically for whatever cover they could find. One of them raised his hand in the air; too late, Cormack realised that the hand held a signal pistol. He aimed and fired the Browning in a single motion; the man cried out and slumped back, but the flare was already soaring up into the sky. With a brilliant flash, it exploded far above him, bathing the scene in an incandescent glare that would be seen miles away. . .

Cormack swore and then unslung his Sten; the time for silence had gone. He reached down to his belt for a grenade; as he did so, Schelhaas and Woodward opened up, raking the stretch of sand below Cormack with a murderous hail of fire. One German threw up his arms in agony as the bullets tore into him; the other two still surviving scrambled desperately out of sight behind a low dune.

Cormack primed the grenade and then lobbed it behind the dune, just as one of the Germans came into view again, sprinting over to the left. The grenade detonated and Cormack heard a high–pitched scream of terror and pain, abruptly cut off.

The last German was still on the move about twenty yards from Cormack; he was making a run for it. Cormack rose to his feet and drew a bead on the running figure. Slowly, carefully, he squeezed the trigger and maintained the pressure as he poured a three-second burst into the fleeing man. The soldier seemed to stumble in his run, arching backwards, his body shuddering under the impact of the bullets. He turned round, still on his feet, face contorted in agony; then fell slowly backwards.

Cormack let the Sten fall to his side, fighting off the feeling of despair that threatened to overwhelm him. The whole bloody thing was going wrong; the alarm had been well and truly sounded now. If they didn't get through the perimeter fence in the next two minutes or so, they never would.

He took a deep breath, nerving himself and then ran to the opening he had made; with half-a-dozen savage cuts, he had enlarged it sufficiently. He signalled to the others.

As arranged, they came through one at a time, Woodward first, scrambling awkwardly through the gap. Then Lena, in a low crouching run, smiling at him as she bent down to crawl through the hole in the fence.

Cormack waved his arm again and saw Marika beginning her run; too late, he saw a movement out of the corner of his eye. As he turned his head, the night was rent by the vicious stuttering of a Schmeisser. Marika cried out and came to a dead stop, a look of shocked incomprehension on her face as she looked down at the growing stain of red on her chest. Then the Schmeisser chattered again and she was hurled to one side as the bullets tore into her.

Cormack spun round and saw the German solder through the fence, already sprinting for cover. Lena muttered a low curse and then fired her Schmeisser in a raking two-second burst. The German threw up his arms and fell forward, heavily. He lay motionless in a spreading pool of blood.

Cormack looked around rapidly. Where the hell had he come from? Had he been part of a back-up patrol or had he simply been nearby and had come to investigate the gunfire? No time for that, now; all that mattered was that they had relaxed their vigilance and allowed him to sneak up on them. And Marika had paid for the lapse with her life.

Schelhaas was bending over her body, feeling for any pulse; as Cormack watched, he released her wrist and stared down at her face for several seconds. With a curiously tender motion, he closed her eyes and Cormack saw him murmur a few words; then, Schelhaas straightened up and ran over to the fence, his features expressionless, composed. He shook his head in answer to Cormack's mute query; for an instant, Cormack saw naked grief in the Dutchman's eyes and then the moment was gone as if it had never been.

"Let's go," said Schelhaas, his voice harsh. "Let's get that bloody plane."

# CHAPTER 19

**VERWIJK AIRFIELD 00.40 hours**

"Oberst Strassner?"

"Speaking, Major Behrens. What can I do for you? I trust it's important, for you to be calling at this hour of the night."

Behrens ignored Strassner's peevish tone; he had been trying to reach his superior for the last hour and a half and Strassner had only just returned from a dinner engagement, so he could hardly complain at being dragged out of his bed. "I wish to request reinforcements at Verwijk, Herr Oberst. I have reason to believe that a group of enemy agents will attempt to penetrate our defences. Certainly, there is a highly dangerous group in this immediate area; they've already successfully attacked the Gestapo headquarters in Leiden."

"Yes, we've been receiving reports about that." Behrens was convinced he could hear a note of smug satisfaction in Strassner's voice. "Do you have any solid evidence they're coming your way?"

"No, Herr Oberst. But—"

"And you have—what? Sixty men in your security squad at Verwijk? Surely that should be sufficient, Major?"

Behrens took a deep breath. "With respect, Herr Oberst, we have five kilometres to guard. Twelve men per kilometre is hardly excessive under the circumstances, especially as half of them are on weekend passes. I'm trying to round up the men in Leiden, but I have only forty men available at the moment."

There was a silence at the other end lasting for several seconds. "Why do you think they might try to get into the airfield?" asked Strassner eventually.

"They could be after the Liechtenstein radar, Herr Oberst," said Behrens. "There's already been one attempt—"

"Yes, yes, I know all about that," said Strassner testily.

"Well, this particular group have been in Holland since Friday night, that we do know, but they've stayed in this area. They've had plenty of time to contact the local Resistance and set up a second attempt. The fact that they've stayed in the Leiden area indicates that they're after something round here." As he spoke, Behrens realised that he was repeating, almost verbatim, Kreissner's theories; he'd never liked the man, but in this instance he'd spoken good sense.

"I see. Well, if you think they're after the radar, then put guards on each aircraft equipped with it."

"I can't do that as well as patrol the perimeter, Herr Oberst. I don't have enough men. I'm only guessing about the radar; they might have something else in mind. Blowing up the fuel tanks or taking a look at our telecommunications gear. Anything. I have to keep them off the base altogether, but I need more men."

There was another lengthy pause, during which Behrens vaguely realised he was holding his breath, before Strassner gave his decision. "I'm sorry, Major. This is all supposition on your part. You'll have to manage with what you—"

Ziegler burst in abruptly. "Herr Major! There's shooting over by the western perimeter! A pitched battle by the sound of it!"

"Halldorf!" Behrens bellowed, putting his hand over the receiver. The beefy Oberleutnant hurried in, his face pale. "Get over to the western perimeter and report—fast!"

"At once, Herr Major!"

Behrens lifted up the telephone again and heard Strassner's voice, demanding to know just what in the name of heaven was going on? "I'm sorry, Herr Oberst. We are all too late, it seems. They're trying to get in, right now." He slammed the phone down and turned to Waltke. "Can we depress the anti-aircraft searchlights enough to light up the airfield itself?"

Waltke thought for a moment. "I don't think so, Herr Major. But we do have one or two vehicles with smaller lights—we could use them."

"Then get them over to the fence. I want to be able to see those saboteurs. I want all the maintenance area floodlights turned on, and get every spare vehicle over to the aircraft parking areas with their headlights on—I want this place lit up like a fairground."

Cormack sprinted across a thirty-yard gap and came to a halt behind a stack of fuel drums. He looked around and then gestured with his arm; immediately, he saw Woodward beginning his run. The other man was breathing heavily as he arrived, but Cormack ignored him and beckoned again after checking that the coast was clear; seconds later, Lena had joined them and Schelhaas was on his way.

Cormack consulted his watch; two minutes to go until the 'diversion' commenced, a low–level bombing raid on the airfield by twelve Mosquitoes, who would be flying in at tree-top height to avoid radar detection. The raid had originally been intended as a diversionary tactic while Cormack and his party had gone through the fence, but they had been obliged to move in ahead of schedule. The attack would still serve a useful purpose, spreading chaos and confusion to cover the actual theft, but, by the same token, Cormack reflected, they stood a very real chance of being killed by their own bombers. Especially standing next to a pile of fuel drums. . .

He tensed: he could hear them, very faintly; aero engines coming rapidly closer, the sound increasing steadily in volume. He searched desperately for their next cover, but there was nothing between them and the nearest Ju88, a hundred yards away except for an anti–aircraft battery at half that distance. It was manned; the odds of him making an undetected approach in the time remaining were non–existent.

So the fuel drums would have to do, after all. Cormack had a vivid mental image of what would happen if they went up; the four of them would be instantly incinerated in a flaming holocaust. He pushed the thought to one side impatiently.

"Get down!" he hissed. The drone of the Mosquito engines was now only too evident; the anti–aircraft gun was already swivelling around as the air-raid siren began to wail. Cormack could hear excited shouts; abruptly, the clamour of the Rolls–Royce engines was deafening as the Mosquitoes flashed past overhead, barely a hundred feet up.

And then the bombs started falling.

The R/T crackled into life; Behrens snatched up the

microphone as he heard Halldorf's voice.

"Halldorf to Command Post. I'm at the fence. Over."

"Behrens here. Report."

"Eight men dead, Herr Major. One enemy casualty, a girl. She's dead as well."

"Any sign of the intruders?"

"Negative, Herr Major. But there's a hole in the fence."

Behrens muttered a curse. They were inside and they'd had five minutes to take cover. And he still did not know for certain what they were after; he would have to take a calculated gamble. "Get over to the parking area immediately, Oberleutnant." He put down the microphone and looked out of the window. "Where are those lights, for God's sake, Waltke?"

"I countermanded that order, Behrens," said a curt voice behind him. Behrens spun round and groaned inwardly; it was von Mahrendorf, the Staffel CO. "What the devil is going on? What was all that shooting? And why do you want my airfield illuminated for any Allied bomber to see?"

"Enemy agents," said Behrens shortly. "They're inside the base, somewhere."

"They're what?" exlaimed von Mahrendorf incredulously.

"You heard," Behrens snapped and turned away. "Ziegler, contact all patrols and have them concentrate on the aircraft parking area. Maintain a guard on the Control Tower and the fuel dump. And, Waltke, I want those damned lights on—now! Understand?"

"Yes, Herr Major."

"What are they doing here?" demanded von Mahrendorf accusingly.

"They must have forgotten to tell me," retorted Behrens. "I am assuming that they are after the Liechtensteins on your Ju88s."

"And if they're not?"

"Then I'll be bloody wrong, won't I? And I have no doubt that you'll be able to say that at my court-martial, but,just now, I am rather busy, so if you'll excuse me—Ziegler, get the car ready!" he shouted, striding towards the door.

He stopped dead as he heard the unmistakable whine of the

air-raid siren, punctuated suddenly by the rhythmic thumps of a solitary anti–aircraft gun. There was just enough time to discern the sound of aircraft engines before he heard the first explosions. . .

"Go!" yelled Cormack as the bombs started expoding at the western end of the field. He began to run, followed by the others, heading straight towards the anti–aircraft gun emplacement as it opened fire, pumping tracer shells up into the night at the fast–moving bombers. The gun crew were oblivious to everything but their targets; the first they knew of Cormack's approach was when he opened up with the Sten from about twenty yards away. All four Germans died within seconds of each other, mown down by a merciless hail of fire from Cormack and Schelhaas.

"Get under cover!" Cormack yelled as he hauled the gunner out of his seat, throwing him to one side before taking his place. He traversed the 40mm gun, bringing down the barrel until it was pointing directly at the fuel drums they had just left. The bright tracers curved out across the gap as he pressed the firing button, to smash into the drums.

There was an eye–searing flash as the fuel detonated in a raging fireball; Cormack slid out of the seat and crouched down next to the others behind the sandbags. He peered over at the nearest Ju88, clearly illuminated by the blazing fuel, and then looked around.

No–one was in sight; presumably, they had all taken cover when the bombs had started to fall. The front of the nearest hangar suddenly erupted into flames as a bomb smashed squarely into it; another fire was growing and spreading over by the perimeter. And the bombs were still coming down, the noises of their separate explosions blending into a single continuous cacophony that battered mercilessly at the eardrums.

Cormack tapped Woodward on the shoulder; the pilot nodded. Cormack vaulted over the sandbags and set off for the Ju88, fifty yards away. He glanced back; Woodward was following him, about ten yards behind. Good enough; Cormack continued to run towards the aircraft in a low crouch, coughing as a plume of smoke drifted past, enveloping him. Thirty yards to go, twenty, another bright flash as a lorry was blown to smithereens over to the left and then a monstrous black shape hurtled past overhead; one of the Mosquitoes.

With a sudden ice–cold certainty, Cormack knew what was going to happen. He skidded to a halt and then began to run back towards Woodward, his mouth opening to bellow a warning to the pilot. A giant invisible hand lifted him up and hurled him forwards as the bomb exploded somewhere behind him. He cartwheeled crazily in mid-air and landed on his left foot, crying out as he felt a searing pain in his left ankle. The leg collapsed under him, sending him crashing to the ground.

Jesus! That was too close for comfort . . . He could taste blood in his mouth, could feel a wet stickiness against his leg, which was throbbing painfully; a piece of shrapnel must have hit it, he thought detachedly. Damn lucky it wasn't worse . . .

Bloody hell. Woodward. Was he all right?

Without thinking, Cormack tried to pull himself to his feet; as his weight came onto his left leg, he felt a white-hot shaft of agony spearing through his ankle. Unconsciousness came almost instantly, blanking out the pain in merciful oblivion, even before he could cry out.

Schelhaas ducked behind the sandbags as the bomb detonated, but not before he had seen Cormack thrown bodily through the air and Woodward reel backwards, falling heavily. He crouched down behind their cover as earth and stones pattered down on Lena and himself, his ears ringing from the blast, his mind racing.

If Woodward had been killed or incapacitated, then they were finished; Cormack, he knew with dispassionate logic, was not as vital now as the pilot. Their only way out now was by aircraft; Woodward was, quite literally, indispensable. If he were dead. . .

The instant the deluge of debris was over, he peered out over the sandbags: Woodward was rising shakily to his feet, dazed, apparently, but with no signs of any serious injury. Woodward looked round and saw Cormack, who was lying ominously still. The pilot reached the motionless figure in half-a-dozen rapid strides and bent over him.

Schelhaas sensed a movement beside him and looked down to see Lena lifting herself up from the ground. She was white–faced and trembling, but seemed to be unhurt. As if from a great distance, Schelhaas became aware that the sound of aircraft engines was fading away; the raid was over, had lasted perhaps two minutes in all. Two minutes, but the airfield was devastated.

And then he saw a movement in the distance and froze. A half–track was heading towards them, about four hundred metres away. It had a searchlight mounted behind the driver; not that they needed it, thought Schelhaas. The entire airfield was lit up by the flames from the wrecked hangar and the fuel drums. And, if the half–track kept on its present direction, those on board could hardly miss Cormack and Woodward. . .

Schelhaas yelled at Lena, "Go and help Woodward! There's some Nazis coming—I'll hold them off!"

Lena's head whipped round, her eyes widening as she saw the half–track; it was coming almost straight towards them.She scrambled to her feet, scooping up her Sten.

"Good luck, Vim!" she shouted above the din and then clambered over the sandbags.

Schelhaas climbed into the gunner's seat and wound the training handle, bringing the long barrel round until the half–track was firmly centred in the sights. Although he was totally unaware of it, his face was split in a feral grin as he pressed the firing button. The tracer shells stabbed out through the darkness, over the half–track, and then into the bodywork as he corrected the range.

The vehicle swerved to one side, but Schelhaas followed it round, remorselessly, pumping the 40mm shells into it, seeing German soldiers leaping panic–stricken for safety. Then the half–track blew up. One of the soldiers fell forward as the explosion caught him; he picked himself up, his back and shoulders ablaze. He staggered away, a human torch, arms beating in vain at the flames; he fell again, onto his face, but still he was moving, crawling across the tarmac.

Schelhaas ignored him; others were escaping, running for cover as he swung the gun around, raking the area to the right of the burning vehicle. One of the running men was thrown to one side as the tracers ripped into him, but then, as if by magic, the only Germans in sight were those who were lying motionless on the ground.

Schelhaas released the button and slid out of the seat. Time to go, he decided; he could make them keep their heads down for a while, but if he remained in his present position they could whistle up reinforcements and encircle him. He looked around and saw that Lena and Woodward were supporting Cormack between them. The nearest Ju88 was a blazing wreck; the bomb must have landed almost on top of it, but the three figures had already passed it and were heading for the aircraft beyond.

For perhaps a second, Schelhaas was tempted to go after them; they could be at the aircraft within half a minute. But the Nazis would be right behind them and Woodward needed time to start the engines, taxi to the runway and take off. He had to give the pilot that time. . .

Deliberately, Schelhaas turned his back on his three companions and surveyed the situation. The nearest hangar was only about ninety or a hundred metres away with plenty of cover around it: crates, packing cases and so forth. Good enough.

He loosed off a short burst from his Sten in the general direction of the blazing half–track and began to run towards the hangar.

Cormack was still unconscious as Woodward and Lena reached the Ju88; they deposited him gently on the tarmac and Woodward began to unfasten the clips on the access hatch in the rear section of the fuselage. He gestured to Lena to remove the chocks from the wheels; she nodded and ran to obey.

He swung the hatch open and then bent to lift Cormack; Lena came running back to help him. They manhandled him awkwardly through the narrow hatch, ignoring his low moan of pain and then they set him down again on the maintenance walkway, propping him up against the side of the fuselage. Then Woodward scrambled out through the hatch again, returning half a minute later with a first-aid kit which he had taken from the cockpit.

He bent over Cormack and was about to tear the trouser leg open to take a look at the wound when he was unceremoniously pushed aside by Lena. He stared at her in surprise.

"You get the plane started," she said in heavily accented but comprehensible English. "I'll see to him."

Woodward nodded and then spoke slowly, to make sure

she understood. "If his leg hurts, there's morphine in the syringe. Give him the full amount. Understand?"

"Yes. Now go!"

"Good luck," he grinned and, before she could reply, he had gone.

She turned round quickly as Cormack groaned loudly and she saw his eyes flicker open.

"Lena . . ." he moaned.

"It's all right, Alan. I'm here. Just relax." She bent forward and kissed him briefly on the lips.

Gradually, he began to take in his surroundings; he was inside the aircraft, but had no idea how he had come to be there. He could only vaguely remember the explosion, a fragmented, disjointed impression of flying through the air, and pain in his leg . . . His leg! He looked down and saw the blood, but there was surprisingly little pain now. Which was a bad sign with that much blood . . .

He looked around the dark interior, hearing the roar of the twin engines as they burst into life; Woodward certainly wasn't wasting any time, he realised distantly. The aircraft lurched forward as Woodward opened up the throttles.

And then Cormack realised that Schelhaas was nowhere to be seen. "Where's Schelhaas?"

Lena shook her head, refusing to answer.

"Where is he?" he repeated and then it hit him. Schelhaas was still out there, still alive . . . "Where is he, Lena? Tell me!" he yelled.

"Some Germans were coming. He's drawing them off."

Cormack stared at her. Oh, bloody hell, it was France all over again. Elliott going off into the dunes, sacrificing himself as a decoy and now Schelhaas was doing exactly the same . . .

"No!" he shouted incoherently and began to scramble to his feet, only then remembering, too late, what had happened when he had tried that before . . . He cried out as his ankle buckled under him and fell back, gasping hoarsely. The pain, Jesus, the pain! Make it stop, for God's sake, make it stop . . .

With a hand that was rock–steady, Lena plunged the syringe into Cormack's leg. Almost instantly, the pain receded, to be replaced by an exquisite numbness. Carefully,

Lena withdrew the needle.

"What the hell was that?" Cormack shouted above the rising clamour of the engines.

"Morphine," Lena yelled back. "Woodward told me how much to use."

"Hope to hell he knew what he was doing."

"He certainly seemed to."

Cormack nodded in understanding; Woodward was in an aircraft again, in his own familiar world. Now, he was the professional and Cormack the helpless amateur. Not only helpless, but immobile; Cormack knew beyond all doubt that there was nothing he could do to help Schelhaas now.

Schelhaas loosed off another short burst from the Sten and dashed across to the next cover, a pile of crates. He guessed that perhaps six men were after him—one less now, he thought, with an almost savage exhilaration, remembering the look of shocked surprise on the Nazi's face as Schelhaas had come round the corner of the hangar, cutting the German down before he could even cry out.

He rammed another ammunition clip into the magazine and glanced around the crates in time to see a shadowy figure flitting across a gap about forty metres away. They were getting closer, but he had succeeded in drawing them away from the aircraft . . . He looked up at the pile of crates and grinned. Slinging the Sten over his shoulder, he began to climb upwards rapidly, nimbly. The pile was only about five metres high and within seconds he was lying full length on the top crate looking down on the scene below him. He unclipped two grenades from his belt and placed them on the wooden planking, in easy reach. The bastards would be passing below him within minutes . . .

Schelhaas did not have to wait long. He could see his pursuers quite clearly as they stalked their quarry, darting from one piece of cover to another. One stopped directly under him, looking cautiously around. He did not look upwards, however; even if he had, he would have been unlikely to have seen Schelhaas.

There were two more men hiding behind a crate, twenty metres away; the German below him had moved past and was standing with his back to Schelhaas. Perfect; Schelhaas pulled the pin out of one grenade, counted to three and then threw it just behind the two Germans. Before it had landed, he had armed the second and was lobbing it gently towards the single Nazi, just as the first detonated.

The soldier must have heard or sensed something; he turned and stared horror–struck at the object that bounced and rolled towards him. He lifted one leg to run and then the grenade exploded, the blast driving him against the crates like a crumpled rag doll.

A movement out of the corner of his eye made Schelhaas look over towards the runway; he almost whooped with joy as he saw a solitary Ju88 taxiing past the other parked aircraft. Woodward had done it, had got the bloody engines going! Which meant he had to move fast if he were to reach the plane before it took off; they would not, could not, wait for him. And the bombers had gone; soon, the All–Clear would be sounded and the Germans would start emerging from their underground shelters.

It was time to go.

Behrens waited until the sound of the Mosquitoes' engines was fading into the distance and then came running out of the shelter with Ziegler close behind. This had been no chance raid; it must have been timed to coincide with the attempt to break into the base. The mere fact that the British had sent Mosquitoes just to attack an unremarkable Luftwaffe airfield like Verwijk indicated that something was afoot.

He looked around the base, taken aback by the devastation. The bombers had achieved almost complete surprise and had pressed home their advantage with consummate skill. He could see three night fighters on fire; Number Two Hangar had been almost entirely flattened and the Control Tower was a blazing inferno. In rather less than five minutes, Verwijk had been virtually completely neutralised as an effective Luftwaffe base. Although, he realised, they had missed the east–west runway; it was completely untouched as if on purpose.

As if on purpose . . .

Dear God, no. They couldn't be. Not even the British . . .

Still incredulous, he saw the lone Ju88 moving slowly towards the eastern end of the runway. Jesus bloody Christ . . .

"They're stealing one of the damned planes!" he yelled to Ziegler. He looked around frantically and saw Mundt's Kubelwagen parked only fifteen metres away. Mundt, he knew, always kept the Spandau fully loaded . . . "We'll try to cut them off!" He gestured at the car and Ziegler nodded, understanding at once. They sprinted across, Behrens leaping into the back as Ziegler grabbed the starting handle, which he cranked viciously.

The engine coughed into life and Ziegler jumped into the driver's seat. Behrens almost lost his balance as Ziegler let out the clutch, the tyres screaming as he spun the wheel, foot flat to the floor.

Behrens automatically checked the gun and flicked off the safety-catch, cursing as the car lurched and bucked across the uneven surface. This was sheer bloody insanity, he told himself; the Spandau was a heavy machine gun, but its bullets would not be able to do much damage to a Ju88. But there was always the chance of hitting a fuel tank or of blowing out a tyre. Anyway, he was damned if he was just going to sit and watch them fly away with that bloody radar . . .

They were closing the distance rapidly now; Ziegler had pushed the speed up to nearly seventy k.p.h., and the night fighter was looming larger and larger in the Spandau's sights.

Schelhaas scrambled hastily down from the crates and broke into a run, firing a rapid burst behind him as he pelted across an open stretch before sliding to a halt behind a petrol tanker. Time for the last act, he decided, priming his final grenade. He rolled it under the lorry and sprinted away; he had gone thirty metres or so when there was a deafening roar and he felt a blast of heat on his back, but he did not look back, because the Ju88 was only a hundred metres away now. It was moving from left to right in front of him, but was already beginning to turn at the end of the runway. The hatch at the rear of the plane was open and he could see Lena's face framed in the opening. Seventy metres, sixty . . .

Suddenly, he heard a car engine behind him and looked around to see a Kubelwagen hurtling across the grass. It was coming straight towards him . . .

Cormack leaned back against the side of the fuselage, eyes half–closed. He could feel nothing at all in his left leg below the knee; Lena must have given him just about the full dose. He was faintly drowsy; it was suddenly very tempting to close his eyes, let it all slip away, just for a few seconds . . .

He sat up with a start. For God's sake, this was no time to doze off!

Forcing himself to concentrate, he looked across at Lena, who was leaning out of the open hatchway, peering anxiously beyond the tailplane.

"What's happening?" he asked, suddenly angry at his own immobility.

"There's been shooting over by the hangar and some explosions, but I can't see much else."

"Schelhaas?"

Wordlessly, she shook her head. Then she tensed. "There's a car coming towards us!"

Jesus . . . Cormack leaned forward and twisted himself round, gasping at the pain in his ankle. Slowly, he began to drag himself across the deck, cursing his useless leg. He had to see what was going on . . . He picked up his Sten and hauled himself to the hatchway.

"There's Vim!" Lena exclaimed excitedly. "Over there!"

Cormack was lying on his stomach now, his head by the hatch; he saw it all. Schelhaas was sprinting towards the plane, with the car hurtling towards him; the Dutchman suddenly turned and saw the Kubelwagen. He skidded to a halt and brought his machine gun up.

"The lights, Ziegler!" Behrens yelled as he swung the gun round, lining it up on Schelhaas. The headlights came on, full beam, transfixing Schelhaas; he put his arm in front of his face in reflex action to shut out the glare. Behrens fired a long burst that tore into the Dutchman, ripping him open from his left hip to right shoulder. Schelhaas reeled and staggered backwards, driven by the impact of the bullets, yet he would not go down, even though his chest and stomach was a mass of blood. And Ziegler was going straight at him . . .

"Look out, Ziegler!" Behrens shouted, but it was too late; probably Ziegler had intended to hit him. The Kubelwagen smashed into Schelhaas at over forty miles an hour. Behrens ducked involuntarily as Schelhaas was thrown high into the air;the body seemed to come right at him as it cannoned off the bonnet, before falling to the ground behind the car in a limp, boneless fashion.

Behrens straightened up, glancing backwards at Schelhaas' body as it rolled grotesquely behind them; he dismissed it from his mind as he swung the Spandau back towards the Ju88, now only fifty metres away.

"Vim!" Lena screamed. "Vim!"

Dear God in heaven, how many more? thought Cormack, horrified. How many more had to die for this bloody radar?

"Get that car!" he yelled as he lined the Sten up on the Kubelwagen's windshield. He pressed the trigger, but the car suddenly swerved to one side. Cormack swore and tried again, hearing Lena's Sten clatter into life at the same time as the Ju88's engines began to rev up; Woodward was taking off,he realised distantly. All they had to do was to hold this bloody car off for perhaps twenty seconds and they were clear . . .

The aircraft was already picking up speed; Ziegler spun the wheel and pressed his foot to the floor again, turning parallel to the night fighter as Behrens saw the gun flashes from the hatchway; he opened fire, raking the fuselage,trying frantically to keep the heavy gun lined up on the hatch as the car lurched crazily to and fro on the tarmac. With a feeling of despair, he realised that the Ju88 was beginning to pull ahead . . .

And then, for perhaps a second, Behrens was right on target; Lena screamed in terror and pain as four bullets scythed into her, throwing her backwards so that she crashed into the opposite wall of the fuselage. Cormack twisted round in horror and saw her stretch out her hand towards him, her lips working soundlessly as she tried to speak . . .

"Lena!" he yelled, desperately, seeing the mass of blood across her torso. For a last time, she stared into his eyes, still trying to say his name and then her head lolled lifelessly to one side . . .

Cormack stared numbly at her; she couldn't be dead . . . She couldn't! "Lena!" he sobbed helplessly.

Lena . . .

He rammed another ammunition clip into the Sten's breech and with almost inhuman calm aimed it at the car's windshield, not even reacting as the Spandau opened up again. Cormack steadied himself and squeezed the trigger, holding the shuddering gun remorselessly on the target until the magazine was empty.

The windscreen disintegrated in a shower of flying glass fragments. Ziegler screamed and reeled back, clutching at the bloodied mess that had been his chest. The car slewed violently to the left and, responding instinctively, Behrens leapt out half a second before it flipped over. He hit the tarmac and rolled over in a welter of arms and legs, hearing the grinding, crashing sounds as the car cartwheeled crazily along the runway, breaking up with each impact. There was a blinding flash as the fuel tank exploded and then there was nothing left of the Kubelwagen but shapeless fragments of flaming wreckage sliding across the tarmac.

Behrens finally stopped rolling and tumbling after about thirty metres; incredibly, he was still conscious, but his face was contorted by the agony in his right leg, which lay smashed and broken, the knee bent at an impossible angle. Waves of unconsciousness were beating at his brain, but he refused to give way to them. Not yet; there was still one thing he had to do, had to know. He pulled himself round, crying out with the pain, and looked towards the western end of the runway.

It was a text book take-off, he noted with professional approval; the Ju88 simply seemed to drive up an invisible ramp and was airborne. The pilot pulled up the undercarriage before he was even ten metres up, and roared over the perimeter fence with only feet to spare. And he wasn't climbing, Behrens realised; he was going out over the dunes at practically zero altitude so as not to be picked up on any radar screens. A damned good pilot, Behrens thought admiringly as he watched the night fighter, with its fully operational Liechtenstein radar, disappear into the western sky. He would make it, Behrens knew; from the Dutch coast to England was only about thirty minutes' flying time.

Behrens stared into the sky to the west, long after the sound of the Ju88's Jumbo engines had faded; then, he lay back wearily, closed his eyes and, at last, allowed himself to melt into oblivion.

Cormack laboriously closed the hatch and then crawled slowly over to Lena. Gently, he cradled her head against his chest, completely unaware of the tears streaming down his face. His eyes stared blankly into infinity.

# EPILOGUE

Behrens was released from hospital two weeks later, absolved from all blame for the loss of the Ju88 and its Liechtenstein radar. It was decided at the subsequent investigation that the 'extreme negligence' of SS–Sturmbannführer Kreissner had made Behrens' task virtually impossible; the verdict was perhaps unsurprising, considering that it was a Luftwaffe Court of Inquiry that passed it . . .

Cormack spent several weeks in hospital but consistently refused to answer any questions concerning the operation. In fact, the only person he would talk to at all was Woodward, who became a regular visitor; anyone else was utterly ignored. The day after the plaster on his broken ankle was removed, Cormack absented himself from the hospital and disappeared without trace.

## AUTHOR'S NOTE

The following is an extract from *The Secret War* by Brian Johnson (BBC Publications, 1978):

"The secrets of Liechtenstein were further revealed when on 9 May, 1943, a Ju88 . . . landed at Dyce Airfield, Aberdeen, equipped with the FuG202 Liechtenstein radar. There remains a mystery about this aircraft, which is preserved at RAF St Athen . . . not only was its arrival expected but, according to one report, it even had an escort of RAF Spitfires. Whatever the reason, the gift of an operational Ju88 was a windfall for TRE and the radar was soon evaluated . . ."

